Praise for Patricia Frances Rowell

A Dangerous Seduction

'Rowell creates a wonderful Gothic atmosphere,
using beautiful Cornwall and its history of smuggling
and shipwrecks to enhance her story.'

—*Romantic Times*

A Perilous Attraction

'Promising Regency-era debut…
a memorable heroine who succeeds in capturing the
hero's heart as well as the reader's.'

—*Publishers Weekly*

A TREACHEROUS PROPOSITION

Patricia Frances Rowell

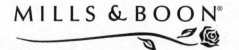

MILLS & BOON®

DID Y   ?

If you did,   orted
unsold and   lisher

All the char   ation
of the autho   e
same name
individual k.   .e
pure invention.

First published in Great Britain 2006
Harlequin Mills & Boon Limited,
Eton House, 18-24 Paradise Road, Richmond, Surrey TW9 1SR

© Patricia Frances Rowell 2005

ISBN 0 263 84654 7

Set in Times Roman 10½ on 12 pt.
04-0606-84520

Printed and bound in Spain
by Litografia Rosés S.A., Barcelona

Award-winning author **Patricia Frances Rowell** lives in the woods of northern Louisiana with her husband, Johnny, in a home they built themselves. There they enjoy visits from their collective seven children, numerous children-in-law and eight grand-children, as well as making friends with the local wildlife. Please stop by her website at www.patriciafrancesrowell.com to visit.

Prologue

Yorkshire, England, April 1796

"But, Papa! Timothy is my friend!" The little boy's lips quivered in spite of his determination to forbid them.

His father glared at the older boy standing beside him. "Your friend, do you think? Now what would a great boy of thirteen years want with a lad not quite eight? What have you given him?"

The younger boy's gaze dropped, then slid sideways toward his friend, guilt in every muscle of his small body as he stared at the straw on the stable floor.

"Ah!" His father folded his arms.

The boy lifted his chin. "I only gave him my soldiers, Papa. Tim doesn't have any."

His father's eyes narrowed as he studied the ragged Timothy. "And a boy your age likes to play with toy soldiers?" Suddenly he barked, "Let me see what is in your pockets."

The older boy made a break for it, sprinting for the stable door, only to be captured by an under groom and hauled back before he had made good his escape.

The boy's father grasped him by the collar and shook him. "Your pockets."

Reluctantly, Timothy turned his pockets outward and two gold coins fell into the straw. The man stooped and retrieved them, his icy stare never leaving Timothy's angry face. "So you steal from your *friends?*"

Timothy lifted his chin defiantly. "He's not my friend!" He kicked straw at the younger boy. "You aren't my friend. You're just a *baby.*"

He turned and ran for the door again, and the boy's father let him go. After the boy had disappeared from sight, the man knelt beside his son and looked into his tear-filled eyes. "I'm sorry, Vincent, but there is a hard lesson you must learn. When one has the power and wealth that will someday be yours, one must always be on guard. Always. The world is filled with people who will let you think they like you, but who, in fact, only want what you have. Do you understand?"

The boy nodded, his mouth firming into a hard line.

"Yes, Papa. I understand."

Chapter One

London, England, April 1814

Vincent Ingleton, Earl of Lonsdale, leaned his shoulders against the stained wall, arms folded across his chest, and studied the lady's face where she sat by the bed. Tired. Tired and sad. He narrowed his eyes and looked more closely. No, not sad exactly. In truth, she showed very little grief. Just an abysmal weariness. Little wonder in that. The man dying in the bed had not made her life easy.

Hardly even bearable for a lady of her breeding.

Vincent wrinkled his nose at the smell of blood and mildew pervading the room. The dying man coughed and fumbled at the bedclothes. "Diana?"

She reached out and took his hand while the doctor wiped blood away from his patient's lips. "I'm here, Wyn."

Vincent sighed and bowed his dark head. She had always been there when Wynmond Corby needed her. No matter what he had done, Lady Diana had been there for her husband. No matter how little Wyn had provided, she had always been a gracious hostess for him, quietly welcoming his friends into their home, even as Corby finally descended into these cramped, grubby quarters. She had been there for him.

No matter how little he deserved her.

But who was Vincent to say who deserved love? He had not much experience with that thorny subject.

He glanced at the two other men quietly conversing against the adjoining wall. Men like Wyn seemed always to have friends, even though he hadn't two coins at a time to rub together in his pocket. And why not? He constantly had a quip on his tongue, a laugh in his eyes, the heart to put his horse at any fence in the country. Perhaps that was why Corby was, in fact, the only one of his old friends with whom Vincent still associated, very nearly the only friend he had.

The only one of them who had never sponged off him.

But having friends had not stopped someone from slipping a blade between Corby's ribs.

The softest of sighs brought his gaze back to Diana. In spite of the fatigue, she looked as she always did, calm and serene, the small pool of candlelight in the dark room setting her smooth, pale chignon aglow. Even in a worn, dull-gray gown, she was beautiful. Truth be told, Vincent knew the reason he spent so much time at the Corby home had as much to do with Lady Diana's company as it did that of her husband.

But of course, there was the other, more important, reason.

A barrage of coughing from the bed caused him to straighten and step closer. Blood spattered the sheets, and the doctor and Diana both moved quickly to lift Corby higher on the pillows. He gurgled and coughed again. Vincent and the two other men converged on the bed and gathered around the foot.

"Friends…dear…" Corby's whisper made them all lean closer. He coughed again. "Please…" Another cough.

More blood. "Care…Diana…my…my chil…" His eyes closed, and Vincent thought it was over, but Wyn rallied for one more breath. "I've…not…done…well."

The next cough brought forth such a quantity of blood that the watchers knew no living man could have given it up. Wyn's blond head rolled to one side and the doctor let it fall back against the pillows. "May God rest his soul."

The stocky, sandy-haired man some years Vincent's senior bowed his head. "Amen."

"Amen." The lanky younger gentleman standing next echoed.

The widow covered her eyes with one hand.

Vincent closed his eyes, clenched his teeth together and said nothing.

"Well…" The larger man took a long breath and a step away from the bed. "That's that…" He walked to Diana and placed a heavy hand on her shoulder. "Of course, my dear, you must not worry about the future for a moment. It will be my pleasure to see that you are provided for, just as Wyn asked. I will make arrangements and send a carriage for you as soon as the funeral is done."

Something in the man's voice pulled Vincent's attention away from his moment of grief. He looked up sharply, his gaze focused on Diana's face. This time he had no trouble at all identifying her expression.

Fear.

He moved around the bed in her direction. "Perhaps we should discuss this further, St. Edmunds. You might find it a bit awkward to explain those…er, *arrangements* to your wife."

St. Edmunds turned a glare on him. "I can deal with my wife."

"I'm sure you can, but it might also be awkward for Lady Diana."

The tall man hesitantly opened his mouth to speak, running his fingers through his straight, light brown hair.

Vincent glanced at him. "Sudbury?"

The Honorable Justinian Sudbury studied his shining boots thoughtfully. "Going to be dashed awkward for all of us."

"Gentlemen." Diana stood and stepped away from St. Edmunds's hand, her mien dignified. "I appreciate your concern more than I can say, but it is quite unnecessary. I will care for myself and my children. None of us need be embarrassed."

At that moment the door opened and a snaggle-toothed, slatternly old woman shoved into the room and peered at the body on the bed. "So the cove's finally stuck his spoon in the wall, has he? So who's going to pay me the rent what's due?"

Diana opened her mouth to answer, but the woman was looking at the gentlemen. Vincent shifted his gaze from Diana to the landlady. "What's the damage?"

She named a figure and Vincent's eyebrows shot up. "Don't try to gull me, old woman. These rooms are not worth a quarter of that."

"Ha! They are when I ain't been paid for four months— and another month due. Hadn't been for the little ones, I'd have put 'em out last month."

So much for no one's being embarrassed. Vincent glanced at Diana. She lifted her hands in a helpless gesture. He pulled his purse out of his coat pocket and counted the amount into the old woman's hand and added an extra coin. "There. That will cover the next month." He took a step toward her. "Now get out."

Suiting the action to the threat, she made for the door. "Aye, ye black-haired devil. I'm going."

Vincent returned to the discussion at hand. St. Edmunds

and Sudbury were looking at Diana who was looking down at her clasped hands. Even in the dim light, Vincent could see that her cheeks were crimson.

"Thank you, my lord. Your kindness will give me the opportunity to make plans." She still did not look at them.

"Nonsense!" St. Edmunds frowned. "We all know in what case you stand."

Sudbury nodded. "Wyn was a very good fellow, but… No sense about money. Always under the hatches. Can you go to your family?"

"I'm sure that I can." An expression of uncertainty flickered across Diana's face. "I will write to my cousin immediately."

Vincent gave that notion some thought. Not bloody likely. When her father had died, the title and estate had gone to a distant cousin—one who had not spoken to her family in years. And Wyn's older brother was no less profligate than Wyn had been. No, someone was going to have to see to her welfare. Damn Wyn and his charm and his prodigal ways and his horses and his women! Damn him for putting her in this humiliating position.

Damn him for getting himself killed.

With an effort Vincent pushed the ache out of his heart. He would deal with it later. Now he must think. St. Edmunds could not be allowed to take control of Diana and her life. The man might be Corby's friend, but he was not Vincent's.

And Diana was wise to be afraid of him. Not only were his intentions highly questionable, St. Edmunds had a certain reputation amongst the libertines of London. Women did not fare well at his hands. Why Corby had let him dangle after Diana…

But that was neither here nor there. He needed to get her out of the room. They could hardly continue to discuss this delicate question before her as though she were a child who did not understand. "Lady Diana, are your children still sleeping? I thought I heard a cry."

"Surely they are—it is well after midnight—but I should make certain. Meanwhile, you gentlemen will be more comfortable in the parlor. I shall just be a moment." She left the room in a soft swish of skirts and Vincent turned to the doctor, reaching once more for his purse.

"Sir, I appreciate your assistance this evening. Can you further oblige me by having Mr. Corby made ready for burial?"

"Certainly. I regret that I could not be of better use, but a sliced lung…" The doctor shook his gray head sadly.

"Yes." Vincent handed him several coins. "If this is not sufficient, send word to me at Lonsdale House, and also apprise me when it is done."

The doctor bowed and left the room, and the three remaining men pulled themselves into a circle. St. Edmunds cleared his throat. "Now see here, Ingleton. It's good of you to take care of these matters, but don't think for a minute that it changes anything. I have told Lady Diana that I shall care for her, and I shall."

Vincent folded his arms, drawing together his dark eyebrows. "And I have told you that I do not believe that is a suitable course of action."

St. Edmunds sneered. "And I suppose you believe *you* are a more suitable guardian—with *your* reputation?"

"At least I do not have a wife."

"I say," Sudbury intervened. "Why don't we ask Lady Diana? Ought to be able to chose who's to take care of her. I would but…pockets quite to let, myself."

Both of the other men favored him with annoyed glances. "You heard what she said," St. Edmunds snarled. "She'll insist that she can manage, but we all know she cannot."

"No." Sudbury sighed. "Can't see how she could. Not a feather to fly with. Went through his fortune and hers, too. Four months' back rent…!" He shook his head in disgust. "A governess, do you think?"

"With two children hanging on her skirts?" St. Edmunds grimaced. "Not likely. That is why I shall send my people…"

"No." Vincent made no attempt to be conciliating. "If you send your carriage the whole of the ton will immediately draw unflattering conclusions about Lady Diana. I will see to it some other way. And that fact need go no further than this room." He turned to glare meaningfully at Sudbury.

"No, no," Sudbury hastily assured him. "Not a word. On my honor."

St. Edmunds's broad face had turned an angry red. He took a step toward Vincent. "Damn you, Lonsdale, I know what you really want."

Vincent stopped him with a cold stare.

Sudbury shuffled his feet uneasily. "Come now, my lords. No way for gentlemen… Great God! His body lies dead in this very room."

"Very well." Vincent reached again into his coat pocket. He pulled out his hand and opened it. "We'll settle it as *gentlemen.* What do you say to a game of hazard?"

"Throw dice?" St. Edmunds's eyes took on a crafty look. "For a woman?"

Vincent made no answer. He just stood, his expression hard, and tossed the dice in one hand.

St. Edmunds laughed uneasily. "Well, I suppose gambling is nothing if not a gentleman's sport." His eyes narrowed. "But not with *your* dice."

"As you wish." Vincent let the implied insult pass. A mere diversion. St. Edmunds also had a reputation where dice were concerned. Not that anyone ever accused him outright of cheating. He was much too good a shot and much too vindictive to chance a duel. But Vincent's past had long ago taught him how to deal with cheats.

His mouth crooked up slightly on one corner. "But hazard will take too long. We have only minutes before Lady Diana returns. I suggest one roll of the dice each—high number wins. I will roll with your dice, and you may roll with mine."

Sudbury nodded sagely. "Bound to be fair."

Vincent handed his dice to Sudbury. "If you will give these to Lord St. Edmunds…"

St. Edmunds eyes became slits in his face. "What are you about, Lonsdale?"

"Apparently you believe my dice too likely to win. I offer them to you. I will use yours." Vincent's crooked smile flickered briefly.

Fury and suspicion strong in his face, St. Edmunds reluctantly reached for the dice in Sudbury's palm. Vincent held his own open hand between them. "If you will first give me yours, my lord.…"

St. Edmunds slapped them into Vincent's hand and grabbed the pair Sudbury held, speaking between his teeth. "Very well. Roll."

Vincent nodded and went to one knee on the splintered floor. The others followed him down. He shook the dice and tossed them into the space between them.

Sudbury bent for a closer look. "Six! Two treys."

St. Edmunds smirked. "Surprised, Lonsdale?" He cast Vincent's dice and scowled.

"Three!" Sudbury called out. "Lonsdale wins."

Vincent retrieved his own dice and left St. Edmunds's on the floor.

"Surprised, St. Edmunds?"

* * *

Diana slipped into the room she shared with her children. Not since Bytham was born almost four years ago had she slept in the bed in which her husband's body now lay. Sometimes she wondered if he had ever noticed. She tucked the covers snugly under her little son's chin, smoothed his golden curls, and moved to his sister. Six-year-old Selena lay sprawled out of the cover, the flaxen hair splashed across the pillow mirroring her mother's. Diana straightened her in the truckle bed, covered her and kissed her rose-colored cheek.

Dear God, how she loved them. The only lasting gift that Wyn had ever given her. The tears she had not shed for their father now sprung into her eyes. What would happen to her babies? In spite of her brave words, she had no idea how she might care for them. But almost anything would be better than to accept Lord St. Edmunds's offer. She had not a doubt as to where his *arrangements* would lead.

No, as difficult as it would be, she would write to her father's cousin. As the present head of the Bytham family he should be obligated to help her, but considering the long-standing feud between him and her father, she doubted that he would. At the very best she would become an unpaid servant in his house, and her children… She could not imagine what their lives as despised poor relations would be. She might even be separated from them. Oh, dear heaven.

Poor little fatherless mites! If Wynmond had been a poor husband, in many ways he was a worse father. Worse because, like most people who knew him, his children adored him. And he spent only enough time with them to ensure their adoration, disappearing for weeks at time afterward.

And he never understood that. In his way, he did love them—just as, in his way, he had loved her. The children would miss him. They would grieve as she no longer could. What comfort might she offer them? What would she tell them about their lovable, irresponsible father?

She went to her own narrow bed and felt under the mattress, sighing in relief. The last terrifying, precious gift of money still lay where she had hidden it. If indeed it could be called a gift. She prayed it had not been sent by Lord St. Edmunds. If he was the one who knew… An icy fist closed around her stomach.

She closed her hand tightly around the few remaining coins, the metal biting into her skin, the shame of possessing them gnawing at her heart. They would feed them, barely, for the next month, the month's reprieve that Vincent Ingleton—to her complete surprise—had bought for her. Such a strange man. Dark and cold, with the face of a hawk. She had heard whispers about him, gossip of a misspent youth, a cruel nature. But Diana could hardly picture the man carousing. He had never been anything but solemn and polite in her presence. Solemn and polite and cold.

But three gentlemen awaited her downstairs. She must go to them. Blood stained her shabby gray gown, but Diana could not find the strength to change it. Perhaps they would go soon.

Go and leave her to her dead husband and her fears.

All three men rose politely as Diana came into the parlor, although St. Edmunds's expression remained dark. He was not accustomed to losing. Neither was Vincent. But unlike St. Edmunds, Vincent took care not to underestimate his opponents.

He ignored the man and directed his question to the lady. "How did you find the children?"

"Sleeping, as I had hoped." She rubbed her temples as though they ached. Sighing, she sank into a threadbare chair. "Thank you, all of you, so much for coming. I will let you know when I have made the funeral arrangements."

"Anything at all I can do…" Sudbury leaned to kiss the hand she extended as he approached her.

"Thank you. I appreciate your kindness."

St. Edmunds cleared his throat. "Of course. If I may render any service at all, you have but to send word." He glared at Vincent. "Your servant, Lady Diana…my lord… Sudbury."

With a nod at Vincent, Sudbury followed St. Edmunds out the door.

When Vincent sat rather than follow them, Diana sent him a startled glance. With an effort he dredged up his crooked half smile. "I have persuaded Lord St. Edmunds to let me assist you with your future plans."

The look of relief which rewarded that statement flickered after a moment and one of wariness replaced it. Not quite knowing how to reassure her, Vincent glanced down at the floor, only to see a cockroach emerge from under his chair. With an oath, he brought his boot down on it.

"Oh, I'm so sorry." Once again color flooded Diana's cheeks. "I cannot get rid of the creatures, no matter how much I clean. I find them everywhere."

"And little wonder, in this hole." Vincent stood and walked to where she sat, and stood looking down at her, forcing down the anger that rose in him. "My lady, you are not to blame for the roaches any more than you are to blame for the unpaid rent. I knew Wyn. I knew him well, and my heart is sore for the loss of him. But I also know his nature. He should never have brought you to this." He glared around the room. He'd be damned if he would leave her here. "And I see no reason for you to stay here another minute. You are not even safe in this neighborhood. And with a dead body in the next room, the cockroaches and rats will… You cannot stay. Go and gather up what you need for yourself and the children, and I will take you to a hotel."

"That's…that's very kind, my lord, but not necessary. I have survived here very—"

"Diana, spare me." Vincent glowered in her direction. "You have survived, but only that. The moment that hag of a landlady spreads the word that you are now alone, you will cease to have any security at all." He softened his tone. "I understand your pride, but you must remove your-self and your children from these quarters. Now go and col-lect what you need. I promise you will be safe with me."

And *from* him, more was the pity.

She sat for a moment more with eyes closed and one hand pressed to her mouth. At last she drew in a deep breath and stood. "You are correct, of course. For months I have slept with a pistol by my hand. I will go with you. My concern must be for Selena and Bytham. If you will wait, it will take only a few moments."

Vincent watched her through the door and began to pace the small room. Why had Wynmond Corby done this to her, to his children, to himself? Vincent shuddered. He had been so close to following the same path, so close to bring-ing himself to utter ruin. And he still wasn't sure why.

Nor exactly why he had mended his ways, for that matter.

"I believe this will do for a day or two." Diana came into the room dragging two small valises. "Now I must get the children up and dress them."

"May I help?" Vincent moved toward the bedroom. "I know very little about youngsters, but perhaps I can assist."

The first smile he had seen since he had helped carry a bleeding Wynmond Corby home softened her face. "It is not that difficult. Perhaps you can get Bytham into his clothes. He is such a heavy sleeper—it will be a struggle."

His brief smile answered hers. "Surely I will prove equal to stuffing a small boy into his britches."

Her eyes twinkled for an instant. "We shall see."

He had done surprisingly well with it, Diana thought as the hackney turned into St. James and headed toward Fenton's Hotel, even if his lordship's previously crisp neck-cloth did now hang around his neck in crumpled folds. Thank heaven he had been willing to help her. She felt completely unequal to the task of wrestling with a cross, half-asleep, small boy. Getting Selena, now sleeping, slumped between them on the seat, dressed had almost proved more than she could do. When had she last enjoyed a sound night's sleep? Diana could not remember. She roused herself when she realized his lordship was speaking to her.

"I desired the doctor to have the body prepared for the funeral. If you will tell me what you want, I will convey your wishes to him."

"Oh, thank you." Diana struggled to focus. "You are very kind. Right now I am not sure…" She rubbed at the pain in her temple.

"You needn't think of it now. Tomorrow is time enough for that." Vincent shifted slightly to move the dozing Selena away from his pocket, retrieved his overworked purse once again, and settled the child back against him, holding her upright. He removed a few coins and handed the purse to Diana. "There should be enough here to provide for any services you need tonight and in the morning. I had rather not be seen handing it to you."

How thoughtful of him, even though Diana had little doubt that his championship of her would soon be all over London—with the attendant gossip. She should not take any more money from him. She really should not. But the pittance she had in her purse would hardly cover a night at Fenton's, let alone meals for the children. Once more she must bite her tongue and swallow a large chunk of her pride with it. "Thank you, my lord. I will repay you as soon as I am able."

He stared at her for a moment with sharp black eyes, and Diana experienced a twinge of alarm. Then he shrugged slightly. "Of course. In the meantime, until you have made your plans, I will settle with Fenton's."

The carriage drew to a stop and Vincent opened the door. He took Bytham from Diana and helped her down, then gave the boy back to her, lifted her daughter into his own arms and paid the driver. As they made their way into the hotel, Selena snuggled her face against his neck.

Diana collapsed onto the nearest sofa while her escort approached the desk. In a matter of minutes, the child draped limply across his shoulder, he had arranged for rooms with a parlor, turned the luggage over to the porter, instructed a maid to assist Diana with the children and seen the three of them upstairs.

And in a few more minutes he had invited her to send for him if she needed him, promised to call on her on the morrow and bowed himself out of the room, no doubt relieved to be rid of the three of them.

Diana fell into bed in a blur of fatigue.

Chapter Two

There was nothing for it.

He would have to ask for her help. And God! How he hated to do it.

Hadn't he caused enough trouble for her in the past? Vincent trotted up the stairs of the town house and lifted the knocker. A dull booming on the other side of the door rewarded this effort and immediately thereafter a startled face appeared in the portal.

"Why, Lord Lonsdale! We haven't seen you this age." The tall, white-haired butler stepped back and bowed Vincent into a small but elegant entry.

"Good morning, Feetham." Vincent nodded at the butler and handed his hat and gloves to a footman. "Is Lady Litton in?"

"I'm not sure, my lord, but I will inquire." Feetham nodded at the footman who disappeared up the stairs.

Vincent carefully schooled his face to show no expression. What the butler meant was, of course, that he did not know if his mistress was willing to see Vincent. The footman reappeared in a matter of minutes.

"Her ladyship is in the morning room," he reported. "She asks that you come up."

Vincent nodded to Feetham and followed the footman back up the stairs and into a cheerful chamber, bright with sunlight.

The dark-haired lady on the sofa, a lady only a few years Vincent's senior, smiled warmly and held out a hand. "Vincent! What brings you here?" A tiny wrinkle formed, marring the perfect skin between her eyes. "Is something amiss?"

"No, my lady." Vincent bent and kissed his stepmother's smooth fingers. "At least not…"

"Well! Will wonders never cease?"

Vincent turned toward the fair-haired gentleman who had just sauntered through the door and bowed. "Good morning, Lord Litton."

"We haven't seen you since Helen and I married." Adam Barbon, Viscount Litton, extended a hand, which Vincent shook.

"For which, I am sure, you are suitably grateful." Vincent tried to smile.

"Now, Vincent, don't talk so. You know you are welcome here." Vincent was relieved to hear that. He had not been sure. Helen Barbon reached for a fresh cup on the tray just provided by the footman. "Do you still take your coffee black?"

"Yes, ma'am, thank you." Vincent took the cup and marveled that she truly seemed to mean what she said. How could anyone be that forgiving? But he had hoped she would be. Otherwise, he would not have come.

Had it not been for Diana, he would not have come at all.

He only hoped his stepmother's new husband would find himself able to command an equal degree of forbearance.

His lordship grinned. "I'll hold my gratitude in abeyance until I discover what has brought you here *this* time."

Vincent took a sip of coffee, struggled with the words and finally choked them out. "I need your help."

One of Litton's eyebrows rose. "Do you, indeed?"

"I would not ask… I dislike troubling you, but…" Vincent felt his mouth tighten. "I am not asking for my own sake."

"Heaven forfend that you should ask your family for help."

The sarcastic tone caused Vincent to look at his stepfather more closely, his eyebrows drawing together. He half rose. "If you had rather I not, I will immediately relieve you…"

Litton waved the comment away. "Oh, sit down, sit down. Tell us who needs what."

"Pay him no mind, Vincent." Helen reached out to place a calming hand on Vincent's sleeve. "You know how he is. We are happy that you asked. Now…who needs our help?"

Setting aside for the moment that he had never understood how Adam Barbon *"is,"* Vincent directed his gaze at Helen. "It is a lady."

"A lady?" Litton looked at him with renewed interest. "I begin to have hope."

Vincent felt the blood heating his cheeks. "You misunderstand me, my lord. Not…not *my* lady."

"Hmm." Litton held out his cup for his wife to replenish.

"Who, Vincent?" Without asking, Helen took Vincent's cup and added hot coffee to it. "Is it someone I know?"

"I'm sure you at least know *of* her. I am speaking of Lady Diana Corby."

"Ah. Yes, I have a slight acquaintance with her. One does not see her out anymore."

"Little wonder in that." Litton helped himself to a pastry from the tray. "With that wastrel for a husband, she could hardly afford it."

"Lady Diana no longer has a husband." Vincent looked back at two pairs of startled eyes. "Wynmond Corby was killed last night."

"Oh, my. How awful." Helen covered her mouth with one hand. "He left her with small children, I believe."

Vincent nodded.

"I don't suppose he left anything to care for them?" Litton looked at Vincent, eyebrows raised.

"No, sir. That is the difficulty. Lady Diana is allowing me to assist her temporarily." His face got warmer as his stepfather's eyebrows rose higher. The devil take him. It had been hard enough to leave her last night without… "Now, my lord. Damn it, Litton, that is not the way of it!"

Helen sighed. "Don't tease, Adam."

"No, no. I'm not teasing." Litton sobered. "It is just very… How did this come about, Vincent?"

Vincent related the whole sorry tale.

"And he had no will?" Litton studied Vincent seriously.

Vincent shook his head. "Apparently not. Wyn always did seem to think he would live forever."

"Damned irresponsible young jackanapes!" Litton scowled. "With a wife and children and he…"

Vincent nodded. "Just so. But this is the first thing he has ever asked of me—and perforce the last—and I intend to oblige him."

"And the lady herself?" This time Litton's expression was not sardonic, simply inquiring.

"She is a very fine lady." That was all that Vincent intended to say about *that*.

"I see." Litton pondered for a moment, his expression speculative. "It is going to look very havey-cavey, you know, your providing for her. I suppose you can afford it?"

Vincent waved the question away. "Oh, yes, but it may not come to that. She intends to write to her cousin. It is *his* duty as head of her family."

"Won't do it." Litton shook his head. "Her father was

the only Bytham worth his salt, and his cousin hated him. So what will you do?"

"For the long run, I cannot yet say. That is why I need your help. The rooms where they were living are infested with cockroaches, rats and a corpse. Lady Diana could not stay there with the children. I took her to Fenton's for the night, but that is not a good situation, either. It would be, however, much worse to bring her to *my* house."

He could never trust himself for that.

"Of course," Helen broke in. "I understand what you need. Bring her to me. She and the children may stay with me until she can make other plans."

"I would be very grateful. I hope it will not be for long." Vincent sighed with relief. "I will see to the funeral, but it would be a great kindness if she had someone with her."

"She will be more than welcome. I will write her a letter immediately and invite her. You may carry it to her when you leave."

Helen went to her desk, pulled out stationery and began to write. Litton gazed at Vincent speculatively. "Do you need help with the funeral?"

"I think not, but thank you."

Litton nodded silently, but continued his contemplation of Vincent. Vincent began to feel uncomfortable. Well, *more* uncomfortable. He wondered if the man was remembering the brawl Vincent had provoked between the two of them. Or the time that he— He shoved the thought aside. There were so many unpleasant things Adam Barbon might be thinking about Vincent's past. It was a wonder he tolerated him in his house at all.

But Vincent had had enough of his taciturn scrutiny. "You have another question, my lord?"

Litton shook his head. "No. I was just thinking how little we know of you now."

Vincent smiled. If only his lordship knew *how* little.

* * *

By the time the knock sounded on the door of their rooms, the children had completely exhausted the entertainment possibilities of Fenton's Hotel. Had she been there alone, Diana would have been reveling in the luxury of the service, the fine furnishings, the wholesome food. The basic cleanliness. It had been so long since she had enjoyed those comforts.

But cooping youngsters up in a hostelry with little outlet for their energy presented a challenge. Diana was nearing the end of her wits as to how to keep them occupied for the rest of the day. At present she had them working in their copy books in the sitting room, but they would soon grow restless.

They knew something was wrong.

She had not yet found the courage to tell them about their father. The crushing reality of her situation had simply drained her of the strength needed to find the words. What could she tell them about what would now happen to them? She didn't know.

Even the stipend Wyn had earned at the Foreign Office was now gone. Or what she had seen of it. It had been little enough, but it had paid her a small household allowance. Sometimes. And the rent. Occasionally. How could Wyn have gotten four months behind? The position should have provided for their basic needs, but had it not been for the other money...

Oh, God! And what was she going to do about *that?*

And what must she do about the man standing in the door? Other than invite him in.

"Good morning, my lord. Come in. Children, say good morning to Lord Lonsdale."

Bytham and Selena jumped to their feet and chorused

a "Good morning, my lord," accompanied by a marginal bow and a creditable curtsey. One advantage of the small home to which they had been accustomed was that they often saw visitors, as children in a larger house did not. Diana could depend on them to know their manners. Besides, she knew the newcomer offered a welcome distraction from copying.

She gestured them back to their work. "Please sit, my lord. Should I ring for some tea?"

"No, thank you. I just had coffee with my stepmother. I have come to bring you this note from her and to discuss…" He glanced at the children. "The other matters."

"Some wine, then?" When he shook his head, Diana took a seat at one end of the comfortable sofa and he sat in a chair at her elbow.

She took the note and glanced at the name in the corner. "Lady Litton is your stepmother? I had not realized that."

"Yes, she married Litton quite a while after my father died."

She broke the seal and perused the message. "Oh! Oh, how kind she is. She invites the children and me to stay with her." She met his lordship's expressionless gaze over the top of the note. "I'm sure that you brought this about. I appreciate your thoughtfulness, but… How can I—a virtual stranger—impose on her with two children?"

His expression did not change. "How can you not?"

"How indeed?" Diana studied her hands where they lay in her lap. "I cannot stay here at your expense—and certainly not at my own. I cannot return to our rooms. They have likely been stripped by now. I cannot go to my cousin without knowing he will take us in—and in truth I have no confidence that he will. Oh, God, Vincent! What am I to do? There is always St. Edmunds, I suppose, or someone like him, but…"

He gazed at her intently, as though to see into her mind. "I cannot believe that you are willing to seek a protector."

"No. No! My children… Do you know what that would mean to them?"

"So accept the invitation for now. We will discover a solution to the problem in time."

Feeling something brush his sleeve, Vincent looked down to find himself gazing into the upturned face of little Selena where she leaned against the arm of his chair. Storm-gray eyes, the image of her mother's, stared back at him.

He cast a startled glance at Diana, but before she could speak, Selena blurted, "You carried me. I remember."

Vincent remembered, too. Never having been around children, he had never had an experience quite like it. The weight of the soft little body on his arms, the trusting little head on his shoulder, the sleepy murmurs. Surprisingly pleasant, in spite of the awkward circumstances. Would he ever hold a child of his own? A moment's sadness flowed through him. It did not seem likely.

"Selena…"

Before her mother could send her back to copying, the girl hurried on. "Where is my papa?"

Alarm shot through Vincent. How the devil was he to answer *that* question? He cast a frantic glance at Diana, only to see a moment of panic on her face. In an instant it was gone, leaving the tranquility he had always seen there—and deep, dark circles under her eyes.

She held out an arm to her daughter. "Come here, Selena. Bytham…come and sit with Mama."

The small boy slid off his chair and slowly crossed the room to his mother while his sister edged closer. Both youngsters clearly sensed the distress of the adults. For a heartbeat Vincent allowed himself to feel relief that it was not his place to tell them their father was dead.

And then he recollected the moment of consternation that had broken Diana's calm. She knew no more what to say than did he. And she looked to be at the end of her endurance. He should at least support her. Vincent moved to sit beside her on the sofa and lifted Bytham onto his lap. The wiry little boy squirmed himself into place, and Selena climbed up beside Diana. Diana drew in a deep breath. After a second's hesitation, Vincent lost the battle within himself and slipped an arm around her shoulders.

After a moment she took one hand of each child and pressed a kiss on it. "I have something sad to tell you, children." Her voice choked a bit and she swallowed. "Your papa…your papa is dead. We will not see him again."

"Not ever?" Selena's diminutive brows came together. "Never?"

"No, my dearest. That is what it means to be dead. He has…he has gone away into heaven."

Vincent wondered briefly if that had, in fact, been Wynmond Corby's destination. He hoped so. For all his shortcomings, Wyn had been a loyal friend.

But how could he have done this to his family?

Selena's face puckered. "But I don't *want* him to be dead. I want him to come back!"

She burst into tears and Diana pulled her daughter into her lap, resting her cheek against the child's hair and rocking her gently. Tears streamed down her own cheeks. Bytham, not quite understanding, but seeing his mother and sister in tears, began to wail. Diana freed a hand to clasp one of his, and Vincent held him closer.

God! How could these tiny beings stand such loss? How could Diana bear to see her children so unhappy? She had already borne so much. What could he say or do for her? Able to think of nothing else, Vincent circled the three of them in his strong arms, willing his strength to shelter them.

Only later did he feel the tears on his own face.

* * *

Strange. Vincent could not remember the last time he had shed tears. In fact, he could not remember the last time he had felt any strong feeling for someone else at all. He made a policy of *not* having strong feelings for others. That way lay danger. Detachment provided a much better wall against the world.

But Diana was different.

He had known that for months, watching her contend with the miserable circumstances of her life—always calm, always patient and kind, always lovely. Had he actually embraced her? How often in recent weeks he had longed to do that? To comfort her. To offer her protection. To feel her sweet body against his.

But his relatively new, carefully nurtured sense of honor would not let him. Even had she not been the wife of his only friend, he would not have done it. Not even if he thought that she would have someone like him. His own existence remained too precarious. He must be careful.

This afternoon the children sat primly across from them in the carriage, dry-eyed but tense. Diana had dressed them in their best—Selena in a simple white dress and Bytham in short britches and jacket. Vincent wished they would smile. How did one play with children and make them laugh as he had seen Wyn do?

Vincent had no idea. His father had taken him fishing from time to time and taught him to ride and hunt and other manly arts, but he had never been one to play. Perhaps the burden of so many children lost, so babies buried, had taken the joy out of being a father for him. But he had always defended and forgiven Vincent's every misdeed.

Even when he should not have.

Especially when he should not have.

Vincent's gaze shifted to Diana. She stared out the carriage window, apparently lost in thought. At least he was able to bring her to the Litton mansion in the comfort and discretion of the Litton carriage rather than a dirty hackney. No one would think ill of his escorting her there.

Or perhaps they would. He could not put a stop to that. The ton always hungered for something to gossip about. If he and Diana did not come upon a solution to her problems soon, society would find a great deal about them to discuss.

One more thing to be careful about.

As the carriage pulled up before the stylish house, Diana dragged her gloomy thoughts away from the unprofitable channels they had followed for the last night and day. There was no benefit in going over and over the same ground until she had heard from her cousin. Perhaps he would prove to be more magnanimous than everyone expected, and the anxiety would have been for nothing. In the meantime, she would take advantage of Lady Litton's hospitality to give her attention to her children's disrupted lives.

The carriage door opened and Vincent Ingleton stepped out and turned to assist her. As she leaned forward, their gazes met. The intensity in his black eyes suddenly took her breath. Why had she never noticed… Flustered, Diana paused. He was hardly what the world would call a handsome man—too dark, too angular, too… Too what? Too predatory. That was it. Much too much the bird of prey. And he was looking at her…

How?

Before she could decide, his strong hand grasped hers and helped her to the ground. She stepped back and watched him lift the children out, aware all at once of the muscles moving under his black coat and the way the sunlight glistening off his ebony hair set colors dancing amid the shining locks.

Who was this man? This man to whom she had entrusted herself and her little ones? Abruptly, Diana realized how little she knew about Vincent Ingleton. Only that he had been Wyn's friend. That he treated her courteously.

That he had summarily taken the decisions she should be making from her.

While she was sorting through these disturbing reflections, he had picked up Bytham in one arm and offered her the other. Cautiously she took the arm and Selena's hand, and he led them up the stairs and into the entry.

"Lady Diana. Welcome."

Diana turned toward the feminine voice. Good heavens! *This* was Lord Lonsdale's stepmother? She could not be but a few years older than he was.

The lady approached and held out her hand. "I am so sorry to hear about Mr. Corby's death."

"Thank you. I cannot sufficiently express my gratitude to you for inviting us to stay." Diana accepted the extended hand and had her own patted gently.

"I only hope I may make this terrible time a bit easier for you. Do you know my husband, Lord Litton?"

Diana smiled at the gentleman who had emerged from a doorway and was presently engaged in tickling Bytham's ear. Bytham, finding himself surrounded by strangers, was overcome with a fit of shyness and hid his face against Vincent's shoulder.

Lord Litton left off the tickling and bowed. "Your servant, my lady. Who is this fine fellow and this lovely maiden?"

"My son, Bytham, my lord, and my daughter, Selena."

Selena managed a bashful curtsey, but Bytham apparently decided that good manners were beyond him at the moment. He clung tighter to Vincent.

"Oh, dear." Diana smiled ruefully. "I fear he needs a nap."

"Of course." Lord Litton patted the boy's shoulder. "He'll come about."

Diana thought she detected something wistful in his expression, and that of Lady Litton, as well, when they smiled at the children. Lady Litton gestured to a young woman standing a few feet away. "Alice will take them upstairs and get them settled."

The maid stepped forward and offered her hand to Selena, who cast a doubtful look at Diana, but took the hand. Vincent attempted to shift Bytham to the floor, but stopped when the child let out an unhappy shriek.

"It is the strange surroundings." Diana held out her arms. "Here, give him to me. I'll go with Alice."

But Bytham was having none of it. He fastened his arms around Vincent's neck and hung on for dear life.

"Bytham!" Fatigue and worry made her voice sharp. What was she to do with the little rascal? "Now, Bytham…"

Lord Litton let out a crack of laughter. "You seem to have an admirer, Vincent. One who especially admires your neckcloth."

Vincent looked down at the chubby fist clutched in the ruined folds of his starched cravat and grinned crookedly. "Obviously a man of good taste. He liked the one I wore last night, too. Never mind, Diana. I shall carry him up for his nap. But what should I do if he does not wish to nap?"

Diana lifted her hands helplessly. For some reason she just could not focus on the problem. "I—I don't… I'm sorry, my lord. I better come with you."

"Never mind." Vincent seemed to sense her exhaustion. "I will rely on my own resources. Bytham and I will settle it between us."

Diana nodded gratefully and followed Lady Litton to the drawing room.

* * *

In the end the resources Vincent relied on were a sugar cake provided by Alice and a promise of a ride in the park on a real horse. He had always found that there was nothing like bribery to achieve one's ends. Descending the stairs to the drawing room, he tried, with limited success, to straighten his neckcloth. It was coming to his attention that children were a mixed blessing.

At the door of the drawing room he encountered Diana and Helen on their way upstairs. Litton intercepted him. "They are off to discuss mourning clothes—a clear indication that you and I should repair to my club."

His club? His lordship had never before invited Vincent anywhere, let alone to a public place. Of course, Vincent had never given him much opportunity. What might this portend? "Thank you, my lord, but after my recent engagement with Corby's heir, I fear I'm not fit to be seen abroad."

Litton made short work of the objection. "Never mind that. It will only take a few minutes to put you to rights. You may borrow one of my stocks."

Considerably astonished by this magnanimous offer, Vincent made the necessary restorations and the two of them strolled off in the direction of St. James Street. More than a little wary, Vincent responded politely to the commonplace conversation initiated by his stepfather and wondered about the real purpose of the overture.

As they turned into the busier streets, the crowds thickened, forcing them to slow their steps. A man wearing a shabby brown coat and boots made a misstep as he approached Vincent and lurched into him. "I say! Sorry, guv'nor."

Vincent regained his balance and the man tipped his hat and continued down the street without looking back. Vincent made a grab for his pocket.

"Purse still with you?" Litton stopped and followed the man with his gaze. "Shall we give chase?"

"No." Vincent patted all his pockets. "I seem to have everything."

"Amazing. Of course, had he taken your coin, he would have passed it to a confederate by now."

"Undoubtedly."

They walked on in silence for a few more steps before Litton cleared his throat. "I cannot help but wonder, Vincent…"

Ah. The real purpose of this jaunt at last. "Sir?"

"You were close friends with Corby since you came down from Oxford, were you not?"

"Yes, sir." No need saying more than necessary.

"I have heard some talk about him—talk unbecoming his position at the Foreign Office." Litton glanced at Vincent, his eyes narrowed.

"Oh?"

"Come now, Vincent. You are bound to have heard it, too. Did Corby support the return of Bonaparte to the throne of France?" Litton stopped walking and turned to look at Vincent.

"He never said as much to me," Vincent replied with complete truth and no hesitation.

Unfortunately, Adam Barbon was a difficult man to deceive. He gazed at Vincent from under lowered brows. "Is that so?"

"Yes, sir."

After a moment Litton's expression cleared and he started walking again. Several steps later he glanced at Vincent. "I suppose this is none of my affair. What the devil am I to you? A stepfather by marriage or some such cockamamie thing?"

Vincent shrugged. "I haven't the slightest notion."

"Nor do I, but Helen and Charles and I—such as we are—are all the family you have. I have been a bit concerned that you may have involved yourself in that business. No, no…" Litton held up a restraining hand as Vincent opened his mouth. "You needn't answer. I don't wish to trap you into an admission—nor necessitate a lie. It is just that…well, we are not unaware of the changes you have made. We would hate to see anything happen to you such as happened to Corby."

Indeed? They considered themselves his family? Had followed the changes in him? He didn't know they had noticed. Vincent did not know what to make of that. "I… Thank you. I appreciate your thought. However, I assure you that I am no supporter of Bonaparte. On the contrary. I very much wish to see him remain on Elba. Or much farther afield than that."

Once again what he said was completely true.

As they stepped up to the door of Litton's club, he slipped his hand into his pocket, just to be sure.

The crinkle of folded paper assured him that the note that had been passed to him was still there.

Chapter Three

Diana sat before the window while she combed her damp hair and wondered what to do until bedtime. Already the small wisps around her face had dried to their silver-gold hue, but it would take the thick, waist-length mass an hour more to dry so that she could braid it for bed. For the first time in years she had had a real bath in a real tub—one for which she had not carried up the water nor carried it away nor set up the screen. In the rooms she shared with Wyn, she had nowhere to wash but the crowded kitchen.

She must beware of becoming too accustomed to such luxury. She had no idea how long her stay here would last, nor what would follow it. But for now she would revel in the fact that her children were tucked safely away between clean sheets in the care of a nursemaid, and that a clean bed awaited her clean body.

Somehow Lady Litton—no, not Lady Litton. She had asked Diana to call her Helen. Somehow *Helen* had found the mourning clothes she had worn after Vincent's father had died, presenting them with the diplomatic comment that it would be a waste to order more for Diana. Only minor adjustments had been required for Diana to use them. Most of them were black, of course, but still much finer and more stylish than what she had been wearing.

She looked well enough in black—not that anyone would be seeing her. Except perhaps the Earl of Lonsdale. Diana flushed at the thought. Now why should she think of Vincent Ingleton in that context? True, he was being very kind to her, but only as a friend of Wyn's.

Wasn't he?

Surely what she had seen in his eyes did not mean…

He had never seen her except in stained, worn-out clothes, exhausted with caring for her children in the face of daunting poverty. Try as she might, it had become impossible to keep up appearances. She was far too thin. So worn-looking. How could he possibly want her?

Before she could come to any conclusion on the matter, a light tap sounded at the door. She called, "Come in," and one of Helen's maids put her head through the door.

"I have a note for you, my lady. A boy brought it 'round to the kitchen a short while ago."

Diana's heart went cold. Not another note! How did he know where she was? What did the wretch want? What could he *possibly* want? She was only too afraid that she knew. Her hand trembled as she took the paper, but she managed an automatic *thank you* as the maid curtseyed and took herself off. Carefully, Diana broke the seal and held the letter nearer to the candle.

My dearest Lady Diana—
My condolences on the loss of your husband. A great tragedy for you, I'm sure. But I see that you have been taken under the aegis of Lord Lonsdale. How fortunate for you.

And for me. I believe the time draws near that you may repay me for the little gifts I have provided. And

*of course, for keeping my knowledge to myself. That
has become even more important now, has it not? So
difficult for Selena and Bytham to lose both their father and their mother. Who knows what their future
might become?*

*I believe your, ah—association?—with Lord Lons-
dale will provide just the opportunity I have been
seeking. As always, I expect you to maintain your silence on these matters as I have maintained mine.
I'm sure you understand the necessity.*

*Until then, I remain unwaveringly yours—
Deimos
P.S.—I have included no gift, as it is obvious your
every need is being provided.*

Diana crumpled the note and dropped her face into her
hands. Damn him. Damn him! Always a threat in every sentence—and now also innuendo. As though she and Vincent… But then, Deimos, whoever he might be, had always
made her feel like a whore. She very much feared he intended to use his gifts to make her one. Had she but known
who he was, she might have flung the money back at him,
even if it meant starving. But that was fantasy. She could
not let her children starve.

And she did not know who he was.

Deimos. The Greek god of fear. He had chosen his so-
briquet well. The fear of what he knew ate at her every second of every day. Fear for herself. Fear for her children.

How dare he use their names!

How *dare* he sully their sweet innocence with his poi-
sonous pen. If ever she discovered his identity…

Perhaps she was capable of killing.

The man in the shabby brown coat tipped his chair back
against the wall and took a long pull from his tankard of

ale while Vincent sketched circles in the cheap liquor spilled on the greasy table. "Nay, my lord. I ain't found out who done it yet, but it wasn't none of our lads. Wouldn't be no reason for us to do it. Too easy to get information from him."

Vincent nodded glumly. "He talked of everything he knew. Try as I might, I could not shut him up."

"Aye. It was his mouth what killed him, I'll warrant. Might even have been the culls at the Foreign Office."

Vincent considered the realities of the intelligence trade. "That's possible. But the whole debacle is their doing. They should never have exiled Bonaparte to Elba in the first place. Much too close to France. Too easy for him to escape—and escape he will, soon or late."

"He will if Lord Holland and his set have their way, such a fine fellow *they* think him to be." Vincent's companion rocked his chair to the floor with a snarl. "But there are those of us who remember what that bastard cost us, first and last." He spit on the floor.

"We shall confound them. He must be contained." Vincent stood. "I've several more people to talk to tonight. I'll be around the hells. You can find me if you have more to report."

His companion nodded and Vincent put on his hat and walked to the door. Standing in the portal, he let his gaze drift casually up the street and then down. He saw no one but the usual crowd that patronized the cheap taverns along the way, but still, he stepped out cautiously. He had not gone half a block when a hackney rumbled around the corner toward him.

Instinct took over and, without thinking, Vincent dropped to the dirty cobbles. The knife sailed over his head and buried itself in the wall of the building behind him. Chips of plaster rained down on him. The driver whipped up the horses and the conveyance disappeared down the street. Vincent rose, brushing dirt off his clothes.

Damn! That was close.

At last Wynmond Corby was in the ground and, Diana prayed, at peace. Vincent Ingleton had taken care of the obsequies and his stepmother had taken care of her. All of Wyn's friends had paid their respects, to him and to her, and gone on their way. Now Diana could only wonder at the huge void within her, empty of any emotion at all with respect to Wyn.

Its very absence made her heart ache. When had she stopped loving him? When had she sustained that loss without even knowing it? She could only hope that in the few days' respite while waiting to hear from her father's cousin, a modicum of peace would also find *her*.

Bytham had been clamoring for a trip to the park since Vincent had promised it to him, but the funeral had intervened. Alice offered her services, but Diana had cared for the children herself for many years. She just could not put them in the hands of someone else.

They were all she had in the world.

Society decreed that she should remain in seclusion, mourning her loss, but that seemed redundant. She had long ago mourned the loss of the man she thought she had married—the laughing, golden-haired boy, the shining young man of promise. Now she just wished to learn what her life was to be. And to feel a few days of freedom lest she learn that it would be a new sort of prison.

Helen did not chide her when she donned a black pelisse and gloves. Suitable clothes for the children had also appeared as if by magic. Where Helen had found those, Diana had no idea, but she told herself that she did not have too much pride to accept used clothes.

She lied.

She *did* have too much pride. She just had little choice.

She was a Bytham of Bytham House, the daughter of an earl, and by God, she would hold her head up, come what may. She hated seeing her babies swathed in someone else's black, their brightness dimmed, but she would not forget who they were. Who *she* was.

The three of them set out for the park afoot, enjoying the easy walk in the summer sunshine. As they strolled through the patterns of shade along the park walks, Selena picked dandelions out of the grass and Bytham tugged on Diana's arm.

"Look, Mama, a butterfly. Look, Mama, a bee. Look, Mama…" Everything was wonderful to him. Before, they had lived too far away to come to the park often, the price of a hackney too dear. Diana found herself laughing with him. How long had it been since she'd laughed? Had taken time to feel the breeze on her face?

When they came to a bench beside a green lawn, Diana released her son's hand and sat. "You may play here for a while, Bytham, but do not go far from Mama. Selena, stay close by."

The automatic chorus of, "Yes, Mama," greeted these instructions and the children raced off onto the lawn. Selena soon abandoned her flowers in favor of helping her little brother chase the fleet of butterflies. She was such a lively child. Someday she would have to learn the manners of a demure young miss, but Diana hoped to put that off as long as possible. Why trammel such a free spirit?

After several minutes she saw that the children had moved across the grass and were nearing one of the carriage roads. She stood and strolled after them. "Selena, come back now. Bring your brother with you."

"Yes, Mama." Selena caught Bytham's hand, but he snatched it away from her. "*Come, Bytham.*"

"No! I want the yellow one. *I* can catch it!" He raced off after his latest quarry, Selena in hot pursuit.

"Bytham!" Diana looked at the road and saw a dark, closed carriage approaching. She started toward them, almost running. "Come back."

The coach was getting nearer and Diana felt a strange sense of panic. That was not the kind of carriage that one used for the park. Perhaps it was just passing through, but… She lifted her skirts and ran in good earnest. "Bytham! Obey Mama at once!"

Hearing the urgency in her voice, Bytham stopped uncertainly and looked in her direction. The carriage pulled to a stop opposite them. The door opened and two rough-looking men got out. Bytham, who had been confronted with far too many strangers for his comfort of late, ran toward Diana. The men started toward the children.

"Selena, run!"

Selena ran, dragging Bytham along with her. Fear put wings to Diana's feet, but she could see that the men would likely reach her children before she did. *Oh, God. Help.* She must have help. She began to scream.

At that moment she heard the hoofbeats of a horse in full career. Glancing up, she beheld Vincent Ingleton astride a sleek black horse, bearing down on them at a dead run.

"Vincent! Vincent!" Diana reached Selena and Bytham at the same time as the men from the coach. She tried to scoop both children into her arms, but one of the ruffians shoved her away. She tripped over the train of her skirt and sprawled backward on the ground.

"Vincent!"

Diana came to her hands and knees, struggling with the encumbering fabric. As one of the men grasped Selena, Diana abandoned the attempt to rise and flung herself at his ankle. He stumbled and, turning, kicked her grasping hands. She fell to the ground again, this time on her face. He picked up a shrieking Selena and ran for the coach. By now the other man had seized Bytham. Diana finally made it to her feet and ran after them. Dear heaven! She would never catch them.

And then Vincent came thundering down on them like a stooping hawk. The man holding Selena dropped her unceremoniously and sprinted for the coach. Bytham's captor, better supplied with determination, tucked the kicking boy under one arm and followed. Vincent turned his mount to intercept him.

Diana heard the rattle of wheels and another set of hooves coming toward herself and Selena. She pushed the child behind her and turned defiantly, only to see Justinian Sudbury in a whiskey pulled by a sturdy chestnut, cutting across the lawn, also in pursuit of the kidnappers.

"Bytham, Bytham." The whisper came out on a sob. They were taking him away! Diana knelt and locked her arms around Selena. They would have to kill her to get her daughter!

As she watched, the men angled away from Vincent and Sudbury, and the coach pulled forward to meet them. The man without a burden dived into the coach, the one carrying Bytham running not far behind.

For a heart-stopping second, Diana thought her son would be thrust into the coach, but as she watched, Sudbury pulled his tiny open vehicle into the road to block the way. The driver of the coach hauled on the reins and dragged his pair around in the other direction. Vincent swooped in and, leaning precariously from the saddle as he passed, plucked the boy out of his captor's arms.

Vincent swung his riding crop with all his strength. The kidnapper howled and sprawled on the ground. Vincent turned his horse and started back. The man scrambled to his feet and made a desperate bid for the coach, but Vincent's mount quickly closed the distance. Just as his fingers were reaching for the would-be abductor's collar, an arm clothed in blue superfine emerged from the window of the coach with something in its hand.

A pistol!

Vincent jerked the reins sharply and his black reared in protest while Vincent leaned his body across Bytham's. A shot rang out. The running kidnapper went down, rolling heels over head. The arm withdrew into the coach and the vehicle thundered off around a curve and out of sight.

For a moment Sudbury seemed about to give chase, but pulled in his horse as Vincent drew up beside him.

"Let them go." Vincent settled the weeping child in front of him on the saddle and patted his shoulder awkwardly. "I need you to help me get Diana and the children home."

"Bytham!" Diana's all but hysterical voice sounded at his stirrup. Vincent looked down to see her clutching Selena with one hand and reaching for her son with the other. The boy leaned down and Vincent lowered him by one arm to his mother. She fell to her knees and clasped her children to her, all three of them sobbing.

Vincent drew the horse pistol from his saddle and dismounted. Standing over them, he called to Sudbury, "May I make use of the whiskey?"

"Certainly. May have to squeeze. Nice bit of riding, Lonsdale." Sudbury moved his small carriage nearer. "What the devil was that all about?"

"I wish I knew." Vincent scowled in the direction the escaping coach had taken. "Lady Diana, you and Selena need…" He paused when he realized she had not moved. "My lady?" When he still received no response, he went down on one knee beside her. "Diana?"

At last she lifted her head and looked in his direction, her eyes glazed with shock and a large area of skin scraped from her cheek. "My lord?"

Fury welled up in Vincent. They had hurt her. They had marred that perfect face. Let him but get his hands on them… But now he must get her safely away. Vincent clenched his teeth and forced his anger down. "Can you stand?"

She nodded, but did not get up. Placing an arm around her, he stood, bringing her with him. Selena and Bytham clung to her, their heads buried in her skirt. He took the boy into his own arms and nudged Diana toward the carriage. "Can you and Selena climb in?"

"I—I…" The vague expression in her eyes cleared. "Yes. Of course." Never letting go of the girl, she managed with Sudbury's help to get them both into the whiskey. Vincent mounted again before handing Bytham down to her.

It would not do to be on foot if his supposed ally proved false. He barely knew Justinian Sudbury. For all Vincent could say, the man might have been on the scene to supervise the abduction, never expecting help to appear. In fact, when Sudbury first came bowling across the lawn, Vincent had feared he intended to reinforce the kidnappers.

Damn! He did not want Diana and the children in the man's carriage. But he could not carry all four of them on his horse.

He *could* ride behind with a pistol discreetly trained on the back of Sudbury's head.

And he did.

Diana's knees would scarcely hold her. Ever since she had disembarked from Justinian's carriage at the Litton residence, she had been shaking. No matter how hard she tried to control it, she shook. And she would *not* let the children out of her sight. When Alice offered to take them upstairs, Diana's heart lurched into her throat.

So they had all assembled in Helen's elegant drawing room where she had ordered restorative viands to be served. The children had been indulged with hot chocolate and cakes, and Diana indulged herself with a large glass of sherry. Exhausted, Selena leaned against her where they sat on the sofa, but Bytham insisted on occupying Vincent's lap.

His lordship appeared resigned to the destruction of yet another stylishly tied neckcloth and was keeping her son supplied with sandwiches from a plate on a table by their chair. Between the two of them, they had made impressive inroads on Helen's supplies. Cream cheese and jelly smeared her son's face, and a liberal amount of it had transferred itself to the starched cravat.

Diana looked at him appreciatively. "Thank God you happened to be in the park. I cannot imagine what I would have done had you not arrived so fortuitously. I am once again more indebted to you than I can ever repay."

Diana caught a whiff of horseradish as Vincent shook his head and selected a sandwich of thinly sliced roast beef. "Not at all. I am happy that I was there, but that was not an accident. I had promised this ambitious gentleman here that he might have a ride on Blackhawk if he would be good and nap. I did not wish to fail in my word, so when I learned that you had gone to the park, I went in search of you."

"Still, I am very grateful." Diana accepted a second glassful of the sweet, amber wine from Lord Litton. What a luxury to have all she wished, even if her head did swim a bit.

Litton topped off Vincent's glass and returned to his seat. He glanced speculatively at his stepson. "The question is, who were those people? Unlikely that it is a kidnapping for ransom. There must be some other motive."

Diana emitted an unladylike snort. "I cannot imagine who would be so poorly informed as to believe I could pay ransom."

Vincent's dark gaze bored into her. "Then what?"

"I…I have no idea." Oh, dear heaven! Could this be the work of her unidentified tormentor? But why would Deimos take the children? He already held the most terrifying threat against her. Still, she dared tell them nothing about *him*.

At that moment Feetham appeared at the drawing room door and addressed Helen. "Lord St. Edmunds, my lady."

Vincent, narrowly preventing Bytham from wiping his hands on his stock again, set the boy down and came to his feet. Lord Litton followed suit. St. Edmunds hurried into the room on the heels of the butler. Vincent scowled. The lord wore a blue coat. But then, so did half the gentlemen of London.

St. Edmunds sketched a hasty bow in Helen's direction and turned to Diana. "Lady Diana, are you well? Are the children unhurt? I just heard the most appalling tale."

Diana could not like the man, no matter his show of concern. Still, she strove to speak politely. "Thank you, my lord. We had a very narrow escape. Had it not been for the intervention of Lord Lonsdale and Mr. Sudbury, my children would have been taken from me."

"Terrible. Terrible." St. Edmunds pulled a handkerchief from his pocket and wiped his brow. "I could not believe my ears."

"And just where did *you* hear of the matter?" Vincent's eyebrows lowered and his voice was cold.

"At White's, just this quarter-hour ago. I came at once." St. Edmunds stuffed the handkerchief back into his pocket. "I'm sure the episode is all over London by now."

"No doubt." Lord Litton offered the newcomer a chair and provided him with a glass of sherry. "We were just discussing the matter. Clearly a case of ransom."

At that, Vincent's eyebrows rose as high as they had been low a moment before. He did not stop glaring at St. Edmunds, but he did resume his chair. When Bytham would have climbed back into his lap, Vincent stopped him with a look and a gesture that sent him back to Diana. He then glanced speculatively at Litton.

So did Diana.

At his comment, St. Edmunds's brow puckered. "Ransom? Do you think so? I would have thought…" He glanced at Diana and apparently decided on diplomacy. "Well, I suppose there is no saying."

How should she respond? Clearly, Vincent Ingleton harbored hostility toward St. Edmunds. And was that suspicion in his black eyes? Diana settled for shrugging. "*I* could not say, my lord. I am quite baffled."

"You should never have been allowed to go abroad without a footman." St. Edmunds returned Vincent's glare pointedly. "I trust you will not do so again."

"She will not."

At the vehemence in his tone, Diana gave Vincent a startled glance. Bristling for a heartbeat, she was on the verge of telling both their lordships that she would make her own decisions just as she always had, thank you very much. But could she, in truth? She feared the forces gathering around her might be beyond her ability to withstand.

Vincent had thought the man would never leave. St. Edmunds had prated on about the terrors of the city, the insanity of the royalty and the incompetence of the Foreign Office. Not that Vincent didn't agree with him on all counts. But he did not like the man, and he did not trust him any further than he could heave his very solid body.

In the end he had Litton's smooth manner to thank for ridding them of the loquacious lord. Thank the gods. Vincent had found himself ready to end the interview with a sharp shove down the stairs. But then, social skill had never been one of his strong suits.

No doubt the reason he had just buried his last friend.

"Well, now." Litton returned from seeing St. Edmunds to the door and resumed his seat. "Where were we?"

Vincent allowed himself a wry smile. "Contrary to more recent comments, I believe we were just saying that this attempt on the children was *not* done for ransom." Bytham, evidently sensing the tension in the room lift, climbed down from the sofa and wriggled his way up onto Vincent's knee again. Vincent let him come. He was growing to like the troublesome little sprat. But he had not wished to be encumbered by a child while St. Edmunds was in the room. The man made him wary.

Litton returned the grin, then sobered. "No, it cannot be that. But I think Lady Diana is safer if no one has reason to think otherwise. Clearly, this is the work of desperate men. Otherwise they would not have killed one of their own."

A tense silence filled the room.

Vincent drew in a long breath and it out slowly. "True." He turned his gaze to Diana. "Can you truly think of no reason for this?"

She hesitated a heartbeat too long. "I... No. It does not make sense."

"Did Wyn ever talk to you of his doings at the Foreign Office?"

"Sometimes." Her brow creased in thought. "Do you think this may have something to do with the business he did for them?"

"Do you?" Vincent waited.

She sat as if lost in thought for a minute, then raised her gaze to his. "I cannot think what."

Litton cleared his throat. "Did your husband ever mention Bonaparte? Anything about his exile?"

"He may have. I…we…" Her cheeks turned pink. "He was very busy. I did not see much of him."

Had she wished to? Vincent knew Wyn spent little time at home. Had Diana waited alone, longing for his company? Had she loved him that much? Or had his neglect taken its toll on her feelings? He hoped it had. It would make things easier for her.

That is, easier if he could protect her from her husband's enemies. She must know something that threatened them—something that Wyn had told her. Could she truly not know what?

His stepfather gave him a penetrating look. "Well, someone clearly considers Lady Diana to be a danger to them. This must be an attempt to control her. They will not stop with one attempt. What will you do now?"

Vincent glanced across the room at Diana. "I will take her away."

She sat up, suddenly straighter. "What? What do you mean?"

"You cannot stay in London. That should be evident. I will take you elsewhere."

Alarm filled her face. "But where can I go?"

"Yorkshire, I think."

"Good." Litton nodded. "There you have a choice— You can go to Inglewood or you are welcome to go to Three Oaks."

"Or to Wulfdale," Helen spoke up. "Charles and Catherine would be willing to help."

Diana looked from one to the other, puzzled and sounding on the verge of panic. "Where is Inglewood? Who are Charles and Catherine?"

"My brother and his wife. They live in the area of Inglewood, which is the Lonsdale estate," Helen replied. "Charles and Adam are best of friends."

But Vincent knew where he would go. He would go to his own place, his own stronghold. There he would keep her safe. He glanced down at the little boy dozing on his lap. "Diana, the children are exhausted and so are you. Come, I'll carry Bytham up. We will discuss our plans on the way."

"I'll send Throckmorton to keep watch over them so that you will rest." Litton stood as Diana rose reluctantly. "You will not worry with *him* on duty."

"Thank you. You have been so kind." Diana's breath caught and she quickly covered her mouth with one hand, tears visible in her lashes.

Helen smiled. "Our pleasure, dear. Now do go up and rest."

Vincent guided Diana out of the room and up the stairs to the nursery door. "We will leave late tonight, as secretly as possible. I have…business I must attend to first. You need to pack everything we can carry in one traveling coach. I don't know how long we will be gone."

She paused outside the nursery door. "I suppose we must go. I cannot risk the children again."

"No. Whoever did this has shown that they do not scruple to take a life. Since they failed to take your children hostage, their next attempt may be to kill you."

He watched the blood drain out of her face as she tried to answer. "If only I understood…"

He studied her expression. "Are you sure you do not?"

Her gaze fell to her hands and she shook her head. Vincent reached out and took her chin between his thumb and finger, lifting her face to study it for the truth. Instead the impulse to kiss her almost overpowered him. He hastily turned her face to the light. The scraped place on her cheek was beginning to bruise, as well.

Someone would die for that.

Chapter Four

As she stumbled along the narrow, odoriferous alley, a chilly breeze brushed against Diana's cheek, eliciting a small shudder. She started as somewhere in one of the mews a dog barked, only to be silenced by a sharp command. The setting moon shed but faint light over the way, and Diana, encumbered by Bytham's limp form in her arms, tripped over a loose cobble.

Lord Litton's firm hand on her elbow steadied her and she glanced at Selena, half asleep in his arms. In spite of his burden, his lordship moved through the night with a watchful eye, followed closely by the exceedingly large footman called Throckmorton.

Diana viewed this addition to the party with mixed feelings. The presence of a veritable giant with the battered features of a former pugilist might prove comforting—if she could believe in his loyalty. Loyalty to *her*. But could she? At this point her enemies might be anyone. She had been forced to put her faith in Vincent Ingleton and Lord and Lady Litton, but were they truly her friends? They had been so kind, she could hardly think otherwise, but now… In the night, in the dark of the alley, she couldn't be sure of anything.

Where were his lordship and his burly henchman taking her?

She had not seen Vincent since they had parted at the nursery door. Her baggage had been taken away hours earlier in Litton's coach, and he assured her that they were going to meet Vincent.

But why were they proceeding in this clandestine fashion?

For that matter, was she wise to cast her whole dependence on Vincent as she had been doing? She had hardly proved herself a good judge of character in the past, she thought wryly. Diana had never quite understood Lonsdale's motives in removing her from her home so precipitately. She began to wish herself back in the safety of the Litton town house—or even her own former quarters.

She wanted to seize her children and bolt.

But that represented no more safety than her present destination.

Whatever it might be.

No, for now she must trust, warily perhaps, but trust in someone. Not far ahead, tucked up against the mews, the outline of a dark coach loaded with trunks emerged from the gloom. The coachman in his powdered wig and top hat slumped on the box as if dozing. At the sound of their approach he sat up and peered down at them. Lord Litton opened the door and lifted Selena onto the seat. She murmured a drowsy protest before curling up and again sinking into slumber. He then took Bytham from Diana so that she could enter. For a moment she hesitated, afraid to let the children be separated, even for a moment.

Apparently sensing her uncertainty, he stepped in front of her and placed the boy on the other seat, then turned to help her, patting her gently on the shoulder. "Do not be afraid, my lady. All will be well."

Diana nodded mutely and settled herself beside Selena. She felt the carriage rock as Throckmorton climbed onto the box and the lamps flickered into light. A moment later the coachman startled her by climbing inside. Before she could question this unorthodox procedure, he shrugged out of his greatcoat and tossed his wig aside.

"Vincent!"

He grinned his crooked grin. "Just so."

"But why this masquerade?"

"For your safety. And mine. There are reasons you needn't…" He glanced out the window as the coach lurched forward. "I don't want us to be followed."

The carriage rounded a corner and set off at a brisk trot. "Is Throckmorton driving? He is coming with us?"

"Aye." A crease formed between his black brows. "It seems so. Litton insisted I bring him. Throckmorton has been in his employ for several years. Litton says he is reliable and very…useful."

"But you do not sound as though you are pleased."

"I don't know him well enough."

"Do you not trust him?"

He gave her an appraising look and replied gravely, "I don't trust anyone."

In fact, Vincent had no real reason *not* to trust the redoubtable Throckmorton. He just found it healthier to be wary of all comers. But he had to admit that the reinforcement represented by the footman might prove invaluable if it came to a fight.

He only wished he could completely trust *Diana*.

She was obviously holding something back whenever he asked about possible enemies. But what? He sat opposite her in the coach with the boy sleeping beside him on the seat. Diana leaned wearily in the corner with Selena's head on her lap. Vincent hated the dark bruise on her cheek. In a few hours he would see that she had a chance to rest.

She sighed and looked at him. "Where are we going, my lord?"

"To Inglewood, eventually, but I do not want to go directly. I'm sure that whoever is harrying you will look for us there sooner or later, but I hope to delay their finding us until I am ready for them. It will be easier to protect you there than it is in London—and much easier than to do so on the road. When they find us, we will know who they are."

Diana pressed a closed hand against her mouth. "Why, Vincent? Why are they doing this? Why would anyone take my children?"

"I am not perfectly sure, but, as Litton said, it must be that they desire a way of controlling *you*." He studied her expression intently. "What do you know, Diana? And whom would it harm?"

"I don't *know!*" Her voice rose on a hint of impending panic. "It must be something someone thinks Wyn told me, but we did not spend much time together. He was always very…busy."

Vincent nodded. Certainly her husband had neglected her. But that did not mean the garrulous rascal never talked to her. "He is bound to have said something. Some reference to some group of people perhaps?"

She stared thoughtfully out the window for several heartbeats. "I cannot think… Well, yes. He once or twice said something about 'St. Edmunds's people,' as though I would know who he meant, but I don't. Except for his lordship, of course."

"Did he ever mention Lord or Lady Holland?"

"Well, yes. We used to be invited to their home, and Wyn would go. I—I had stopped going into society. I could not afford…" He could not see the embarrassed flush in the dark, but he could hear it in her voice. "Why are you asking about them?"

"They are admirers of Bonaparte. There are some English folk who would like to see him replace the Bourbon king."

Diana shook her head. "Who replaced *him* only months ago? Can no one ever be satisfied? How many English lives were lost fighting him?"

"Far too many, and if any attempt to restore him is made, there will be many, many more."

Diana glanced down at her daughter and smoothed the pale hair spread across her lap. "I would that my children might grow up in a peaceful world. I cannot bear the thought that one day Bytham might have to go as a soldier."

"If I have anything to say in the matter, at least he will not have to fight Bonaparte." Vincent leaned forward and peered out the window into the dark. "I need to be able to see. Excuse me."

Before she could ask him questions he wished to avoid, he pounded on the roof of the carriage. It came to a jolting halt and he donned his wig and coat and got out and climbed onto the box with Throckmorton. At least here he would not be so painfully aware of her presence as in the close confines of the carriage. Would not have to inhale her subtle fragrance. Not have to fight the impulse to touch her, to take her in his arms and devour her soft mouth.

They rumbled along at the best speed they could in the darkness for several hours. Vincent was obliged to look sharp to make out landmarks in the gloom. At last he signaled Throckmorton to pull up.

"How far are we from the Ashwell fork, do you think?" he asked of his new bodyguard.

"I dunno, me lord. It's been dunnamany years since I come this way." The big man shoved his white wig aside to scratch his brown-haired pate. "But we ain't come to the Ivel bridge yet. We can turn just past that, but I'm thinking Ashwell's out of our way if you purpose going to Yorkshire."

"We'll get to Yorkshire." Vincent nodded. "Continue."

Throckmorton gave the horses the office to start, and a mile or two later the wheels clattered across the bridge. Another quarter hour brought the fork into view.

"Pull up." Vincent waited until the horses slowed and took the reins from Throckmorton. "Go take a look at that grove to our left. See if there is room to get the carriage out of sight."

"Aye, sir." The big man climbed down and ambled cautiously into the trees. After several minutes he returned. "It'll be tight, me lord, but I think we can make her fit. Ain't no one going to see us in this light." They pulled the coach into the trees, turned it so that it could be driven straight out, and doused the lamps.

And then they sat.

And they waited.

The night wind murmured in the trees and somewhere an abbreviated screech and a triumphant "Who-hoo!" announced that a tiny life had ended as an owl's dinner. Only the faintest starlight illuminated the road. Vincent sat patiently. They would come. He need only await them. And then, between one breath and the next, in the distance hoofbeats sounded. Quickly he went to the horses' heads to keep them quiet.

Minutes later a coach and four barreled past them. It did not even slow at the fork, but continued up the main pike, away from Ashwell. When the sounds of its passage died, Vincent climbed back up and nodded at Throckmorton.

"There's an inn at Ashwell. We'll put up there."

Throckmorton snapped his whip and they headed down the smaller lane.

They pulled into the inn yard shortly before dawn sent her delicate fingers of color across the sky. Stiff from inactivity and sore from yesterday's tussle with the kidnappers, Diana all but fell out of the coach into Vincent's arms. He caught her and righted her, still holding her close and gazing into her face with disconcerting intensity.

"Can you stand?" He kept a cautious hand on her elbow as she backed away from him, flustered by his scrutiny.

Diana took a brace of steps, first one way and then the other. "Yes, I believe so. I was just made a bit awkward by the inactivity."

"And fatigue, I don't doubt. But you can rest soon."

From inside the coach, the children grumbled irritably at being disturbed. Diana smiled. "Alas, my lord, your inexperience with small children is evident. They tend to be early risers, and these two have been asleep all night."

"That is why inns keep maids. We will make use of them." Vincent lifted a groggy Selena out and set her on her feet, then reached back for Bytham.

"But—"

He cut off Diana's protest at the outset. "Either Throckmorton or I will keep watch. We intend to take turns sleeping." He gave her another appraising stare. "You cannot watch them day in, day out, Diana."

"I know." Suddenly the black well of exhaustion and fear threatened to swallow her. "I… I…" She gave it up. "Thank you, my lord."

They entered the inn to find its inhabitants already astir. The short, portly landlord and his tall, sturdy wife came bustling to meet them, only to stop short when they saw Vincent. The wife turned in her tracks and, signaling to a wide-eyed maid who had emerged from the kitchen, disappeared with the girl into the rear of the inn. The landlord held his ground, but eyed Vincent and Throckmorton warily.

"Good morning, Biggleswade. I trust I find you well?" Vincent nodded politely.

"Ah…" The landlord made his bow, one eye on Vincent and one on Diana. "Yes, m'lord. I enjoy tolerable health. And your lordship?"

"Very well, thank you. I believe it has been several years since I stayed here."

Biggleswade's expression indicated that it might suit him better for it to be a bit longer yet, but he answered courteously enough. "How may I serve your lordship today?"

"As you can see, we have been traveling all night. We require a parlor and adjoining rooms for the lady and the children and another room for me close by. Can you oblige me?"

"I… Yes, m'lord. We have the rooms." He cast a suspicious stare at Throckmorton's battered face. "And your…uh…?"

"He and I will make use of the same room." Vincent turned to Diana. "Would you like a tray brought to your room?" Without waiting for her nod he went on, "And we will need a maid to care for the children while the lady sleeps."

"Aye, m'lord." The landlord glanced around for his wife. Finding that she had decamped, he bowed and started to follow.

"And, Biggleswade…" Vincent spoke softly, but the man spun around with a start. "I would prefer that no questions be answered about our sojourn here, should anyone ask."

"Oh! Oh…aye, sir. Of course."

A few moments later Mrs. Biggleswade reappeared and, with a surly look at Vincent, invited Diana up the stairs. Now what was this all about? Diana glanced at Vincent but his somber countenance revealed nothing. She followed the woman up to an adequately furnished parlor and collapsed into a chintz-covered sofa.

By now the children were wide awake and wanting to explore their new surroundings. As she considered the futility of sending them back to bed, a light tap sounded at the door and a girl appeared bearing a tray with tea, hot bread and butter and milk. It smelled heavenly. Diana had not realized how hungry she had become. Anxiety had left her hardly able to eat a bite the evening before.

The children quickly converged on the table as the young woman set down the tray, and the maid and the inn-keeper's wife helped them into chairs. Diana took her own place gratefully and, in a very short time, served by the ladies of the inn, they emptied the plates.

As she finished her second cup of tea, another tap sounded on the door and Vincent strolled into the parlor. His rumpled black locks lacked their usual neatness and a dark shadow covered his cheeks and chin. He had discarded his neckcloth and coat, but in spite of his disheveled appearance, Diana's breath caught in her throat.

Or perhaps because of it. The loosened collar showed the sculptured lines of his throat, and his rolled sleeves revealed his forearms lined with veins across the ridges of muscle. How had she never noticed in months past that he was an attractive man? Had she been that caught up in her own problems?

Apparently so.

The innkeeper's wife scowled, folded her arms across her ample bosom and stepped in front of the young maid, who eyed Vincent warily. He ignored her and addressed Diana. "Are you ready to rest? If this young lady—" he nodded at the maid "—will take the children for a walk, I will accompany them."

The landlady bristled. "Abby has plenty of work to do and don't need to be traipsing off with *you*. If you need help, I'll watch the little ones."

Vincent bowed gravely. "Thank you, Mrs. Biggleswade. I would appreciate your time."

Mrs. Biggleswade nodded, the suspicion in her eyes increasing as she glared at Diana's injured cheek. Selena and Bytham jumped down from their chairs and—as soon as Diana had reminded them—expressed thanks for the breakfast. They followed Vincent and Mrs. Biggleswade out of the room, Diana's anxious gaze trailing after them.

Surely they would be safe with Vincent. Hadn't he, himself, stopped the kidnapping? Surely that meant... But Diana knew she didn't entirely believe in his intentions. He had said that her enemies wished to take control of her—but was that not exactly what he had done? The way he looked at her at times made her wonder what he *truly* wanted of her. Still, as he had so accurately observed, she could not watch them day and night. Her eyes threatened to close even as she followed the maid into the adjoining room.

"The bed is freshly aired, m'lady. I saw to it myself." The girl went to the window and drew the drapes. "Just let me help you with your gown."

Diana turned and let the young woman unfasten her dress. She had no idea where her trunks had got to, so she climbed between the sheets in her shift, and the maid pulled the bed curtains to. Diana lay for a moment, listening as the girl closed the door and then listening harder for some sound from her children. She thought she heard Selena's merry laugh just before she plunged into oblivion.

She had no idea how long she had slept. She waked to a sliver of light and the hiss of a whisper. Opening her eyes, she discovered the source of the whisper to be none other than Mrs. Biggleswade peeking between the bed curtains. "M'lady. M'lady! Wake up. Do you need help?"

"Wh-what?" Diana sat and rubbed at her eyes, trying to dispel the cobwebs fogging her brain.

"Are you needing help?" The woman cast a hasty glance

over her shoulder. "It is all right. His lordship has gone in to sleep, and the other one went out to the privy. Abby has your little ones safe in the parlor." She reached out and quickly touched Diana's face. "Did he beat you?"

"What? Oh. Oh, no. It was not his lordship."

"We'll help you." The older woman's face wrinkled with concern. "We know *that* one from before. Cruel, he is, and wicked. Do you need help to get away from him?"

"I—I don't know."

And, to her horror, she didn't. Here she was, racing away from everything she had known with a man of whom she had only casual acquaintance. Racing from what and to what? Suddenly a sound from the doorway to the parlor caught her attention. Mrs. Biggleswade whirled, scowling defiantly.

Vincent stood there, gazing at them soberly. He didn't speak, and Diana, having no idea what to say, didn't, either. The landlady folded her arms and stood, stalwart, between him and Diana.

Diana drew a deep breath. "Thank you, Mrs. Biggleswade. I appreciate your concern, but I require no further assistance."

"Well, you just sing out if you do." The tall woman brushed by Vincent and went into the parlor.

Vincent watched her retreat with something in his eyes that Diana could not quite identify. Sadness? Certainly something of the sort. Strange. He turned back to her. "I just came to tell you that I am going to sleep for a while. Throckmorton will keep watch. If you wish to go outside, he will accompany you. I do not believe anyone will expect to find me—and therefore you—at Ashwell."

"Thank you, my lord." Diana, suddenly bethinking herself of her state of undress, pulled the covers up to her chin. "I feel quite rested now. I may go for a stroll myself."

He stood gazing at her for several moments. Then, in a perfectly even voice he said, "If you do not wish to continue, Lady Diana, we will, of course, turn back."

Silence ensued for several more moments. And Diana made her decision. "Back to what?"

He nodded. "Just so."

And with that, he turned and went back through the parlor to his room across the hall.

Vincent disciplined himself to fall asleep because he knew he must if he were to be as alert as the situation demanded. But it was not easy. Diana's answer to the landlady echoed in his mind. *Do you need help? I don't know.* She did not trust him. Which was hardly to be wondered at. He did not trust her, either. She knew *something* she would not tell.

But there was another pain in his heart. He knew all too well how he had earned Mrs. Biggleswade's enmity. He had made his peace with her husband as best he could this morning, paying for certain damages to the inn and adding a large gratuity by way of apology for his behavior on his last visit. But it would be many a day before the landlord's wife forgave his past treatment of her daughter.

Vincent wondered if he would ever forgive himself.

He had worked so hard in the last four years to overcome his richly deserved reputation—trying to correct every obligation, going into the service of his country, risking his life—but it never seemed enough. Time and time again a new set of circumstances forced him to confront it. He feared he would never live it down, never regain his self-respect. And now it had touched Diana.

And she didn't know if she needed help against him.

The image of her in the bed, thick fair hair pouring over her soft bare shoulders grew behind his closed eyelids. He had not intended to intrude—until he'd heard the stealthy conversation. Then he had stood immobile, captured by her uncertainty and the curve, just visible above the shift, at the top of her breasts.

Vincent's body began to grow hard. How could Wyn Corby have neglected such an enchanting woman? How had he missed the glowing spirit beneath the tranquil exterior? Had she been his, Vincent would have sheltered her from every hardship, protected himself and her from the forces that had left her a widow and threatened her still. If he made her his own...

But he could not do that now. He was in too deep.

He was as much threat to her as Wyn had been.

He woke as the fading light and the rattle of pots and pans from below stairs proclaimed the dinner hour. Vincent rang for hot water, and washed and shaved. Throckmorton had brought up his trunk. Vincent selected a fresh shirt, but decided against a cravat. It hardly seemed necessary on a secretive flight across the country in the dead of night. If they met someone, he could always put on his coachman's garb.

He sauntered across the hall to Diana's parlor, nodding to Throckmorton at his post by the door. In the parlor he found a freshly washed and brushed Selena, and sounds from the adjoining bedchamber indicated that Bytham would soon join them.

Or perhaps not.

He heard Diana's calm voice firmly announce, "Bytham, if you do not allow me to finish washing you, you will have to eat your dinner alone in here."

An unintelligible response from Bytham was lost in Selena's giggle. "Bytham does not like to have his face washed."

"I see." Vincent did his best to remember what having

his face washed as a small boy had been like. Probably he had not cared for it, either. He smiled at the girl. "Did you have a pleasant day, Miss Selena?"

"Oh, yes! We had two walks today—one with Mrs. Biggleswade and you this morning, and one with Mama and Throckmorton this afternoon. Throckmorton picked flowers for me, and Abby showed me how to make a wreath for my hair." She darted across the room and retrieved a rather wilted offering. "See?"

Vincent turned the flowers over in his hands. So this is what little girls did on an afternoon walk.

"I like being in the country." Selena took the wreath and plopped it over her fair curls. "Outdoors is much more fun than indoors."

At that moment a small form came speeding across the room and launched itself at Vincent's knees, grasping them with wiry, young arms. "Whoa!" Vincent staggered and reached down to dislodge his young admirer, lifting him into his arms. "Who is this very clean fellow? I haven't seen him before."

"It's me! Bytham! Can we go outside again?"

"*May* we go outside." Diana followed her son into the parlor. "And no, you may not. It is time for dinner. Good evening, Lord Lonsdale." She held out a welcoming hand.

She had changed her black dress for one of lavender, and smoothed the wild mane of hair into a demure knot on the nape of her neck. The circles under her eyes had faded a bit, but the bruise on her cheek stood out clearly against her white skin. Vincent set Bytham on the floor and took the hand she extended. When his fingers closed over it, she winced.

Vincent quickly loosened his grip and examined the back of the hand. It was also bruised and the knuckles were scraped. He looked at her questioningly.

She withdrew the hand. "Yesterday. The man kicked me."

Rage roared up in Vincent. He waited until he could master it before answering, "Forgive me, Lady Diana. Had I been but a little sooner…"

She looked at him in surprise. "It is not your fault. If you had not come—" She broke off and sighed. "Was it only yesterday? It seems like a lifetime."

"A great deal has certainly happened in the last two days." Vincent held a chair for her to be seated. "I would like for you to be able to rest tonight, but I dare not stay. It will be dark as soon as we have finished eating, and I want to be on the road again."

"Whatever you think best. Oh, dear!" She made a futile grab for Bytham's fork. "Oh, Bytham! You are dripping sauce on your shirt. Oh! No…don't…wait…" Bytham looked down ruefully and smeared the drips around liberally with his napkin. His mother sighed and smiled at Vincent. "Too late."

Vincent laughed out loud. "I never realized how hazardous parenthood can be."

"Well, it is if one is obliged to provide all the care one's self. Never mind, Bytham. We will change your shirt." She turned a serious gaze on Vincent. "But never think that I begrudge it. These two are the joy of my life."

"I can see that." Vincent wondered for a second if she would ever have room in her heart for anyone else. Was it filled to capacity with love for her little ones and grief for Wyn? He had not seen her weep, except when Bytham and Selena had. But she was not a tearful sort of woman. Thank God.

He could not have borne watching her weep for another man.

So… They had joined forces. Excellent! He had begun to fear that his investment in her had been wasted. What need to extract confidences from the wife of a man who talked of everything he knew? A pity, in a way. It would have been so much more entertaining to extort them from her.

But Lonsdale was much more important to him than her fool of a husband had ever been. He needed all the information he could garner about that gentleman's activities. And the woman would now provide it. He had watched her, had seen the terror he had so carefully cultivated in her grow. She dared not refuse.

No, having control of a beautiful woman was never a waste. He would have his opportunity to enjoy her yet.

Chapter Five

Alone in the dark again, Diana braced herself against the jolting of the carriage as they rattled through the night. Thank goodness the children had fallen asleep. They had been so excited by the prospect of running away in the night that she'd thought they never would. Dressed in their black clothes, she could not see them, but could perceive their presence only by their soft breaths, the dim lightness of their little faces and the warmth of Bytham's head resting on her lap.

At Vincent's request she had also donned a black pelisse. Clearly he hoped to make them invisible—but to whom? They had seen no sign of pursuit since they had hidden in the trees the night before. And who was to say the coach that had passed them had any interest in them?

But on the other hand, who could say it had not?

The problem that most occupied her thoughts, however, was the question of why Mrs. Biggleswade had thought she'd needed help to escape Vincent. And that he had beaten her. What experience had they of him that would cause them to suspect that? Perhaps the rumors she had heard of him were true. Had she simply traded one danger for a greater one?

That was difficult for her to believe in light of the courtesy he showed her—even with the perplexing gaze he occasionally bestowed on her. But that he had motives about which she knew nothing, she had no doubt. Dear God, what a tangle! How was she to ever get herself and her dear ones clear of it?

A sudden thump drew her attention to the window. She gasped as a pair of booted legs rested for a moment in the opening then slithered forward into the carriage. A moment later the rest of Vincent followed, whispering, "It is only I."

Stilling her startled heart with a hand to her chest, she slid over to make room, and he sat beside her on the seat. "You frightened me."

"Forgive me. I didn't want to take time to stop. We are on the main pike. It would be better to stay to the back roads, but I fear we would still be on them this time next month if we did. We should be in Leicestershire by morning. Is all well with you?"

His angular profile, barely visible against the window, turned toward her. She could feel his breath against her cheek where they were crowded together on the seat, and suddenly Diana became aware of the warmth of his thigh pressed against hers. She drew in a sharp breath and his smoky, masculine scent welled up in her nostrils. Oh, my!

"I—I…" For a moment she could not remember what he had asked. "Oh. Yes, I'm fine. I only find it a little tiresome to be riding alone in the dark."

She tried to move away from him a little, but a lurch of the coach rocked her back against him. He slipped a hand behind her, gripping her shoulder to steady her. "Damn these ruts!"

A deeper hole rolled them back the other way. Vincent grasped the handhold and pulled her against him to prevent her falling onto Bytham. In the next heartbeat it became very quiet in the carriage. Both of them had stopped breathing. The road leveled out and Diana found herself looking up into the shadows of his face. They sat thus for several heartbeats, his face coming nearer and nearer. At last she heard a strangled whisper.

"No."

And he hastily left the coach by the same means he had used to enter it.

As they passed through the crossroads, the hair on the back of Vincent's neck lifted. He signaled Throckmorton to pause and considered his choices. Which way would a pursuer expect him to go?

If the pursuer did not already know.

The certainty that he was being watched grew in Vincent. Had he been on the watch for someone, he would pay close attention to the crossroads. Very close attention.

"Which way, me lord?" Throckmorton peered into the darkness uneasily.

"I don't think it matters. Don't look about too hard. Just drive on for a bit."

Throckmorton flicked the reins and headed down the westernmost lane. Vincent climbed onto the roof of the coach and stretched his long frame out between the trunks, watching their back road for several minutes. The moon having set, he saw nothing in the faint starlight. Nor did he hear anything.

But the prickles along the nape of his neck refused to abate.

He returned to the box. "Pull over to the edge of the road."

Throckmorton complied and Vincent descended and opened the door. "Diana, I want you three to get out of the carriage for a little while. Can you manage?"

"I suppose so." He could hear the puzzlement in her voice. "But what about the children? They are both asleep."

"We will carry them." He beckoned to Throckmorton. "Take Selena. I'll carry Bytham."

"But…why?" Diana clasped his shoulder to anchor herself as she climbed out. "Won't it seem odd if someone sees the coach sitting here empty?"

"If their intentions are innocent, they will think no more of it than that the driver is answering a call of nature. If their intentions are otherwise, we will be ready for them." Vincent ushered her away from the road, up the bank and through the smaller trees, gripping her arm to help her up the slope. Throckmorton scrambled after them easily, Selena's weight appearing to bother him not at all.

When he found a huge oak tree, Vincent pulled Diana behind it. He kicked away what debris he could and looked about for unfriendly residents. A futile exercise. How would he see any small creature, friendly or otherwise, in the shadows of the woods? He had no choice but to lay Bytham on the ground and hope that nothing bit him. Throckmorton followed suit, propping Selena against the tree.

The boy muttered groggily and then subsided, but Selena rubbed her eyes, mumbling a querulous, "Where are we?"

"Shh!" Diana quickly knelt beside her daughter. "We mustn't make a sound. Can you be still as a mouse?"

"Uh-huh." The girl leaned her head against her mother's shoulder, already dozing again.

"Good." Vincent patted Diana's back encouragingly. "We won't be here long. Stay behind the tree. If you hear gunfire, get down on the ground."

"Gunfire! Where…where are you going? You will not leave us here alone?" The anxiety in her voice was clear. Little wonder.

"Only for a few minutes. Here…" He reached into his

pocket and pulled out his second pistol. Fumbling in the dark, he found her hand and pressed the gun into it. "Only use this if you must." He smiled wryly in the dark. "And for God's sake, try not to shoot me or Throckmorton."

She caught his arm. "This is not necessary, my lord. I have one of my own in my pocket."

He took the pistol back, startled. "You know how to use it?"

He sensed her nod rather than saw it. Good. An extra weapon might make all the difference. He drifted silently back down the bank. Beside him the big man moved with surprising stealth. They put out the lamps and took up positions a little distance apart not far from the carriage, concealed in the shadows.

They had not long to wait. As soon as they had hidden themselves, the muffled throb of distant hooves floated toward them on the wind. In a matter of minutes three dark silhouettes could be seen outlined against the stars. The trio approached the carriage cautiously and dismounted.

One of them peered inside while the others cast around for signs of life. "Ain't here. Where do you reckon they're at?"

"In the bushes, like as not. Spread out and 'ave a look." The three of them edged carefully into the woods.

Vincent waited, every muscle tense, his ears straining. One of them was almost within arm's reach. Closer. Just a little closer. Vincent sprang, bringing the butt of his pistol down on the searcher's head with a resounding crack. The man crumpled to the ground.

Silence ensued. All sounds of motion ceased. Even the breeze stilled. Vincent held his breath. At last a whisper came through the darkness. "Jake?"

Throckmorton moved. The second man shrieked as the big hand came out of nowhere and spun him around. The boxer's sledgehammer fist connected with the pursuer's jaw, and the man toppled backward full-length on the ground. And didn't move.

Diana crouched behind the tree listening to the confusing sounds coming from nearer the road. And to the rustling in the undergrowth moving toward her up the hill. Wiping damp palms on her skirt, she peeked cautiously around her tree. She could not see from her hiding place who had ridden up, but she had heard several voices— voices that were not those of Vincent or Throckmorton. Then something had happened. She had heard a pair of thuds and a cry.

But who had cried out? Had it been one of her protectors? Were she and the children alone, stranded in the woods? God forbid! She held Selena closer.

The disturbance in the brush moved closer. Diana grasped the pistol in one hand and placed her other one firmly over Selena's mouth. The girl squirmed, but subsided when Diana tightened her grip. Just then a dark form rose up on the other side of her oak.

Who was it?

He was not as big as Throckmorton. Broader than Vincent?

The indistinct shape leaned one shoulder against the side of the tree, breathing heavily. He was not twelve inches away! In spite of herself, Diana uttered a strangled gasp.

The shape jerked back violently. "Gorblimey!"

Diana pulled the trigger.

Suddenly the woods were full of commotion. Selena pulled away and screamed. Diana grabbed frantically for her daughter's arm. "Get down!" She shoved her to the earth.

Stumbling footsteps crashed away through the underbrush.

Other footsteps pelted up the hill.

"Diana!" Vincent burst around the trees. "Are you all right? Where is he? What happened?"

"I have him, me lord." Throckmorton's voice rumbled through the dark.

Diana dropped the pistol and threw herself into Vincent's arms, sobbing hysterically.

"I didn't mean to kill him. I didn't mean to kill him. I didn't mean to kill him. I didn't—"

A considerable time had elapsed before Vincent was able to quiet Diana's sobs and convince her that the man was not dead—a fact that seemed to make little difference to her uncharacteristic panic. By that time Selena was crying, too, and even Bytham had waked, clamoring loudly about something Vincent could not interpret. It was not until he had managed to calm both ladies that he recognized in the boy's complaint the demands of a genuine call of nature.

Vincent's unmarried state began to seem more desirable by the minute.

He put Diana and Selena in the carriage and carried the boy to a spot of relative privacy. In spite of his tension—or perhaps because of it—Vincent could not stop chuckling. It was so damned anticlimactic!

By the time he had dealt with Bytham's situation, Throckmorton had stanched the brigand's wounded arm and tied him and the still-unconscious others, seated, against various trees. The wounded man complained bitterly all the while.

"I say, mate, you can't leave us 'ere like this!"

"Oh, aye. I can." Throckmorton straightened from his task. "Someone will be along in the morning."

He looked questioningly at Vincent who hesitated for an instant. By rights he should shoot them. Very likely one of them had been the surviving ruffian who had hurt Diana, and he had promised himself... But Vincent could not envision killing three men in cold blood in the presence of Diana and the children. There were some things even *he* would not do.

"Correct. Any brass on them?" He put Bytham in the coach where a still-trembling Diana sat, clutching her daughter to her breast.

Throckmorton held up a small purse. "A bit."

"Take the coins and leave the purse. That should slow them down." Vincent gathered up the reins of the horses their adversaries had ridden. "You drive. I'll ride one of these and lead the others. They might prove useful later."

In fact, he intended to dispose of the mounts at his first opportunity. They would provide bright flags to their pursuers, proclaiming the party's whereabouts. But perhaps if the bastards *thought* he had kept the mounts, they would waste time looking for them for just that reason. He could not afford to let them get so close again. The thought of one of their number getting close enough to Diana for her to shoot him made Vincent weak in the knees.

After passing several lanes leading off the main road, he had Throckmorton turn east on one of the narrowest. Sure enough, a mile or two down the path, a farm was just becoming visible in the first rays of sunlight. The farmer, a provident soul, was already making his way to the byre. It took the negotiations of only a few minutes for Vincent, muffled in his coachman's wig and coat, to establish that his master had suffered an accident on the road. Money changed hands and Vincent was assured that the horses would receive the best of care in the barn—out of sight— until Vincent returned for them.

Which would be never.

When they went to earth, the sun had climbed well above the trees. Vincent had owned the house for two years,

but had stayed there only a few times. Not even his associates knew of its existence. What no one knew, they could
betray under no amount of duress, nor even inadvertently.
The small manor lay at the end of a long curving drive surrounded by trees and approached by narrow lanes. One
would have to know where it was to find it.

He had never been so glad to see it.

"As long as we are at Eldritch Manor, we are the Honorable Mr. and Mrs. Greenleigh," he informed Diana as the
carriage pulled up to the door. "The staff knows me only
as an eccentric gentleman who prefers buying houses to
staying in inns. Which, come to think of it, I am."

The solidly built, fair-haired caretaker appeared on the
steps hastily buttoning his coat. His wife, a pleasantly plump
woman with salt-and-pepper braids wound around her head,
bustled out to meet them while a half-grown boy hurried
forward from the stable to take the horses. Diana climbed
down wearily, but predictably Selena and Bytham jumped
out and gazed eagerly about at their new surroundings.

"Look, Mama. We are still in the country." Selena
clapped her hands in approval. "May we go for a walk?"

Diana sighed. "Not now, dear. We must have breakfast."

"After breakfast? May we?" The girl bounced on her
toes. "May we? Please? Please?"

Diana had long since lost the energy to deal with im-
portuning. She said shortly, "Selena, do not beg. It is not
ladylike. Later we will see."

The housekeeper stepped in to her rescue, patting Selena kindly on the back. "You will have a walk, my dear,
as soon as you've eaten your porridge. My daughter, Fanny,
will take you so your poor mama can rest, and you may
visit the stables with Aidan. We have kittens, don't you
know." She turned to Vincent. "You never said you had a
family, Mr. Greenleigh."

Vincent nodded cooly. "No, Mrs. Cobbs. It is a recent event."

Mrs. Cobbs turned to Diana. "Ah! So good to meet you, Mrs. Greenleigh. Had you let us know you were coming, we would have made ready, but no harm done. I've still time to bake and I can get another girl from the village to help out. You look quite done up, ma'am." She spared a reproachful glance for Vincent. "And little wonder, traveling through the night this way. But I'll send Fanny up to air your room right now so that you may nap later. You come straight into the breakfast parlor."

Vincent took Diana's arm and steered her toward the house, past a well-tended flower bed and up well-scrubbed stone steps. Mrs. Cobbs gathered the children in and took them off for a quick meal, chattering to them amiably. Vincent led Diana to a comfortable room with a breakfast table and windows overlooking rolling green pastures dotted with white sheep and a pair of brindle cows.

"What a charming place!" Diana removed her black pelisse and tossed it onto a chair. "You own it?"

Vincent nodded. "As Mr. Greenleigh, do not forget," he added softly. "Though I did not buy it for its charm. It affords me privacy when I require it, and the land pays for the staff and makes a few pounds a year. I may someday use it as a hunting box."

He held a chair for her as Cobbs came in bearing a coffeepot and the necessary accoutrements. They waited until he had poured them each a cup and departed, assuring them that there were bacon and eggs on the grill and scones in the oven.

Diana stared out the window in silence as she sipped her coffee, her mind busy sorting what she knew and did *not* know of the Earl of Lonsdale. She had just enough in the former category to make her even more aware of how large the second category loomed. Why did he require such a degree of privacy as to purchase land under an assumed name?

Vincent looked at her in concern. "How are you, Diana? You haven't much to say."

She tried to smile. "I'm tired, I suppose. It has been a rather difficult night."

"It was that, in fact." Vincent returned a ghost of a smile, then sobered. "You did well, Diana."

Well? She had done well? She had shot a man—and she had intended to do so. And that was good? In what had she become involved? Were their pursuers her enemies alone, or were they also Vincent Ingleton's? Surely nothing she knew justified anyone searching for *her* the length and breadth of England. Not even the wretch who called himself Deimos.

Her heart all but stopped when she considered what she might have revealed to his lordship by falling into strong hysterics last night.

She must be more careful. But at the moment she most wanted to regain control of her life and discover from whom her danger lay—some shadowy stranger, the hated Deimos, or the man sitting across the table from her.

She decided to start with him.

"My lord, may I ask you some questions?"

He paused long enough for Diana to fear his answer would be *no*. But at last he nodded cautiously. "I will be as frank as I may."

And how frank might that be? Diana felt the sting of annoyance. She pushed it aside. Perhaps she would be able to evaluate his honesty accurately. If not, she would be no worse off than she now was.

"The people at the inn in Ashwell reacted to you very strangely. They should have been happy for the custom, but obviously they were not. And then Mrs. Biggleswade said she knew you. Offered to help me *escape* you—even thought that you had beaten me. Why?"

Vincent pushed his chair back from the table and stared, frowning, out the window for several minutes while Cobbs and a pretty, brown-haired girl who must have been the ubiquitous Fanny, set covered dishes on the sideboard. When they had gone, he turned back to Diana.

"Because on my last visit there, I behaved very badly." He rose and stepped to the buffet. "Would you like eggs?"

Diana nodded and he began to fill a plate for her. She waited, until she decided that no further response would be forthcoming. This would not do. She would not be intimidated by his scowl and his silence. "Vincent, I would greatly appreciate a bit more explanation than that. What could you possibly have done that was so dreadful? I cannot imagine such conduct in you."

He favored her with his one-sided smile. "That is only because our acquaintance does not extend back as far as four years."

A diversion. She raised her eyebrows and gave him the look that inevitably induced compliance in small children and occasionally in husbands.

Apparently it worked almost as well with taciturn bachelors for, as he set her plate before her and began to fill his own, he offered one more sentence. "Before that time, I assure you, I was the greatest beast in nature." Diana picked up her fork, but left her eyebrows firmly in position. He glanced at her, his own brows drawn together. "You are determined to have the whole wretched tale, are you not?"

Diana did not deign to reply. Vincent set his own plate on the table, sat and spread out his napkin. "Very well, although it reflects very little wisdom—or even intelligence—on my part. And absolutely no honor. Another scone?"

Diana declined this offer with a shake of her head. Vincent helped himself to two more and spread them liberally with jam. He took a bite and then stared into the middle distance while he chewed. "This is rather difficult," he murmured. Another long pause ensued.

Finally he turned to her. "But I agree you deserve an explanation. So… On my last visit to Ashwell—I cannot even remember why I was there—I followed my usual pattern for the time. I drank until I could hardly stand. I accosted young Abby. When she would have fended me off, I seized her, and we both stumbled over a chair. I did not actually strike her, but she fell and suffered a black eye. When her father and the tapper came to her aid, I fought. The men I called friends at the time—I wonder now how even *they* tolerated me—finally restrained me and got me upstairs to a room where I did more damage before I fell into a drunken stupor."

"But…but why?" Diana set down her cup, her brow furrowed. "You are nothing like that now."

"Am I not?" Vincent considered the statement with narrowed eyes. "I wish I could be sure."

Chapter Six

Merciful heavens! Diana fervently wished *she* could be sure. Was it possible that the wary man in whose hands she had placed her family might suddenly turn on her? Become the drunken beast he had described? She had never seen him drink to excess, but if that were his history…

She had been so wrong about Wyn. How could she trust her judgment now? Vincent was gazing at her steadily with…was that a hint of defiance? But to what end? She was hardly in a position to chastise him. All she could say was, "I see."

Hardly adequate to the occasion.

They ate without speaking for several more minutes. At last Diana decided that, there being little she could do at the moment about the question of his lordship's reform, she would approach the subject of even more sinister potential—his use of a false name.

"My lord, there is another matter that I hope you will explain."

He looked up from his plate guardedly.

"What made it necessary to purchase this property secretly?"

Once again his brows drew together. He took a deep breath and let it out again. "I told you, Lady Diana, that I would be as frank as I can. However, I am not at liberty to discuss certain subjects. That is one of them. Suffice to say that I am very happy this morning that I did so."

"Indeed." Diana studied the dregs of her coffee. He poured himself another cup from the silver pot on the table and offered to pour for her. She shook her head and he looked away. Now what? She wanted to know more—a great deal more.

She opened her mouth to speak and he turned a forbidding gaze on her. "Further interrogation, my lady?"

Diana checked, momentarily nonplussed. Apparently his patience had worn thin.

But so had hers.

She summoned her resolve. The safety of the children might depend on his answer. "One other item, my lord."

He looked at her silently, his face set.

"From whom are we fleeing? My enemies or yours?"

His expression became thoughtful. At last he said, "I am not perfectly sure. I suspect they may be one and the same."

Diana was tired. She had lost her toleration for guessing games. She said, with considerable asperity, "In that case, my lord, as I have no idea who mine are, would you be so kind as to acquaint me with yours?"

A bark of laughter escaped him before he became solemn again. He shook his head and reached for her hand. "Forgive me, Diana. I am afraid that anything I tell you may endanger you further."

Diana withdrew her hand and crossed her arms over her chest, gazing at him seriously. "Then, my lord, am I and my children more or less safe in your company than we would be alone?"

He leaned back in his chair. "Again, I cannot be perfectly sure. Some of your danger may, in fact, come from your association with me."

"Then why have you brought us away to this isolated place?"

He sat silent for a long moment. Finally he stood. "I believe, my lady, that it is because I very much wished to."

Vincent rose hastily and left the room before she could react. Now why the bloody hell had he said that?

Beside the fact that it was true.

He had very much wished to see her in his own place, his own house. At his own table. In his own bed. Now that she was here, would he be able to muster the honor to leave her untouched?

But that would probably not come into question. He had, in all likelihood, frightened her completely—if not with his last remark, then with the tale of his past depravity at Ashwell. She would probably not let him come within arm's reach of her again.

He hoped not. It would be easier. More painful, but easier.

She had not let him take her hand.

Vincent shook himself and went in search of Throckmorton. He found his new henchman in the stable, helping Aidan Cobbs groom the horses. "Morning, me lord." The boxer straightened and bowed. "You needing me?"

"Aye." Vincent motioned toward the stable door and Throckmorton followed him out. "You've had breakfast?"

"Oh, aye, me lord. Mrs. Cobbs filled me right up."

"Best not call me 'me lord' while we are here. I am simply Mr. Greenleigh."

"Oh, to be sure, sir."

"Are you up to another ride—an hour and back? I think we will both be able to sleep tonight."

The big man grinned. "I could ride all day, need be, sir."

Vincent nodded. "Good. Need may be someday, but not this one." He leaned against the stable door. "I want you to ride into the second village east of here and call for the post."

"Hmm." Throckmorton rubbed his jaw. "Easy enough. What name?"

"Not mine, nor Greenleigh, either. Ask for Mr. or Mrs. Egbert Johnston." Vincent didn't like the man knowing so much. He still could not be sure of his loyalty, but he didn't want Cobbs to hear the alias or to be seen asking for the post in that village. And he didn't want to leave Diana and the children. "And, Throckmorton." Vincent gave him a stony look. "If anyone at all were to hear of this, I would be most displeased."

"Mum's the word, me—sir."

"Very well. Take the bay hack. He should be fresh. I've not been here for quite a while." Vincent nodded and went back to the house through a side door.

Coming from the light into the dimness of the small entrance way, he did not immediately see the figure coming from the other direction. It took a heartbeat to recognize Diana. She stepped hastily aside to avoid a collision, moving back into a corner of the cramped space.

"My lady! I beg your pardon. Did you wish to see me?"

"Uh, yes, my lord." She glanced about for a way out of the corner.

The wariness in her eyes brought out something bitter in Vincent. Damnation! Had he done anything to alarm her? No. He had been the epitome of honor. Had kept his hands—and most of his thoughts—to himself. For months the desire had been building in him to add his strength and courage to hers, to protect her vulnerability, to take in her in his arms and shield her. And now she feared him. She had no idea what the effort was costing him. Vincent moved slightly, taking a perverse satisfaction in completely blocking her in. He crossed his arms over his chest and raised one eyebrow inquiringly. "Yes?"

For a moment Diana fought the impulse to bolt. He was so tall, so intimidating, so…so *close*. She could smell him. Could *feel* him—even though he was not touching her. She tried to back up, but found herself stopped by the wall.

But of course, he *intended* to intimidate. He did not wish to answer any more questions. But Diana had no intention of *being* intimidated. She wanted answers.

She looked up into his inexpressive face. "My lord—"

"Not here. Do not call me 'lord.'"

The interruption once more deflected Diana's purpose. Confound him. She took a deep breath. "*Mr. Greenleigh…* Oh, the devil with it! Vincent, what did you mean when you said you *wanted* to bring me here? Surely these alarms have not been contrived to that purpose?" His expression changed, but to what she could not say.

"No." He spoke firmly. "No, they have not. Even I would not do that. I believe the danger to be very real. My hope is that by staying here awhile, we will confuse the pursuit. We are too vulnerable on the road. Sooner or later they would catch us. No one but you and Throckmorton knows who I am here."

"How long must we stay?" Diana sensed a softening in his stance, but he did not move back.

"I am not sure of that, either. I have arranged to receive messages that will help me decide. We must eventually go to Inglewood to identify our pursuers and deal with them. Without a doubt, they will be watching for us there, but in time they will become less vigilant. Then we may be able to reach shelter without their being aware of it." His crooked smile flashed briefly. "They cannot possibly watch every way into the estate. I assure you I know ways in and out that they would never think of."

Diana considered this plan. Apparently she was to remain in his lordship's company for some time. She had to know where she stood with him. "Vincent, I still need to know the meaning of what you said earlier—about wanting to bring me here."

He looked into her eyes for a long moment. Finally he let out a breath. "Forgive me, Diana. I should not have said that. It is better that I do not try to explain it. Please be assured that you are in no danger from me. I am not St. Edmunds."

"I—I did not think you were." Had she? Had she thought for a moment that his purpose might be the same as St. Edmunds's? She had certainly wondered, but now... "It is just that I am very confused."

"I know. Try to believe that I mean you no harm. My chief desire is to keep you and Bytham and Selena safe." He touched the scrape on her cheek and for a second his touch seemed to tingle against her skin. Then he turned her face to the light and frowned. "That spot looks red. Is it healing?"

"I haven't really looked." Diana lifted her own hand to the spot, only to find Vincent's still in place. His fingers closed around hers. She studied his face, trying to read his thoughts.

She could not.

He released her hand and stepped back. "Let us ask Mrs. Cobbs for some ointment."

He offered her his arm and she took it.

With more questions raised than answered.

Later that afternoon, after a morning nap in a curtained bed, Diana enjoyed a romp on the lawn with Bytham and Selena. Eldritch Manor was a beautiful, very old house, with warm, rich brick-and-stone terraces. Across the rear, French doors opened from several rooms onto the widest terrace. The lawn stretched the length of the back of the building and a pleasant woodland could be seen at its border.

For an hour she put all the unanswered questions and future fears aside and simply played with her children. Once she thought she saw Vincent watching from a door, but he did not come out to join them. When they had all tired, Fanny had taken the youngsters upstairs for a wash and a rest before feeding them dinner. Thank heaven for the sweet girl. How wonderful to have someone to help her. Now Diana might have another rest herself.

She was just crossing the entry on her way to the stairs when Throckmorton came in the side door. "Good afternoon, ma'am." The big man bowed. "I've just been to pick up the post. This one says 'Mrs.' so I suppose it is for you."

"Indeed?" Diana turned the letter over. Written in a vaguely familiar hand, it was addressed to "Mrs. Egbert Johnston." "I do not believe it could be for me. I know no one by that name."

The footman winked. "His lordship do have some right puzzling ways. But that's the name he sent me after." He bowed again. "If you'll excuse me, ma'am. I've need to speak with him."

"Of course. Thank you."

What in the name of heaven could Vincent be about? An uneasy feeling stirred in her stomach. She would not read the message here. Diana put it in her pocket and hurried up the stairs. Not until she had locked her bedroom door did she withdraw it and break the seal.

An icy hand closed around her heart.

Inside were two notes—one from Helen, asking after her welfare and explaining that she was forwarding the other that had arrived at her house for Diana. Diana knew instantly from whom the second one came.

Stifling the impulse to cast it into the fire unread, she broke the second seal with trembling fingers.

Ah! Most fortunate Lady Diana—
Who could have foreseen such an advantageous situation arising from your husband's demise? Who would ever suspect that his death might open the door for the affluent Lord Lonsdale? Surely no one, unless of course, they know you as I do.

But I am discreet. I would not dream of suggesting anything to the authorities, especially as now you are in a position to return my past favors.

I desire you to observe his lordship for me. That should be simple for you in your present situation. Write down anything out of the ordinary that he says or does—anything at all, anyone he mentions. No detail is too small.

I'm sure you will be happy to provide this trifling service. Especially since your future and that of your charming children depend on it. I doubt even Lord Lonsdale would overlook your past offenses. I'm certain he values his own health.

You may send the information to George Ellison in care of the postmaster of the City of London. I will receive it, just as I am confident this message will find you—as, you may rest assured I will, no matter where you go.
Your faithful confidant—
Deimos

Dear God! And she had thought that matters could not be worse. Now the blackguard intended to accuse her of

Wyn's death. But he could not do that. There had been witnesses. Wyn had been stabbed on the street. Vincent had been there. And Justinian Sudbury and St. Edmunds. A choking wave swept over Diana.

They had all been there when her husband was killed. Diana sank down onto a footstool, her eyes closed.

They had all been there.

At the tap on the door of the library, Vincent turned from staring out the window and called, "Enter."

Throckmorton opened the door and came in, several letters in his beefy hand and a grin on his abused face. "I dunno who this Egbert Johnston may be, but he gets a deal of mail." Vincent grunted and held out a hand. His footman passed over the letters. "His wife got some, too."

"Did she now?" Startled, Vincent glanced into the big man's face. "You gave them to Lady Diana?"

"Aye, sir. She was in the hall when I came in. Should I not?"

"No, no. That is all right. They were addressed to 'Mrs. Johnston,' I collect?" Vincent propped both feet on the desk and leaned back in his chair.

"Aye, sir."

Vincent nodded and thought about that bit of information. He had arranged for Adam and Helen to be able to communicate with them, but somehow he had thought that only Litton would write to him. Another disturbing realization occurred to him. His new henchman understood covert arrangements all too well. He even knew to question the propriety of giving Diana her own mail.

He must watch the man.

"There's another thing you'll be needing to know, sir."

"What's that?" Vincent squinted up from his chair.

"The news everywhere I passed is that a way south

of here three men were found tied to trees with their throats cut."

"The devil you say!" Vincent's boots slammed to the floor and he leaned forward across the desk.

Throckmorton shook his head. "That's the word, sir. Thought you would like to know."

"Of course, I want to know." Resuming his thoughtful pose, Vincent returned his feet to the desktop. "They don't much value their people, do they?"

The boxer said nothing, but his expression turned grim.

Vincent rubbed his chin. "Or is someone else in the game?"

Throckmorton maintained his silence. Vincent hoped that was because he didn't know what game they played.

"I should have done it myself, but… Did you say anything to Lady Diana about this?"

"No, sir. I didn't want to overset her. But the Cobbses already know, so expect she will hear about it soon enough."

"At least she won't be able to lay it at my door." The degree of relief he felt surprised Vincent. He did not want Diana to see him as a brute—even if the shoe fit.

"Will that be all, sir?"

"Yes. Yes, thank you." Vincent's mind had already returned to the question of the untimely demise of the last night's assailants.

"One more thing, sir."

"Oh?" Vincent's wandering attention jerked back to the footman.

"She didn't seem none too happy about that letter."

Diana pulled her shawl more tightly around herself against the cool of the early summer night and found a seat on a stone bench near the balustrade at the edge of the terrace. Tired as she was, she knew she would not sleep. The turmoil in her mind would not allow it.

The full moon hung in a sky lit silver, dimming the stars and painting the landscape in stark black and white. If only the tranquil light could pour into her mind and erase the fear and suspicion. If only decisions could be as clearly marked as the shadows of the trees against the grass.

What was she to do? For years Diana had relied only on herself. It had not taken long to learn that she could not lean on Wynmond Corby. How could she have been such a fool as to have married him?

A young fool. A young, love-struck fool. A fool barely eighteen years old. One with no parents.

What more answer to that question did she need? She had thought that all men were like her father—responsible, dependable, a steadying influence in her life. When he died… Diana shook her head. If she had been seeking to replace him, she had failed miserably. And in so doing, had failed her children. They would never know a father such as hers.

But that was in the past. Now…now she faced problems she never dreamed could exist—certainly not in *her* life—and she didn't know what to do. Everywhere she turned were men she could not trust—men who had designs on her body, men who wanted to take her children away, men who… Dear God!

One man who threatened to send her to the gallows.

As always, she had thrown the note from Deimos into the fire. She could not bear to look at them. But that did not erase the words from her mind. He wanted her to spy on Vincent Ingleton. To spy on the one man who seemed willing to place himself between her and the dangers that threatened her.

A man who might be her most immediate threat.

True, but every feeling in Diana revolted at the thought of betraying him. She would hate herself for practicing that deception. Whatever Vincent's motives, she must deal with him straightforwardly. She would not answer Deimos.

But what if Deimos made good his threats? What would happen to her children if she were taken away? In the first matter, it would be a case of his word against hers. She had never intended to hurt anyone, but who knew what a court of law might decide or who they would believe? That fiend made her every innocent action sound sordid or sinister. Diana felt sick when she remembered the money she had taken from him. What would he make of that?

That he had actually insinuated that she'd had a hand in Wyn's death in order to seduce Vincent had stunned her. How could anyone think that? Wyn had been killed on the street, in the presence… Oh, God. In Vincent's presence. And St. Edmunds's. And Sudbury's.

Had they killed him?

She felt so alone, so tired, so afraid. Diana dropped her face into her hands and began to weep, weeping as she had not done since that awful night. Nay, long before that. Since her love for Wynmond Corby had died. Since her future had slowly disappeared. The well of sorrow overflowed, shaking her whole body as the anguish poured out of her. She had not known it was there. Had not realized how badly she hurt inside.

Suddenly the pain was almost more than she could bear. It crushed her. Diana crossed her arms on the balustrade and collapsed over it in a forlorn huddle.

He pulled the curtain back from the glass and watched her. He had been there for some time now. At first she'd merely sat looking out into the night. Moonlight suited her, Vincent thought. Silvery-gold, calm, mysterious. But as he watched the scene, another thought came to him. Where the moon shone its silver light, all was bright as day, but on the shadow side of the trees lay utter darkness. Nothing at all could be discerned.

Like trees in the moonlight, his Diana was hiding something.

At first he did not notice the shaking of her shoulders. But it gradually increased until he could not overlook it. Vincent gritted his teeth. She was weeping for Wyn. Slowly she crumpled into a ball, wedged between the railing and the bench. Her whole body shook now.

He had been right about one thing. He could not bear it. He could not stand there watching her cry for her dead husband.

He opened the French door and stepped onto the terrace.

At the scuff of boot leather on the stones, Diana drew in a sharp breath and strove for composure. It did not come. Sobs persisted in escaping her control. She had not the strength to shut them off and straighten herself on the bench. She wanted only to crawl inside herself and disappear forever. The warmth of a gentle hand on her shoulder just made her cry harder.

Warm breath against her cheek told her that Vincent Ingleton had knelt on one knee beside her. His hand slid across her back as he pulled her closer. Somehow her face now rested against his shoulder and he was stroking her hair. How long they remained thus, she later had no idea. How long she had wept, how many tears she had shed, faded into oblivion. She only knew that after a time, her sobs diminished to hiccups and the hiccups to sniffles.

At that point Vincent rose and sat beside her on the bench, pulling a serviceable handkerchief from his pocket and offering it to her. His arm remained across her shoulders, holding her close. When finally she had dried her face and recovered enough breath to speak, she pulled back a bit and turned to look at him.

"Thank you. Please forgive me. I did not intend to become such a watering pot."

"Do you miss him so badly?" Vincent didn't want to hear the answer, but something in him compelled him to ask.

"Miss…? Oh." For a moment she sat silent. "You mean Wyn."

"Yes. Do you miss him so much?"

Diana took a deep breath. "I have missed the man I married for many years. Or the man I thought him to be."

Relief washed over Vincent. The tears were not for Wyn. "He disappointed you."

"Yes. And many other people, I suspect."

He thought about that. "I suppose he did. He was always my friend, but I knew I could not depend on him for anything but his loyalty."

"I could not even depend on him for that."

Remembering Wynmond Corby's attractiveness to the opposite sex, Vincent nodded. "But I think he always cared for you."

"I've no doubt he did—in his way."

"I know his way was not very satisfactory. He had no right to squander his fortune—and yours—as he did."

"No, but I suspect he never realized that he was doing it. It never seemed to occur to him that a household required money. His homes had always been there. Someone provided for the daily needs without his ever having to think about it, so he never did." She turned more toward Vincent. "Once when there was no food in the house for me and the children, I asked him for money. He was astonished. He had eaten at his club."

Vincent sighed and shook his head.

"He went out and pawned his grandfather's watch," she continued, "and came and poured the coins into my hands—all contrition. I finally realized that his intellect was not of a high order."

"No, nor his discretion. He was handsome and likeable, but not very wise." Vincent thought of the loose talk that had very probably gotten her husband killed and put his wife and children in danger. Why he had trusted Corby himself? Of all people.

They sat quietly for a space. Somehow his arm no longer encircled her, but he could still feel her warmth against his side. After a few moments he asked, "So what is the source of this distress?"

For a minute or two he thought she would not answer. At last she murmured, "Everything…just…everything." Comprehensive, but not very enlightening. Vincent waited, hoping for further elucidation. Finally she said, "I feel so frightened and alone. I don't know who to trust, which way to turn."

Pain shot through Vincent's heart. He knew she had no reason to trust him. Every reason not to. Still… He reached over and turned her face toward his. "I'm sorry you feel alone. Perhaps one day you will learn to trust me. I will do my utmost not to fail you."

She gazed at him soberly, searching his eyes, not speaking. Her face was too close. Her eyes too deep. Her mouth… Before he realized he would do it, he covered it with his own. She tasted salty from her tears, soft and sweet. Her breath checked. For a moment she leaned into him.

And then she pulled away.

He touched the wound on her cheek and reality intruded. This must go no further. He stood, helping her to her feet. "You are cold. We best go in."

She stepped back and drew her shawl tighter, armoring herself against him. "Yes," she agreed. "We best go in."

And they did.

Chapter Seven

The kiss had meant nothing. A mere impulse on both parts, born of her need for comfort. Diana had been telling herself that ever since she had drunk her morning chocolate.

And she did not quite believe it.

There *was* something growing between Vincent Ingleton and herself. She hardly dared put a name to it. Perhaps it was only that she had been so long without a man's touch. Without any masculine attention, in fact. She had told herself that she didn't need it, that her children's love was enough for her.

And she did not entirely believe that, either.

The last four years had been bleak, cold and very lonely. She was only now beginning to realize just how desolate and empty. The passion she had ruthlessly crushed was showing a spark of revival. She could feel it warming inside her. She was comforted to know that it still lived.

Both comforted and terrified.

She must not let it again lead her into a lack of judgment about a man. If only she knew in what Vincent had involved himself, why he had brought her here, what his intentions were—in what he had involved *her*. He had asked her to trust him. What a huge relief it would be if she could, if she could allow herself to lean on him, both literally and figuratively. But until he became more forthcoming, that was out of the question.

She would not be a fool twice.

As Diana put the finishing touches on her toilette, a firm knock sounded at her door. She opened it to find Mrs. Cobbs with a small, round china pot in her hand.

"Good morning to you, Mrs. Greenleigh." She stepped into the room, her sharp eyes clearly taking in the circles under Diana's. She frowned and tut-tutted under her breath. "You are still looking a bit pulled. You really should let Fanny care for the children and rest more. You may rely on her."

"I'm sure that I may, Mrs. Cobbs. Fanny is a very good girl."

"Oh, aye." Fanny's mother smiled brightly. "She is that. She minds her papa and me well enough, even when she don't wish to." She set the pot on the dresser.

Diana smiled. "I cannot imagine her not minding you."

Mrs. Cobbs opened the small jar. "I've brought you the comfrey salve I promised yesterday. I had none in the still-room, so I made it up yesterday evening." She waved toward the dressing table chair. "Here now, sit down, and I'll put some on your face for you. It does look a mite red."

Diana sat and Mrs. Cobbs returned to the subject dearest to her heart. "Our Fanny is a good lass, but you know how girls are. The Harter boy has taken her eye, don't you know."

"Oh, dear." Diana fervently hoped that young Harter was a good, steady lad.

"She thinks she's old enough to wed, and some would say she is, but I'd not like to see her tied down so soon— babies and all. She'll won't be seventeen until Christmas. Mayhap then."

"I agree. You are wise to hold her back. If I had been older when I…" Diana checked. She must not cast doubt on the story Vincent had told. She settled for, "When I married my first husband, I was much too young."

"As I was. It ages you." The housekeeper stepped back to examine her work. "I should have listened to my ma."

Diana wondered if her own life would have been different had she had a mother's counsel. Or would she have rebelled, as Mrs. Cobbs apparently had done, and married Wynmond Corby in any event?

"Fanny wanted to go to the fires and dancing on May Eve, but Cobbs ain't having none of that." She dabbed a bit more salve on Diana's cheek. "Says he knows too well what goes on at Beltane." She giggled. "And so do I. But Fanny went to the Maypole dance the next day. No harm in that." She stopped as if struck by a thought. "You and the mister could take the children next year. They would enjoy seeing the bright ribbons and pretty girls."

So would Diana. She had not seen a maypole since she moved to London. "I—I don't know." Where would they be next May? She decided to temporize. "Perhaps."

"I don't mean to pry, ma'am, but if there is anything I can do…" The housekeeper gave her a motherly pat on the shoulder and reached to tuck a strand of hair back into Diana's chignon. "I could not help seeing you last night, it was so clear and all. I can see you're still grieving for the children's papa. Why, you're still wearing your weeds! If I may say so, better to put them off and look to the future. Mr. Greenleigh seems a good sort." She turned to the door. "But enough on that head. Cobbs says I try to mother the whole world, and it ain't my place. I best get back to my kitchen."

"I…" Diana didn't know what to say. "You're very kind, Mrs. Cobbs. Thank you."

The woman curtseyed and went out. Diana stared at the mirror for a long while, pondering the usefulness of motherly advice and the comfort of a motherly touch. How would she manage when Selena became a young woman? Would she be wise enough?

Would she still be alive?

Vincent turned his chair so that he could see through the French door in his study. Sunlight shone golden on the soft, green lawn and a light breeze ruffled the leaves of the trees. He could hear Selena and Bytham laughing, and soon they came running into view across the grass, followed by Diana and Fanny. Diana had ceased dressing them in black, much to his relief, and they made a pretty picture on the lawn. He waited a heartbeat and, surely enough, a watchful Throckmorton materialized in their wake. At least the man kept to his duties.

Yesterday's letters lay open on the desk. According to the report from his associate, St. Edmunds's affiliation with Lord and Lady Holland continued to ripen. Damnation! Bonaparte's supporters had to be stopped. Vincent cursed the circumstances that had him immured in Leicestershire when he needed to be in London—at the heart of the investigation.

But some good might come of it. His instincts told him that St. Edmunds feared Diana and her knowledge—and probably feared Vincent himself. The man was not stupid and his sources were, in all likelihood, as good as Vincent's. He knew he was being watched and by whom. Unless Vincent missed his guess, it had been St. Edmunds's people who had attempted the abduction in the park. Having failed to bring Diana under his control by offering her shelter, he had attempted to do so by threatening her family.

And he was still trying. Vincent had little doubt that it

was his lordship's men who had been following them—and likely the lord himself. At least, that would mean he could not be in London plotting, either.

Vincent considered three cut throats. Whoever had followed them, he was making certain his identity remained obscure. Vincent feared, the kidnapping having failed, that its perpetrators would now move to lethal measures. He only hoped that he could lure them out and deal with them when he and Diana reached Inglewood.

Assuming he could get them there safely.

He reached across to the desk and picked up the second letter. Its contents worried him even more than the plans of Lord St. Edmunds.

Vincent's group had completely lost track of Deimos.

No one knew where the assassin now lurked, who he really was, nor where he stood in the present issue. He had once served Napoleon, but how he viewed the Bourbon king remained a mystery. He had been known to change sides.

They had, however, no doubt of his savagery. The notion that it might be not St. Edmunds who hunted them, but Deimos, caused the hair on the back of Vincent's neck to rise. Deimos was infinitely more dangerous.

He was far more cunning.

Vincent suddenly felt an overwhelming urge to seek Diana and the children, to put his own strong body between them and the perils surrounding them. He rose and carried the messages to the fireplace and watched until they became ash. Then he used the poker to reduce the ash to dust. Satisfied that they would never be read by prying eyes, he stood and walked to the door.

A wild pitch from Selena sent the ball sailing over Diana's head. She turned to follow it, only to see Lord Lonsdale, coming across the terrace, stretch a long arm upward and capture the ball before it collided with the glass door. As she watched, he grinned and sent it flying across the wide lawn toward Throckmorton—a mighty heave, indeed. He was showing off, she thought, startled. For her? The thought brought a little thrill of warmth up from her depths.

Laughing, the big footman caught it easily and pegged it back at his lordship. They were both showing off. Diana smiled. With such strong arms to come to her defense, perhaps she would survive this adventure, after all.

A lively game of six-cornered catch ensued. The adults arranged themselves around the children so that they could toss them gentle pitches. Occasionally the men on the outside of the circle would indulge themselves with a more energetic pass, hurling the ball the length of the lawn to one another. Diana and Fanny took their part, alternating short and long throws to each other and the children.

After half an hour, Diana reluctantly called a halt to the game. Bytham was getting wilder and wilder, a sure sign that he was tired, and Selena was beginning to droop. She caught the ball and held up one hand. "I think that is enough for now. Time for a nap, children."

Both youngsters frowned and Bytham stamped his foot. "Don't want a nap! I'm not a *baby*."

"Sir?" Vincent stepped up and lifted Bytham into his arms, favoring him with a stern look. "That is no way to speak to your mother. Apologize at once."

Bytham hung his head and Diana awaited events.

"Well?" Vincent gave the boy a gentle shake.

"I'm sorry, Mama," Bytham muttered and quickly hid his face on Vincent's shoulder.

"That's better." Vincent patted his back and set him on the ground. "A gentlemen is never rude to a lady—certainly not his mother. Now go with Fanny."

Fanny took Bytham's hand and turned to Selena. "Come along, Miss Selena."

"I'm coming." Selena paused to give her mother a quick hug and stopped beside Vincent. "Thank you for playing with us, Papa. I like it here."

Vincent stared at the girl, his jaw sagging. Diana almost broke into a fit of giggles. He looked stunned.

"Wha… What did you call me?" He peered down at Selena.

"I called you Papa. I told Fanny my papa was in heaven, and she said that you were my papa now, so I should call you that."

Fanny smiled in acknowledgment.

Vincent stammered. "I—I… Of course. Quite right. Uh, well, off to your nap now."

Fanny and the children trooped away, followed closely by Throckmorton. Vincent walked to where Diana stood with one hand covering her mouth, her eyes dancing.

"What is so amusing?" His black brows drew together.

Diana chuckled. "The expression on your face when Selena called you Papa."

"Huh." After a moment, Vincent smiled a lopsided smile. "That *was* a bit of a shock. I certainly never thought of myself as a father. But that solves the problem of the children inadvertently calling me Lord Lonsdale. If they did so, the game would be up." He nodded toward the trees. "Would you like to walk?"

"Yes, I would enjoy that." Diana took the arm he offered and they strolled in the direction of the woodland. "You acted as a father just now, you know—a very good one."

For a moment he frowned. Then his brow cleared. "Oh, you refer to my correcting Bytham? I didn't think of it that way, but, yes. Boys need to be disciplined or they grow up to be abominable louts—as I know to my sorrow."

Diana cast him an inquiring glance.

After a few minutes' thought he said, "My father never disciplined me. I was his only surviving child. My mother suffered several miscarriages, and my older brother, Henry, drowned when he was eight years old. I think Papa just could not bear to hurt me in any way."

"That's understandable, I suppose."

"Perhaps, but the result was that I grew into a nasty whelp and a worthless young man."

"Not *worthless,* surely." She smiled up at him.

"Near enough. The episode at Ashwell was not the worst, by any means."

"Was that brought about by the drinking?"

"In truth, no. I always imagined myself with a burning thirst in those days, but I cannot say why. I don't enjoy heavy drinking above half. I think the drink was more of an excuse."

"An excuse for what?"

"To behave like an ass…uh, I beg your pardon, Diana, but that is what I was. And an excuse to test people. In addition to allowing me to behave badly, my father always taught me that others would pretend to be my friends in order to get what I have. I found that to be largely true, so I punished them." He smiled ruefully. "I set out to make myself the most hated man in England. I succeeded only in becoming the greatest brat."

"But not everyone is like that. Many people are true friends."

"I suppose. Wyn was one of the few who never asked me for a shilling. I believed he was my friend."

Diana found herself unwilling to speculate on the loyalty of her late husband, so she changed the direction of the conversation. "But why did you stop?"

"My Uncle Charles gave me a memorable lesson in

honor." Vincent's wry smile broke through his serious expression. "And did me the greatest service of my life."

"Your uncle…Helen's brother? What did he do?"

"He took a riding crop to my backside."

"Oh, dear. How old were you?"

"Twenty-two."

Twenty-two! Not a boy, but a man. Diana walked in stunned silence for several moments and tried to imagine the uncle who could beat Vincent Ingleton like a naughty child. And then she tried to imagine Vincent Ingleton being a naughty child. And then… She could do neither. Vincent seemed so hard. So somber.

So forbidding.

Finally she said, "Your uncle must be quite terrifying."

Vincent looked startled. "Caldbeck?" After a moment's thought he added, "No, not terrifying. He is…very hard to describe. But you will meet him in Yorkshire."

"I am not sure I wish to."

"I have given you a false impression. He is a good enough fellow." Vincent smiled. "But he *is* very formidable. For years I was in awe of him—and therefore hated him. Went out of my way to antagonize him, to be rude to him and to his wife. And Helen…" He stared into the treetops for a moment. "I cannot describe the hell I put her through. She tried so hard to be a good mother to me, but I insisted on treating her as an interloper—someone who would steal my father's affection from me."

He turned back to Diana, a great sadness in his eyes. "I knew how unlovable I was."

The truth struck her like a blow. His grief was not only for the unruly child. He saw himself as a *man* that no one could love. A matching sorrow welled up in Diana. She would always wonder if *she* had been different—better somehow, more beautiful, more outgoing, more lovable—

her husband would have loved her more. What a contrast they both were to Wynmond Corby who had expected everyone to love him, no matter what he did.

Her impulse to reach out to Vincent, to comfort him, died aborning as she recognized the fixed set of his jaw. He would have none of it. His pride would see it as pity. Besides, she was not yet sure she could afford to wish to comfort him, even though he had comforted her last night. She must remain wary.

She became suddenly very aware that the path they trod had taken them out of sight of the house. The trees shaded them completely now. She stepped back from Vincent too hastily and stumbled. He caught her arm and steadied her, gazing into her face, his expression unreadable.

He knew. He knew she was afraid of him. And that she wanted him. Again, he was so near. She could feel the heat of his body. See the heat in his eyes. She tried to draw away, but he tightened his grip and, with his other hand, smoothed her hair away from her face.

For a moment she thought—feared, hoped?—he would kiss her again. He was staring at her mouth. She opened it to speak, shut it again quickly, stared back at him. For a space, time stood still. Somewhere a bird poured its joyous song into the air.

Vincent muttered something under his breath.

"Damnation."

And he turned them and led her back to the house.

She had called him *Papa.* The thought still created tremors of unease in Vincent. Had the chit really come to think of him as her father? Surely not, not in such a short time. But it had not taken Bytham long to begin clinging to him. Perhaps they did miss Wyn. Vincent felt pretty sure that Corby was no more constant a father than he had been a husband, but he had been good with children—including his own. They needed someone. Perhaps they needed Vincent.

But he could hardly see himself as a replacement. His life had grown too dark, too enmeshed with evil and danger. Not the stuff of parenthood. Not the stuff of husbands. He could not bring it into their lives.

Ah, Diana. Vincent stood and began to pace the library from fireplace to window. If only he were free of the menace, if only he could take her in his arms, claim her, keep her, without bringing violence down on her head. Every time he touched her it became harder to let her go. He must constantly remind himself of his honor—that she was under his protection. He could not impose himself on her, even if occasionally he saw an answering spark in her eyes.

Vincent paused and stared into the fire. Had he, in his desire, imagined it? Or had he truly felt a response from her? He must be dreaming. She knew the kind of man he had been. He had told her himself. Possibly she still did not realize just what a scurvy rascal he was. And practicing espionage had only stained him deeper. It had bloodied his hands.

No. She and Bytham and Selena deserved a future, and as much as he might wish to, he could not offer them one.

He might not have one himself.

The next week passed in deceptive peacefulness. Diana could almost forget that they were fleeing for their lives—or alternatively, that they had been cleverly kidnapped. Bytham and Selena blossomed with Mrs. Cobbs's good food and the wholesome country air. Fanny and Throckmorton watched over them, and Diana begun to feel rested for the first time in months. Vincent Ingleton kept a polite distance—both to Diana's relief and dismay.

The only cloud in this idyllic sky was the fact that the

scrape on her face refused to heal. She would have a scar, but, Diana reflected, that would be the least of her worries if she did not survive to tell the tale.

Mrs. Cobbs, however, did not view the matter in that light. "We cannot have you with a scar on your pretty face, ma'am. The problem is, it wants to fester, and I don't rightly know what to do. I'd best send for Old Annie."

They had been standing near the door in the small entry where the light would fall on Diana's face through the glass. They were forced to step back as Cobbs came through from the outside.

He scowled. "What? What about Old Annie?"

Mrs. Cobbs turned to her husband. "We need her. She'll know how to heal Mrs. Greenleigh's face."

Cobbs snorted. "That Cat Anna! Don't like her prowling around. Can't you tend to it yourself?"

"Now, Mr. Cobbs…" His wife shook her head. "You know there is no such thing as witches. Annie is harmless, and she is the best midwife in the shire. If she hadn't been there when Aidan was born…"

"Oh, yes, yes. I know. I've heard it often enough." He waved a dismissive hand. "But I still say she's a crazy old witch. Makes my skin crawl when she has them spells. Well, do what you think best."

With this grudging permission, he took himself off in the direction of the kitchen. Mrs. Cobbs put her hands on her hips and scowled after him. "Never mind him, Mrs. Green-leigh. Men don't much like Annie. Something about her scares them. But she is just an old woman—and a very clever one at that. Just getting a little strange. I'll send for her."

When Old Annie arrived the next day, Diana found herself in agreement with Cobbs. There was something eerie about the midwife, in spite of her simple black dress and spotless white apron. It was not so much the gray hair peeking from under her cap or the fact that very few teeth graced her withered gums. It was in her eyes—an almost feral gleam. Diana fervently hoped she would not be treated to seeing one of Old Annie's "spells."

In Annie's opinion, they had pursued the wrong treatment, as she hastened to instruct them. "Comfrey salve is all very well for healing, but this place has poison needs to be got out. Shouldn't have let it go this long." She scowled disapprovingly at the housekeeper. "What's needed is a fomentation." She turned the frown on to Diana. "You best go up to your room, me lady. I'll fetch it up."

Accordingly, Diana took herself off to her bedchamber. She put on an old wrapper and waited in the chair by the window. A light breeze blew in and sunshine flickered on the sill as the sun flirted with a growing number of clouds. It looked as though they were in for a bit of rain.

Diana glanced around the room. So pleasant. So comfortable with its chintz-covered chairs and stone fireplace. She sighed. Why couldn't they just stay here forever, safe and hidden? The children loved being here. Why couldn't she just shut the troublesome world away?

Pretend she was safe with Vincent Ingleton.

She *felt* safe. He certainly had expended every effort to keep her enemies at bay, had offered her comfort, watched over her children. It would be such a relief to explore that spark between them, to see where that kiss might have led. Diana wanted to simply enjoy his attention and his beautiful person, perhaps even to hold him next to her heart, without fear and suspicion.

If only…

A tap on the door interrupted this reverie and signaled the arrival of Mrs. Cobbs and Old Annie, the former bearing a steaming copper pot. Annie beckoned to Diana. "You best lie down, me lady, and turn your face this way." Diana complied and Mrs. Cobbs dipped a cloth into the kettle. "Mind what you are about, Nellie!" Annie snapped, snatching the cloth into her own gnarled hands. "A burn is worse to heal than a scrape."

"Yes, I know, Mistress Annie." Mrs. Cobbs smiled gently and retrieved the material. "Here, let me help you fold it."

When the poultice had been wrapped to her satisfaction, Annie took it again from her helper. "This will sting, me lady. I used calendula and yarrow. The calendula does smart."

"Ah!" Diana winced as the hot cloth settled over the wound.

"Is it too hot?" Mrs. Cobbs hovered over her anxiously.

"Got to be hot," Annie growled, reversing her earlier ground. "Don't do no good if it ain't hot."

Mrs. Cobbs sighed. "Yes, Mistress Annie. I know."

Diana gritted her teeth against the sting and wondered if the housekeeper gritted her own against the irascible old woman. Annie's knowledge must be valuable indeed to illicit such patience. But then, Mrs. Cobbs had shown herself to be a very kind woman. Her compassion would certainly extend to the cantankerous aging.

Drowsiness descended over Diana. The stinging ebbed as she grew accustomed to the warmth against her cheek and she began to drift off. If only she could just stay here like this…. Safe… Cared for…

If only.

The peace and quiet had begun to chafe Vincent. Almost two weeks had passed without word from London. He had no way of knowing where his enemies were, how close they might be to finding him and Diana. They could not stay here forever without word of strangers in residence getting around the district, and when that information became widespread, they would no longer be safe. No, soon it would be time to move on.

At least the sojourn had given Diana a chance to rest and for the wound on her face to heal. The housekeeper had called for some old crone to come and minister to Diana. Whatever she had done appeared to be effective. The wound seemed to be healing. Mrs. Cobbs worried out loud about a scar, but that made no difference to Vincent.

He would never see anything but Diana's beautiful face.

Somehow, by dint of the greatest effort, he had managed to stay at arm's distance from her. He made it a point not to be alone with her at all. He dined with her, walked with her and the children, played skittles with them on rainy days, and went to his library every evening and stayed there alone until he was ready for bed.

And when he was in bed, he stared at the door that led from his chamber to hers, torturing himself with images of her soft body clothed in nothing but a thin nightdress. Of her glowing hair spread over the pillow. Of the hungry light he had seen in her eyes.

And his fledgling honor prevailed.

He did not go in to her.

Now he paced the library, waiting for Throckmorton to come back with the post. He needed information. But when the footman returned, he had nothing for Vincent, only two letters forwarded by Adam and Helen to Diana. Vincent curbed the impulse to snoop. Diana had said the last message she received had come from Helen, but he had his doubts. It had obviously upset her, as a letter from his step-mother would hardly have done. Perhaps she would eventually confide in him without his having to stoop to reading her mail.

But when he found her in the morning room and gave

her the messages, he came no closer to discovering the source of her earlier distress. She simply thanked him, put the notes in her pocket unopened, and went back to her book, her face tense but expressionless.

Perhaps he would have to snoop, after all.

He made his way through the crowded ballroom, smiling and speaking to acquaintances, bowing to the ladies, and snarling inside. The bitch was defying him! She must be brought to heel. He needed the information she should be providing. How dare she deny him? Women! Sluts, all of them.

He slid past a small, provocatively dressed young woman in the throng. Slut! He stepped back suddenly to tread heavily and purposefully on her slippered foot with the heel of his boot. The bones crunched. When she screamed, he turned to her, all surprise, apologizing profusely. He watched with satisfaction as her escort carried her away.

He would send her flowers tomorrow.

Chapter Eight

Even though Diana had been expecting both letters sooner or later, the messages they conveyed fell with crushing weight. Deimos now vowed to go to a magistrate within two weeks if she did not comply with his orders. She would not do it, of course. She was beginning to realize that he would never leave her alone, even if she did as he directed. He would always want something, would always abuse her.

If he made good on his threat, she would deal with the inevitable consequences when they befell. A possibility—an exceedingly remote one—existed that the authorities would believe her explanation. If only she had never taken Deimos's money! That alone seemed to confirm her lack of character—made it appear that she had some clandestine relationship with the man. With that fact and his wicked tongue, he would surely hang her if he chose.

The other letter, the one from her cousin, put the death knell to her hopes of a respectable life, regardless of Deimos's action. It was hardly a shock. She had expected it, but still… When the blow fell, the force of it numbed her.

A strange calm descended on Diana as she accepted despair. There was no further need to worry about her future.

She very likely had no future. Between Deimos and her pursuers and her homeless condition... Her only concern now was for her children. She must make plans for *their* future—one they would very likely have to face without her.

Diana sent a message that she had the headache and would not be down for dinner. As night closed around her, she was still sitting in the chair in her bedchamber where she had read the letters. She did not bother to light a candle, but sat staring into the darkness, thinking.

The house quieted as its various inhabitants took themselves off to bed. The night deepened. Suddenly, Diana felt desperately shut in by the silence and the dark. She jumped to her feet and felt her way to the door of her chamber. The corridor outside still had candles burning in the sconces. She hurried down the stairs and quietly let herself out onto the terrace.

The moon was dark tonight, but a blazing carpet of stars blanketed the sky. Diana made her way to the bench and sat, marveling at the dazzle above her. She had lived in London so long she had almost forgotten the stars. Under which ones had she been born? They must be hidden far away in some very dark corner of the sky.

Was there somewhere among them a brighter one for her children?

Vincent heard the shuffling of soft slippers on the stones of the terrace. He rose from his desk where he had been sitting in the dark, planning what he would do next. Walking to the window, he peered through the glass. It was Diana, of course. He would know her step anywhere. She sank to the bench and sat staring at the sky. At least, tonight, she was not weeping.

Having her out of doors alone made him uneasy. They were probably safe enough here for the time being, but still… Vincent quietly opened the door, then cleared his throat. He didn't want to frighten her.

"Diana?" He stepped out onto the terrace.

She turned toward him. "Vincent?"

"Yes, it is I." He crossed to her and sat beside her. "Is all well with you?"

For a space she did not answer the question, just sat staring at the sky. At last she said, "Vincent, I need for you to promise me something, if you will."

Startled, Vincent looked at her more closely. "I will if it is within my capabilities. What is it?"

Diana turned and shifted her gaze to his face. "If…if something happens to me, will you care for Bytham and Selena?"

Damnation! What brought this on? He searched for the right words. "Of course, if I am able, but… What has happened, Diana?" But of course, he knew. "There was something in those letters." It was not a question.

She nodded. "My cousin writes that he will not have a…a disgraced woman and her *spawn* in his house. He expresses shock that I have—in his words—*thrown myself at Lord Lonsdale in such a shameless fashion.*"

"The bastard!" Vincent jumped to his feet. "What does he know of the matter? In fact, *how* does he know of the matter?"

Diana shrugged. "I have no idea. But I did not expect him to offer me shelter. This is merely an excuse."

Vincent stalked across the terrace, spun about angrily and stalked back. She watched him calmly as he came to a stop before her. Sudden alarm shot through him. He scowled. "Diana. You…you are not thinking of harming yourself, are you?"

"No." She sighed and shook her head. "I would never do that to my children. But I fear that my enemies may do it for me, one way or another. I must think of the children, plan for them to be cared for."

Vincent sat and ran his fingers through his hair. "Diana, I don't know what to say to you. I—I promised Wyn to care for you and the children, but you must know by now that I would do it for your own sakes regardless of any promise to Wyn." He turned to her and took her hand. "You know I am drawn to you—I cannot hide that—and I am growing very fond of Bytham and Selena."

Diana gazed at him steadily. Skeptically? "But?"

He would have to tell her. Vincent shuddered at the thought that the knowledge might place her in even greater peril. But she needed to know. He reached for her other hand. "Diana, I am not free to make promises to anyone. If I am not very careful, I might not live to see the month out myself."

Her delicate eyebrows rose questioningly. Vincent drew a deep breath and plunged on. "I have placed myself in the service of the Crown—have taken on the investigation of certain matters."

"I see." She nodded thoughtfully. "You have become a spy."

"Yes." He looked into her face, trying desperately to see what she thought of that information. "I am a spy."

"And you are being pursued, also."

"Yes, I believe by the same people who wish to capture you or the children. The situations overlap."

"And are you going to tell me what they are?" Her tranquil expression had not changed.

Dare he tell her? "I am afraid that any further knowledge you might have…" He bounded to his feet. "Ah, the devil with it! It can make little difference now that everyone knows I have you with me." He began to pace again. "As I told you, we fear that there are those who wish to help Bonaparte escape from the island of Elba and return him to power. They must be stopped. If they actually make the attempt, there will be a veritable bloodbath."

She followed him with her gaze. "And Wyn was a part of this plot?"

"I am not sure. St. Edmunds almost certainly is. To what extent he had involved Wyn or exactly what the plan is…I don't yet know. That is what I am trying to discover. Wyn talked admiringly of Napoleon to anyone and everyone, but nothing to the purpose. It was very bad of him, in his position, but try as I might, I could not stop him." He paused before her. "But I am not sure he was included in the scheming. Rather, I believe they were using him to gain knowledge from the Foreign Office. But for someone to be in such a panic about what he might have told you… He must have known something."

"The conspirators may have killed him to keep him from revealing their plans, then."

"Quite possibly."

"And you are equally at risk, because they know you also have knowledge of them."

"Suspicions, more accurately, no real knowledge. Certainly not proof. But I fear that these recent events mean that somehow they have discovered my role in the investigation."

Diana looked up into the stars again, as if seeking an answer to her problem. "So what arrangements should I make for my children?"

Vincent sat beside her again. "Do you have a will?"

"A will? I have never thought about it. I own nothing…"

"But your children."

"Yes, of course. I should have thought of that as soon as Wyn died." She pondered for a moment. "But who would take that responsibility?"

Suddenly, Vincent knew without a doubt. "Adam and Helen."

"Lord and Lady Litton? But…but they hardly know me."

"They have wanted children for several years. Helen has suffered a number of miscarriages. We will write to them tomorrow and include your will. If they don't wish to accommodate you, they will say so."

"You believe I can trust them to…to love Bytham and Selena when I am gone?" Tears hovered on the tips of her eyelashes.

Vincent thought about the question. Suddenly he knew that, as few people as he trusted in this world, he would bet his own life on the love and loyalty of Adam and Helen Barbon.

Why had he never realized that before?

He reached out and brushed Diana's tears away with his thumb. "With all my heart. But do not despair, Diana. We are all still alive, and I intend to keep us that way."

She sighed and he moved to pull her into his arms.

And stopped dead still.

A dark figure drifted toward them across the lawn.

"Shh!" Vincent seized Diana and shoved her toward the house, putting himself between her and the approaching shape. But she didn't move, simply stood staring at the approaching black form. He was at the point of pulling her to the door when she held up a detaining hand.

"Wait. That looks like Old Annie."

"Who?" Vincent squinted into the darkness. "The midwife who has been treating your face?" He sensed her nod rather than saw it.

"What is she doing out this time of night? Perhaps she is ill and needs help."

In fact, the old woman seemed to be stumbling. Vincent cast a wary glance into the shadows of the trees. Surely she could not be in league with his enemies. He pressed Diana back against the wall of the house and walked to meet Old Annie. As he approached her, he could hear a sound coming from her, a soft singsong, rising and falling under her breath. She did not seem to see him at all.

He took her arm. "Mistress Annie, do you need assistance?"

"Hmm-hmm, hmm-hmm." She looked past him toward the house.

He turned to see Diana right behind him. "She doesn't answer me."

"Cobbs said she has spells." Diana came around him and touched the old woman's shoulder. "Mistress Annie, can you hear me? It's Lady… It's Mrs. Greenleigh."

"Dark." The word rumbled up from deep in the woman's chest. "So dark."

"Yes," Diana agreed. "It is very dark tonight."

"The moon." Annie rolled her eyes at the heavens. "Moon dark."

The hair on the back of Vincent's neck rose. He nodded and tried to speak normally. "Yes, Mistress Annie, of course the moon is dark."

"Dark…dark…" Suddenly the midwife spun around, jerking out of his grip. "I hear her."

"Hear who, Mistress Annie?" Diana took hold of her sleeve.

"Black Annis. She walks at the dark moon. She says danger…danger."

"Come now, Annie." Fighting the shiver crawling up his back, Vincent strove for reason. "Black Annis is only a tale to frighten children."

A screech of a laugh erupted into the night. In spite of himself, Vincent stepped back. Annie turned on him. "You wish, you wish. You tell yourself tales to *not* be afraid. But

I know." She turned slowly, scanning the darkness around them. "I know. Named for her I was. She walks. She has ways. She walks hidden ways."

Diana drew back and looked around her. So did Vincent.

"Nonsense." Vincent gave the old woman a gentle shake. This was getting out of hand. "I will walk you home."

"There! There!" Suddenly, Annie flung out a hand. "You see! I told you."

Vincent dropped Annie's arm and grasped Diana's. "Into the house. Now!"

Half running, he all but dragged Diana across the lawn. He vaulted up the terrace steps, bringing her with him, and pushed them both through the door. "Send Throckmorton to me! Get your pistol and stay with the children. Hurry!"

Without a word Diana ran out of the room and up the stairs. Vincent took a double-barreled horse pistol from his desk and peered out into the dark. He could no longer see Old Annie.

Or anyone else.

A thump and a grunt heralded Throckmorton's arrival in the darkened room. Vincent never took his eyes off the lawn. "You go out the front. I'll take the side door."

Throckmorton muttered agreement and slipped off through the house. Vincent felt his way to the side entry. When they had each circled the house without seeing signs of life, Vincent nodded at the woods. They moved off silently.

A chilly frustrating hour later, they gave it up and returned to the manor, having seen or heard nothing but the rustling of the night.

Old Annie was gone.

The incident continued to disturb Vincent the next morning. He and Throckmorton searched again in the daylight, but discovered no indication that anyone other than the old midwife had been afoot the night before. Of course, if Throckmorton had loyalties other than to him… The thought brought chills to Vincent's spine. But so far he had found no reason to believe that.

He called Cobbs to the library and questioned him about Annie. Cobbs grimaced. "Well, sir, I suppose, as my wife says, there ain't no such thing as witches. But if there is, then Old Annie is the one Eldritch Manor is named for."

"Oh, come now, Cobbs," Vincent chided. "The manor is far older than any living person."

"Aye, sir…. At least, I hope so."

Vincent frowned. "In any event, I am not concerned so much about her possible supernatural abilities as her present associates." He raised an eyebrow. "Could she possibly be in league with anyone who might be up to no good?"

"Oh, I wouldn't think that, sir. She's too strange."

"She said last night that she saw someone, heard someone. Said she heard Black Annis." Vincent shook his head in disgust. "But I have no confidence in *that* theory. If she saw someone, they were flesh and blood."

Cobbs shuffled his feet uncomfortably. "I wouldn't be too sure about that, sir. She do have the sight. And the moon was dark. Black Annis—"

"Don't tell me you believe that nonsense? Besides, I'm told the uncanny crone is supposed to live in a cave near Leicester." Vincent's mouth quirked wryly. "Or in Scotland. She seems fairly ubiquitous."

"Leicester ain't that far, sir." Cobbs studied his boots. "If Mistress Annie saw something, it was very likely beyond our ken. I don't believe she would lead anyone here to burgle the place or nothing like that. Wouldn't no one want to come with her."

With that Vincent had to be content. He had to admit that the old woman seemed an unlikely confederate for his pursuers. But had she actually heard or seen anything other than the fantasies of her own mind?

They needed to move on while they could do so unobserved.

He still could not be sure from whom they fled. After he had finally reached his bed last night, it had occurred to him that, while he had revealed his secret to Diana, she had kept hers. She had received *two* letters. And she had mentioned only one. Apparently she still did not trust him enough to confide in him.

Or she pursued a goal of her own of which he had no inkling. Vincent winced. That would be a sharp wound, indeed, to discover that she conspired against him with his opponents.

One from which he might never recover.

But somehow he did not think that was the case. That she genuinely feared for her life, he had no doubt. But whom did she fear, and why? Perhaps she *had* known of St. Edmunds's plans and had already betrayed them to someone. She had feared him from the first. If so, why did she not admit that? Other than the fact that she suspected Vincent himself of a double game.

But Vincent began to think that there was another player—one that had never been mentioned between them, one he might not know. Time would tell. The shadowy menace could not remain hidden forever. But he wished with his whole heart that Diana, herself, would tell him who it was. That she would trust him. That he *could* trust her.

One thing was certain.

Whether he could or not, he still wanted her.

They spent the rest of the day on correspondence. Diana wrote a simple will and a letter to Lord and Lady Litton, begging them to accept the charge of her children should she lose her life. She could only pray that they would.

And that the situation would not arise.

Vincent also composed a lengthy document to be sent to them, but what it was, he did not say. Perhaps it had to do with his business as a spy. A spy! As if she had not enough reasons for anxiety and suspicion. She must watch herself with him. He seemed so kind, and he said he cared for her and the children, but… A spy might be hiding anything.

Tomorrow, Throckmorton would post her letter, and Diana felt an overwhelming sense of relief. Now she could give her attention to defeating her enemies and contriving to stay alive, knowing that if she failed, Selena and Bytham would be provided for.

Ah, but how it grieved her to think of leaving them forever!

After sitting with the children while they finished their supper, Diana kissed her offspring good-night and watched Fanny lead them up to bed. Perhaps it had become a little easier to let someone else tuck them in. They must become more accustomed to the care of others. It would be easier for them if…

But she would not think of that.

When she and Vincent had eaten their own dinner, he disappeared into his study as was his custom. Diana went out onto the terrace and sought her accustomed spot on the bench, seeking solace in the scene. A soft summer sunset had given way to a thick lavender twilight. In the west the tiniest sliver of a new moon poised against the mellow sky, bidding the world a lingering good-night. Just below the slender crescent hung a brilliant, diminutive star, like a lady's diamond earring below her delicate ear.

Diana let the peace of the dusk steal over her. The breeze tonight felt slightly damp and warm, soothing. After a few moments she became aware of Vincent standing behind her. He said nothing and she did not turn. They stayed thus, captive to the spell of the night, watching the moon descend into the void and feeling the soft blanket of the dark slowly wrap around them. He moved closer and rested both hands on her shoulders.

Diana found herself leaning back against him and his grip tightened. Her heart began to beat faster and she could hear his breathing deepen. He stepped over the bench and, straddling it, circled her waist with his arms and pulled her back against his chest.

Last night he had told her that he was drawn to her. She did not know then if she believed that. She did not know now. The chance that he was using her and her children as pawns in some deadly competition was all too real. She had succumbed to the sweet words of love once before.

But tonight it did not matter. There might be very little of her life left to her. She did not want to die celibate and alone. Empty. Tonight she wanted to be filled with the warmth of his body, to smell his smoky masculine scent, the wool and starch of his clothes. To feel the rise of passion.

The rasp of a day-old beard pressed against her cheek. She felt his breath against the skin of her neck. Diana closed her eyes. His arms pulled her closer. The muscles of his thighs pressed against her hips. His lips touched her ear.

"Diana."

A shiver ran through her. She turned in his embrace and lifted her face.

"Ah, God." The sigh whispered through her hair and down the side of her face to her mouth. His lips came over hers, hot, hard, demanding. Diana dropped her head back and his mouth found its way to her exposed throat. Heat pooled in her lower body as she leaned back in his arms.

Suddenly his whole body went rigid. Vincent lifted his

head, his eyes narrow, searching. Then Diana heard it, too. Stealthy footsteps. The rustle of grass. Before she knew what had happened, he had swooped her off his lap and onto the floor between the bench and the balustrade, rolling onto her, his body covering hers.

The footsteps drew nearer. The corner of Diana's eye caught a flicker in the dim light and movement close beside her face. Vincent had lifted himself on one elbow, a pistol in his other hand. Diana lay very still, hardly daring to breathe.

Suddenly the light of a lamp appeared at the door leading into the corridor. A voice called out, "Fanny, is that you?"

"Yes, Mama. We are coming." The footsteps hurried forward.

Diana felt Vincent's weight increase as, all at once, he relaxed. A giggle rose up in her. His lips found her ear. "Shh!"

Diana stifled the giggle, but she could feel the shaking of his own silent laughter. She peered under the bench in time to see two figures, one tall and one small, hasten up the steps to the terrace. The Harter boy.

"You best get in, young lady." Mrs. Cobbs's voice sounded annoyed. "You are supposed to be in before dark. It's well your father is doing accounts."

"I'm sorry, Mrs. Cobbs. I wanted to show Fanny my new foal. It's my fault."

"Huh." The housekeeper's voice softened a bit. "I know very well how it happened, Jacob, but if you want to keep walking out together, you best mind."

"Oh, yes, ma'am. We will," the young man promised earnestly. "Good night, Fanny."

The door closed and young Harter made his way down the steps.

Vincent and Diana stayed where they were until they

heard his whistling disappear into the distance. Vincent lifted himself off her and she sat up.

The chuckles finally made their way out of Diana. "What a sight we must be! The master and supposed mistress of the manor cowering under a bench, hoping to escape detection by a pair of young lovers."

Vincent leaned back against the balustrade, grinning, the pistol held loosely in his hand. "One feels a little foolish."

"Yes. One does." Hysterical laughter began to grow in Diana. After all the tension… She took a deep breath and, with an effort, contained it. "Poor boy. Not even a goodnight kiss."

"Oh, I suspect he had a few kisses. The foal was probably in his byre." He sighed and looked at her, suddenly sober. "Which is more than I had—or should have." He ran his fingers through his hair and shoved the pistol into his belt. "I'm sorry, Diana. I have been struggling to treat you with the respect you deserve. Forgive me. I should not have touched you, but you looked so sad…"

The laughter died in Diana. She stared up at the stars. "Yes, I am sad. I have very little to look forward to, Vincent. And my children… I fear it is inevitable that I will be separated from them—one way or another."

"Diana…" He extended a hand toward her.

She did not look at him. "And you see… My honor no longer matters. I have no reputation any longer. I would take what comfort I may—while I still can. I would shut out the fear."

Something like a growl issued from him.

He reached out and jerked her into his arms.

She came to him easily. For several minutes he was awash with the scent of her, the softness of her breasts against him, the heat of her mouth under his as he pressed her against himself. His starving senses could not get enough of her. She melted into him, matching touch with touch, tongue with tongue, moan with moan.

He slid to the side, laying her down. He stretched out beside her, one knee drawn up across her body. He fastened his fingers in her hair and devoured her face with his eyes and lips and tongue. As she arched her body against him, his mouth moved of its own accord over her throat to the top of the neckline of her gown. There he tasted the swell of her breasts, breathing in the musky fragrance of her skin.

Her moan brought him to his senses. He could not take her lying here on the stones of the terrace floor. Not in the open, vulnerable to unseen dangers. Coming to one knee, he scooped her up and made for the library door. He shoved it open with one shoulder and kicked it closed behind him.

A sofa faced the fireplace. He set her on it and knelt in front of her, lifting her skirt and spreading her knees. Hands fumbling behind her, he found enough buttons to loosen the dress and tugged it off her shoulders. Then he pulled her hips forward against his throbbing erection and buried his face in her bosom. Her fingers tangled in his hair as he covered her nipple with his mouth, and she rocked her hips forward.

He could stand it no longer. He yanked at the buttons of his buckskin britches, undoing the flap. Falling backward, he pulled her on top of him and lifted her onto his straining shaft. He could not go slowly. Every sense screamed for her. He gripped her hips and drove into her, while she tightened around him.

Somewhere in the red haze that engulfed him, he heard her cry out, felt her go rigid. In the next second his own voice burst out of him. Vincent went completely out of control, pumping his seed into her. Waves of sensation swept over him until he fell limply back to the floor.

Diana lay against his chest, exhausted. He fastened his

arms around her and held her hard against him until the ache of the floor against his back and the chill of the dying fire roused him.

"Come," he said, setting her gently to the side. "It is time for bed."

They spent the night in her bed, so that she could hear the children in the next room if they cried out. She fell asleep, her naked back held close against his chest and his hand at her waist. And she woke, sometime in the night, with his hand on her breast and his lips against the nape of her neck. The hand moved, closing over her nipple, sliding down her body, coming to rest between her legs. Pressing. Circling. His shaft pulsed against her bottom.

Diana sighed and turned to him. He slid over her and joined his body to hers, thrusting slowly, brushing his mouth across hers, bending to nibble her throat. One hand stroked her breast. He thrust… And again… Harder… Rocking against her. Circling… Harder…

Diana's scream would certainly have waked the children, and Throckmorton into the bargain, had Vincent not swallowed it, smothering it with his mouth. Mouths and tongues and bodies entwined, he thrust faster and faster until Diana would have cried out again had she been able. She barely heard his muffled groan as her head swam and her heart pounded, the world swirling away into myriad sparkling colors.

He moved to the side and gathered her into his arms, holding her tightly against his chest. Gently he kissed the top of her head and stroked her back. Diana snuggled against him until she heard his breathing grow steady and even as his hand stilled and he drifted back to sleep. Even then she did not move from his arms, but lay awake for some time, savoring the closeness, absorbing his soothing touch. How long had it been since she had been held by anyone? She wanted to stay there forever.

Did she dare? Could he possibly really care for her? She needed so much to believe that someone did.

Chapter Nine

Well, he had done it. In spite of all his honorable intentions. But he could not be sorry for it. If he died tomorrow, at least he would have known her. And she would be cared for. His own will had seen to that. Eldritch Manor and his private fortune would be hers if he met an untimely demise.

Vincent did not flatter himself that Diana would grieve for him. What passed between them last night had been born of his desire and her desperation. She still distrusted him. And he still could not trust her.

He could only want her.

And today he must make plans to protect her. She blushed and studied her plate when he found her in the breakfast parlor and dropped a quick kiss on the back of her neck. He had risen before her and gone to his own chamber, not wanting the maid to find him when she brought Diana's chocolate. Though why it mattered, he could not say. The staff thought them husband and wife.

But he knew better.

And so did she.

Vincent stifled the impulse to reassure her, to tell her that he understood the impulse of the moment, the magic of the new moon. The urgency of fear. That he would expect nothing more from her. He would speak to her about that later, when they had more privacy. Now he needed to inform her of their impending departure.

He settled for patting her gently on the shoulder and sat in the opposite chair. "We need to discuss plans. I have become convinced that we need to move on."

"Oh, dear." She set her cup down and gazed at him. "It is so pleasant here. I hate to leave."

"Yes." Vincent poured coffee into his own cup. "It has been a very comfortable stay, but I am becoming uneasy." He could not afford comfort. "I have become complacent. The episodes of the last two nights have shown me that. We were very vulnerable on both occasions."

"But there was actually no danger either time." Diana set the preserves by his place while he rose and filled a plate from the sideboard. "Most likely Old Annie heard Fanny and young Harter on their evening walk."

He turned, eyes narrowed in thought. "I am not as sure of that as I would like to be." He sat, took a mouthful of eggs and chewed. Swallowing, he added, "Old Annie might indeed have seen or heard someone else spying about."

"How could so old a woman have heard something we did not?" Diana pushed her plate away and leaned back in her chair. "Old persons are usually rather deaf."

"That's true, of course. Still…" Vincent could not quite put a finger on the source of his disquiet. "But she is very familiar with this area. Something out of place might catch her attention, and I do not wish to discount a real threat. No, we must go. I'm sorry."

Diana sighed. "Very well. I suppose you know best."

Vincent wished he could be sure he did. "Who is to say for sure? But I have a feeling…" He could not exactly describe it. "Rather like Old Annie's premonition of danger. Cobbs says she has the sight."

"I would not expect you to credit that." Diana smiled. "It does not seem like you."

"I've learned to believe in my instincts. Perhaps Mistress Annie has learned to believe in hers." He finished his beef and reached for his cup to wash it down. "How soon can you be ready to depart this morning?"

"Today?" Dismay filled her voice. "I… Well, later this morning, I should think. I haven't much to take. Oh, my. The children will be so disappointed. They have become very fond of Fanny and Mrs. Cobbs."

Vincent stood and rested his hand on her shoulder. He would allow himself nothing more. "I'm sorry. Perhaps when this danger has passed, they can return for a visit— though by then, Fanny may have become Mrs. Harter. But I am sure they will enjoy Inglewood once we arrive."

"We are going there, then?"

"Yes. I think the time has come to entice our enemies into the light."

Diana did not recognize the coach pulled up before the main door of Eldritch Manor. Where the vehicle in which they had arrived had been black, this one shone with a rich wood finish trimmed in burgundy. Inside, the velvet upholstery echoed the deep wine.

"Is this your carriage?" She turned to where Vincent descended the stairs carrying a portmanteau carelessly in one hand.

He glanced around for other ears. Finding none, he nodded, his smile sly. "Greenleigh keeps it here."

"I see. What will you do with the other one?"

"I'll send for it, or it will await my return." He shrugged. At that point Throckmorton appeared at the top of the stairs, a trunk perched easily on his shoulder. Diana went out into the soft summer sunshine. At least they would not have to ride all night in the dark, but how she was to keep the children entertained all day in the coach, she did not know.

They were on the front steps, engaged in telling the Cobbs family farewell. At least they seemed pleasantly excited about another journey. Mrs. Cobbs turned as she came out the door. "Ah, Mrs. Greenleigh, we will miss you. Such a shame that you have to leave so soon, but I suppose Mr. Greenleigh's business can't wait."

"No, we have had an agreeable holiday, but we must go. Thank you so much for your kindness. And please tell Mistress Annie that I appreciate her helping me."

"Oh, dear. I almost forgot." The housekeeper fished in her pocket of the apron and withdrew the small pot of salve. "Old Annie says that the comfrey should now help complete the healing. You must use it three times each day."

"Thank you." Diana slipped the ointment into her own pocket. "Perhaps we will see you again before long."

Fanny hugged Selena and Bytham and helped them into the carriage. "Be good children."

They chorused an assurance that they would be truly excellent children until they saw her again. Diana could only hope so. They had a very long ride before them, one for which she wished she had some privacy for her own thoughts. She needed to sort out her feelings about the passionate interlude with Vincent; the fact that she had slept with a spy.

But she would not have that opportunity. Instead she would be sitting next to him in the small space, smelling his scent and feeling the ripple of muscle in his thigh each time he adjusted his position.

Hardly a situation for cool reflection.

He handed her up into the carriage and climbed in behind her. All of them waved vigorously at those left standing on the steps of Eldritch Manor as Throckmorton set the horses in motion. They left the house behind at a spanking pace. In the drive and the lanes, all they could see was trees, but when they reached the main pike, fields and houses became visible, providing something to interest Selena and Bytham. Diana was pointing out sheep and cattle and haystacks for their amusement when the carriage abruptly turned into another wooded lane.

She looked questioningly at Vincent. He smiled crookedly. "Another small subterfuge."

After a few more minutes the coach pulled to a stop. Vincent got out and took his valise down from the boot. Opening it, he retrieved a small signboard with a coat of arms emblazoned on it. Curious, Diana climbed down from the coach, followed by Selena and Bytham. Vincent pointed to two hooks fixed to the door of the carriage that Diana had not noticed before. He hung the sign on them and secured a catch at the bottom.

"Is that the Lonsdale crest?" Somehow it did not look familiar to Diana. Vincent shook his head. "Then whose is it?"

"I have no idea. I suspect that it is no one's." He tested the security of the sign and stepped back to admire it.

"I see. Does this *no one* have a title?" Diana smiled. "Which is to say, who are we now?"

"Lord and Lady Throckmorton, I believe." He gestured at the grinning Throckmorton who had joined them on the ground and was doffing his coachman's coat and wig. He handed them to Vincent, who tucked them into the suitcase out of which he had pulled his own. "His lordship here, will of course ride inside while I drive. He is much too distinctive to be left on the box."

Diana glanced at the children. "Do you think anyone will be misled?"

"Oh, yes. People see what they expect to see. If one does not see an unusually large coachman or a plain black coach, they will not look further at a lord's coach with an ordinary driver."

Throckmorton smiled at Diana. "I ain't had so much fun since I…" The big man hesitated. "Uh, since I took employment with Lord Litton. You won't mind if I ride inside, my lady?"

"Why, no. I'll be happy for your company."

Selena bounced happily on her toes. "We can play that game you showed us."

"Right enough. Now, in you go, miss. Come, Master Bytham."

Throckmorton bundled the children into the carriage and helped Diana up the steps while Vincent climbed onto the box. Diana realized that by now the boxer and her offspring had become fast friends. He had been with them most of every day, even sleeping in the room with them.

When they were settled, the coach made a wide turn and headed back to the pike. Immediately, Selena held out her closed fist, her thumb extended. Bytham chortled and wrapped his hand around her thumb and offered his own to Throckmorton. The big man added his great paw to the stack, closing his hand carefully around Bytham's thumb. Then the three of them repeated the process until their hands were piled six deep. Diana watched, fascinated.

Selena gazed up at Throckmorton. "Knock it off or blow it off?" she inquired saucily.

He grinned at her. "Let's see you knock it off, miss."

Both hands captured, Selena puzzled for a moment, then bumped Throckmorton's fist with her chin. His hand fell limply to his side. She turned to her brother. "Knock it off or blow it off?"

"Blow it off!"

His sister puffed and Bytham's hand flew upward. And so it went until only Selena's little fist was left. Throckmorton peered at her closed hand. "What's in there?"

A giggle. "Bread and cheese."

"Where's my share?"

"The rat got it!"

"Where's the rat?

"The cat got it," shouted Bytham.

"Where's the cat?"

"On the roof," Selena cried, "and the first one to laugh or show his teeth gets... Gets a pinch!"

She immediately clapped both hands over her mouth, her eyes bright. Bytham followed her example. Throckmorton assumed a ferocious scowl. Uncertain whether or not the threat applied to her, Diana decided against laughing. Not that it was easy! They rode in silence for perhaps fifteen seconds before Selena let out a whoop.

"Aha!" Throckmorton gave her cheek a tiny pinch. "We win, Miss Selena."

"I want to gallop!" Bytham announced. He crawled across the intervening space and onto Throckmorton's knees.

"Do you, now? Very well. Hold on tight." The big footman started the familiar rhyme, suiting the action of his knees to the words. "My lord goes riding, a-trot, trot, trot. My lady goes riding, a-canter, a-canter. My young master goes riding, jockety-hitch, jockety-hitch. My young missy goes riding, an amble, an amble." He stilled his knees and the coach grew very quiet as the children held their breaths. Very slowly and portentously, Throckmorton measured his words. "But the groom lags behind...to tipple ale and wine...and must go..."

"A-gallop, a-gallop, a-gallop to make up his time!" Selena joined in as Throckmorton galloped his knees wildly and Bytham held on for dear life. "Now me!" She tugged at her brother.

Diana laughed out loud. "Great heavens, Throckmorton, have they worn you out completely these past weeks? I had no idea."

"Oh, no, my lady. I love the little ones. Don't have none of my own." He set Bytham on the seat and lifted Selena.

After two more rounds of My Lord Goes Riding, Diana took pity on the good-natured giant and called a halt. Rock, Paper, Scissors was not nearly as exciting, but a deal more restful in the confined space. Still, they were all relieved when they pulled into an inn yard for a nuncheon and a change of horses.

Diana had no opportunity either to talk to Vincent or to think about him for the rest of the day. He ate his mutton in the inn stable while Throckmorton ate with her and the children. What arrangements would be made when they stopped for the night? That question was answered that evening, at yet another inn, when Throckmorton, in his role as lord, requested a private parlor with two adjoining bed-chambers and dinner brought up.

Diana sank onto the sofa of the parlor gratefully while the inn servants carried up their trunks. Even the children drooped as they found a place to perch, but to Diana's amazement, Throckmorton looked as chipper as ever. A short while later, Vincent appeared, reporting the carriage to be properly housed.

He took off his greatcoat and she realized that he and Throckmorton wore almost-identical conservative dark coats. They could exchange roles in a moment. She could only wonder at Vincent's planning. Such devious clever-ness again gave her pause.

He might have planned anything.

They ate dinner informally, dismissing the waiters as soon as they brought the food. Diana welcomed the relief from dissembling. Constant pretense wore on the nerves. How did Vincent stand it? He must have had a great deal of practice in his service to the Crown.

After they had eaten, Throckmorton asked leave to stretch his legs out of doors and have a look around. Vincent took up watch in the parlor, but Diana still had no leisure to ponder the change in their relationship. She had to get the children ready for bed.

The usual tussle with Bytham ensued when she attempted to wash his face. Tired and cranky, he jerked away from her and made a dash for Vincent. Diana followed him to the bedchamber door and stood with hands on hips while he climbed into Vincent's lap.

Vincent looked at first one and then the other, eyebrows raised. "Is there a difficulty?"

"He doesn't want me to wash him. Come, Bytham. Mama is tired and losing patience."

Bytham grasped Vincent's neckcloth, stuck out his chin and announced, "Don't *want* to go to bed."

"Here, now." Vincent stood and delivered the miscreant back to his mother. "Let us have none of this, young man." Bytham held on to the cravat and hid his face against Vincent's shoulder.

"Mama-aa!" A weary wail sounded from Selena.

Diana threw up her hands. "I'm coming, Selena. Bytham…"

"You tend to Selena." Vincent followed her into the bedchamber. "I'll deal with young Mr. Corby." He set the boy firmly on the bed and reached for the washcloth.

"Thank you." Diana could not help but chuckle. "You are becoming quite the *père du famille*."

"And nursemaid." He grinned at her, then scowled at her wriggling son. "No, Bytham, you *will* sit still. Stop that at once, or it will be the worse for you."

At this change of tone from his favorite, Bytham gave up resistance and began to cry. Vincent got the child's nightshirt over his head and picked him up, patting his back soothingly. "Now, now. You'll be better for a good sleep." He turned to Diana. "They will sleep in the truckle bed?"

"Yes, I shall take the bed." Diana tied the ribbons of Selena's nightie and gave her a hug. "Into bed with you, miss."

Selena crawled obligingly onto the low bed and Vincent put her brother—sniffling, but drowsy—in beside her. Diana tucked them in and blew out all but one of the candles. She stepped to the doorway, only to find it already occupied by Vincent. He stood staring at her intently, his expression unreadable.

Flustered, Diana stopped. "Thank you for your help. I'm sure this is far more than you bargained for."

"True enough. I never realized how much attention children require. But in many ways, I find it very pleasant. I never expected—" He broke off and moved aside enough for her to slide past him, never taking his gaze from her face. Before she was clear of the door, he halted her with a hand on her elbow. "Diana, we must speak about last night. I—I realize that your…actions were the result of a moment's impulse. However much I would like for us to continue as lovers, I will abide by your decision. If you prefer not to…"

Diana studied his coat buttons and tried to gather her thoughts. "I—I don't know. As you said, it was the effect of the moment. We… There is so much…"

"I know." He brushed the hair back from her face and Diana's breath caught in her throat. "There is too much doubt between us."

Too much doubt between us. Somehow Diana had not realized that he had questions about *her.* But of course, he should. She had not been open with him. In fact, Vincent had possibly been more honest than she had been. She had not exactly lied. She did *not* know who had reason to take the children. Even Deimos did not have that—but she had not told Vincent about him and his threats. But what would he do if he knew? He was an agent of the government, after all. And what if he knew she had taken gifts of money from another man?

The warmth of his body seeped through her clothes where the two of them stood crowded in the doorway. His breath brushed her cheek. She lifted her gaze and found him staring at her mouth. He leaned forward and very gently pressed a kiss on it.

"Let me know your wishes." He stepped into the parlor and she followed. "But I do prefer that Throckmorton sleep in the room with the children. You may have the other bed-chamber and I shall use the sofa in here where I can watch both rooms. Unless…" He smiled wryly. "But be that as it may, I cannot become lost in passion tonight. I must remain alert."

Diana nodded.

She knew, of course, what she wanted.

But she did not know what she would do.

Three days later, as they drew near to Inglewood, Vincent still had no answer from her. Which was, in itself, an answer of sorts. Very well. He would respect the lady's preference. He could not blame her. Even had he been a paragon of virtue, he was not free to claim her.

But his association with her and Selena and Bytham had whetted an appetite he had not known he'd had. He had never before envisioned himself taking a wife, setting up his nursery. He didn't expect to live long enough. But now he had come to value those dirty little hands crushing his cravat. Had found himself listening enchanted to Selena's innocent prattle. Who would protect them if he did not survive?

Who would care for them if he *did* survive?

He did not want to give them up.

Now, however, he must concentrate on getting into Inglewood without being detected. Almost certainly the estate was being watched for their arrival. He could not risk being overtaken in the open. But most likely the search was concentrated on the main approaches. Accordingly he set the coach, not on the road to the Inglewood gates, but down a lane leading to one of the outlying tenant farms.

As they pulled into the dusty farmyard, several children and a number of dogs came tumbling out of the whitewashed cottage to meet them. A moment later a sturdily built man in a farmer's smock appeared in the byre door, eyeing them suspiciously. Vincent climbed down from the box and tossed his powdered wig aside.

"Me lord!" The farmer came hurrying toward them. "I didn't know you right off." He halted when Throckmorton opened the carriage door and got out, looking at the big man warily.

"Claugh, this is Throckmorton." Vincent nodded at the boxer, who stepped forward and extended a hand that Claugh cautiously clasped. "He is new to my employ."

By this time Bytham and Selena had put their heads out of the carriage door. Bytham started to jump down, but quickly retreated as a large dog bounded up to the carriage.

"Bowser! Here." Claugh's dog responded immediately to his master's voice and Bytham peered out again. A towheaded boy in ragged britches, perhaps a year older, had come up to the coach and stood staring at him. When Diana leaned forward to look out the door, he, too, bolted for the safety of his father's shadow.

"Do you have room for the carriage in your byre for a short while?"

The farmer gave Vincent a puzzled look. "Well, aye, me lord. I reckon we could manage… Might be a bit of a squeeze."

"Would you be willing to do me a favor, as well?"

Claugh nodded immediately. "Ye know I would, sir, after what ye done for Rolf here. We wouldn't still have him else—"

"Nonsense." Vincent cut him off firmly. "But I'm happy to see that he is hale again." He tousled the boy's hair. "But here is what I need…"

An hour later a farm wagon pulled out of Claugh's yard, the sturdy farmer himself driving the oxen. In the back Diana, Vincent and Throckmorton lay on the floor amongst baskets of apples from Claugh's cellar. A large ham rested immediately in front of Diana's face and her toes were crumpled by the presence of a wheel of cheese. The straw under her tickled her nose and scratched the back of her neck. Bowser, tongue lolling, guarded the tailgate.

Bytham and Selena thought it a wonderful lark. They had exchanged clothes with Rolf and one of Claugh's young daughters, and were sitting on the bench with the farmer. Selena's pale hair was hidden under a bonnet and Bytham's sunnier curls restrained by a straw hat. Diana had protested against having the children so exposed, but had allowed herself to be persuaded, comforted by the pistols held by both Vincent and Throckmorton—and her own small weapon clutched in her hand. The children would be much happier on the seat than if forced to lie in the cart.

The wagon creaked and groaned its way over rutted roads, across pastures and through newly tilled fields, arriving at last at a gate behind the Inglewood stables. Thence they made their way through the stable yard and up to the kitchen door, where they were greeted by a greatly astonished kitchen staff and a pair of footmen.

"La, m'lord!" A stout, gray-haired woman in a spotless apron came bustling out as Vincent rose from the wagon and brushed away a large collection of straw. "What *will* you do next?"

Vincent grinned. "One never knows, does one, Mrs. Buckden?"

"No, nor never did." She shook her head resignedly. "But, my goodness! Who is this?" Her smile slowly faded as Diana emerged from amongst the apples, her pistol discreetly tucked into a pocket. The woman cast Vincent a suspicious glance.

"Lady Diana—" Vincent helped Diana to her feet "—may I present my housekeeper, Mrs. Buckden. Lady Diana will be our guest for a while. And these are her children, Miss Selena and Master Bytham Corby." Selena ducked her head, but smiled shyly while Bytham scrambled over the seat to shelter behind Vincent in the wagon. Diana did her best to look gracious. Just how did one accomplish that when arriving with the ham in a farm cart?

"How do ye do?" Mrs. Buckden's greeting sounded just a bit chilly. Diana nodded, her heart sinking at the thought of what surely must be running through the woman's mind. Vincent smuggling her into his home…

Vincent's voice hardened. "I'm sure, Mrs. Buckden, that you will be eager to extend aid to one in need of it."

"Ah, of course, m'lord." Curiosity began to replace disapproval on the housekeeper's face. "My lady, if you would, uh, step this way." She looked doubtfully at Diana standing in the bed of the wagon.

"We need to inform the staff that caution is necessary." Vincent vaulted over the side and lifted Diana down, his strong hands warm against her waist. "Where is Rugerton?"

"Here I am, my lord." A tall, thin gentleman whose hair surrounded his shiny pate in a faded gray halo hastened out into the yard. "What are you doing back here at the kitchen? At least you brought extra provisions." He squinted into the cart. "Why didn't you let us know of your arrival?"

"Didn't know of it myself. Lady Diana, this is Rugerton, my steward."

Diana extended her hand. "How do you do, Mr. Rugerton?"

Vincent turned back to set Selena and Bytham on the ground. "Rugerton, would you be so good as to compensate Claugh for his produce? I will explain the situation to you shortly. Mrs. Buckden, where is Nurse Marshaw?"

"Upstairs, I think, my lord, and I'm sure she will want to attend to the children." The housekeeper chuckled. "She is forever complaining that you have given her none to fuss over."

Vincent grinned. "A just complaint, no doubt. If you would fetch her… Throckmorton will assist her in keeping the children safe."

"Oh, dear." Dismay settled on Mrs. Buckden's good-natured face as the boxer climbed down from the wagon. "Are they…? I mean, is there…?"

"There has been a threat to their welfare, yes."

"Oh, my! The poor dears. You just come right this way, my lady, and we will get you all settled in. You won't mind coming through the kitchen?" Mrs. Buckden gestured and Diana started past her, only to be stopped by Vincent's voice, low and intense.

"Lady Diana, welcome to my home."

Chapter Ten

A certain amount of confusion ensued before arrangements satisfactory to Vincent were made for his new guests' accommodations. Nurse Marshaw was a tall, angular woman with iron-gray hair ruthlessly restrained under a starched white cap who had cared for the young Vincent herself. She insisted that the children be housed in the nursery. Mrs. Buckden insisted that Diana should occupy the best guest room, and Durbin, the butler, assumed that Throckmorton would sleep with the other footmen.

None of which suited Vincent. He could not allow his charges to be so scattered over the rambling old mansion, nor to be so far from his own protective presence. By the exercise of much diplomacy, he finally managed to have all of them housed in rooms in the same corridor as his own, without creating—he hoped—undue suspicion. He could, of course, have simply ordered it so, but Vincent had spent the last four years rebuilding relations with his staff. He did not wish to forfeit the respect he had earned one decision, one apology, at a time.

Vincent now awaited Diana's appearance at dinner. He would, at last, have the pleasure of seeing her at his own table. He rose as she glided into the family dining room wearing silver-gray satin, her hair dressed high on her head. The graceful chignon spilled shining curls to caress her neck. Vincent had all he could do to keep his fingers and lips from joining them. He settled for kissing her hand—holding it a bit longer than propriety decreed—and helped her into her chair. At least he could touch her soft skin, let his gaze rest on the mouthwatering curve of her breasts.

At least he had her safe in his home.

He studied her coiffure as he took his own place. "You are very lovely this evening. I've never seen you with your hair that way."

"No, I cannot arrange it in this style without assistance." She spread the napkin in her lap. "Mrs. Buckden sent a maid to help me dress—a girl named Emma. She is quite good with hair."

"Ah, yes. She is Claugh's oldest daughter, I believe. Will you have wine?" He inclined his head at the elderly butler who held the bottle poised near her glass.

"Thank you, yes." Diana nodded, and Durbin poured. She took a sip. "Mmm, delicious. Speaking of Claugh, I heard him say that they would not have Rolf had it not been for you."

Vincent leaned back so that Durbin might pour for him. "An exaggeration."

"Huh." Durbin set down the wine bottle and began carving the ham that sat on the sideboard. "It's no more than God's truth, my lord, and well you know it." He turned to Diana, bushy white eyebrows bristling. "The boy would have died sure as check if his lordship had not brought him here and had Dr. Dalton himself in to look after him." He set a plate of ham and stewed apples before each of them. "One moment, my lady. I'll fetch the bread rolls."

"Your servants seem very devoted to you." Diana sampled the apples.

Vincent grimaced. "They have known me all my life. It is amazing what folk are willing to forgive in those they knew as children."

"Surely you could not have been so bad."

"Perhaps not." He thought for a moment. "At least not as a young child—not as long as I was under Nurse's domination—albeit rather spoilt. For a few years after my father died, however, I was quite odious. I'm surprised any of the family servants stayed with me. Part of my anger was attributable to grief, I suppose, and the rest to the knowledge that most of those I called friend were, in fact, using me."

"Then why did you remain friends with them?"

Vincent pondered that question. Why *had* he tolerated those hangers-on? In his heart, he knew, of course. He decided on honesty, unpleasant as it was. "Abusing them gave me a certain sense of power, I think, and gave them an acceptable reason to dislike me—as I thought everyone must. I feared no one else would befriend me…that there *was* no one I could trust."

"You trusted Wyn." A puzzled expression creased her face. "Yes?"

"I wonder why. No one else saw him as trustworthy."

The truth of the comment startled Vincent into silence. Why had he chosen to place his very infrequent trust in a man on whom no one could depend? Just because Wyn never asked for money? That now seemed a very unconvincing reason. He had, by some obscure process, put himself in a position to prove his belief that no one could be trusted, not even his best friend. He must think about that. But Diana still awaited his answer.

"I'm not sure, myself," he said at last. "Perhaps my trust was misplaced. That is a very unsettling thought."

"Yes, I know. I made the same mistake with respect to Wyn." Sadness crept into her eyes. "But we have to trust someone. We cannot go through life completely alone."

Vincent frowned. "That is true. Even in my…work, I am forced to trust certain individuals, like it or not. My life depends on my judgment—and my caution. As yours does now." He looked at her intently. "But I am reasonably confident of the loyalty of the staff who now remain at Inglewood—that you are safe here."

"You have made amends for the past." It was not a question.

"I certainly have tried." Vincent sat back, staring into the middle distance. "I believe for those at Inglewood, it was a matter of attending to the needs and prosperity of the estate. This is their home, after all. And of course, apologizing to many of them. And—" He broke the sentence off, his smile crooked.

"And what?" Diana gave him a questioning glance.

"Uh—" Vincent grinned sheepishly "—one might say I moderated my entertainments."

She laughed out loud. "My lord, do you mean to say that you held unseemly parties?"

"I think *orgies* is the word." Vincent went back to eating, admiring the blush that suffused her delicate features.

"Oh, my. No wonder Mrs. Buckden looked askance at my arrival. One can hardly blame her."

"Mrs. Buckden knows full well that when I brought women here for that reason, I did not bother to conceal them in a wagonload of apples. At least the apples seem to have been put to good use." He took a large mouthful.

"Yes, and the ham, also. But where is the cheese?" An impish smile lit her face. How lovely. Vincent had seen her smile so seldom.

"Were you wanting cheese, my lady?" Durbin hurried

back into the room and presented a basket of rolls. "I believe Cook has some planned for the next course."

"That will be fine, thank you." She chuckled. "I was sure it was on the menu. Please tell her that the food is quite delightful."

"Oh, I will, my lady. She'll be that pleased, she will. Kind of you to say so." He gestured at the footmen bringing in the next course. They filed in and deposited steaming dishes on the sideboard. "Now, what would you like with your cheese?"

Diana felt uncomfortably full. She had lived on short rations for such a long time, she had to resist the temptation to overeat. Durbin had plied her with far more cheese than she'd wanted, but he had been so eager to please she had not the heart to refuse. If she was not careful, she would soon find herself letting out the seams of her clothes. But no matter, she was still far too thin.

She never ceased to wonder at the numerous platefuls of food Vincent could devour at a sitting without seeming to gain weight. No matter how much he consumed, his body remained lean and hard.

A body she found herself thinking about all too often.

Every courteous touch between them, every hungry glance, set her tingling with almost-forgotten desires. But she dare not succumb to them. Restraint would serve her far better than surrendering to passion. She must keep her wits about her. Her relationship to Vincent was ambiguous, to say the least. Guest? Lover?

Hostage?

She had never been sure. Could she leave Inglewood if she wished? Even if she had somewhere to go? With Throckmorton guarding Bytham and Selena and Vincent watching her… It would not be easily done, if his lordship did not wish it. But that question did not signify. She *had* nowhere to go.

And she was beginning to understand that she did not want to go.

If she were in actuality a prisoner, at least her prison provided not only comfort but luxury, Diana thought as she made her way through several broad, richly paneled corridors to the wing that housed her and the children. She now need not concern herself with cooking or cleaning or even the care of her children unless she wished.

But she did wish it. Selena and Bytham were all she had in the world and the greatest joy of her life. It was for their sake she fought. Without them she might well succumb to the temptation to give up and let Deimos send her to the gallows or allow her unseen enemies to put a bullet through her. It would be so much easier than living with dread and suspicion and poverty.

And she was so tired.

But they needed her. She would battle to her last breath not to desert them. They should be asleep by now, but she could not go to bed without looking in on them, to kiss their little cheeks and listen for a moment to their soft breathing. She would have preferred to share their bedchamber, but Vincent had insisted that Throckmorton stay with them. She nor Nurse could hardly sleep in the same room with him, and she worried about his ability to care for the youngsters at night.

What if they had a nightmare?

She listened for a moment at their door before carefully opening it. All was silent, but a candle still burned. She peeped through the crack to see Throckmorton ensconced in a rocking chair, a book open on his knees, and Selena asleep against his shoulder. As the door opened, he dropped the book, his whole being alert. He lifted a pistol from his lap. Diana froze.

"Ah! My lady. Come in." A grin broke over his face. "I won't shoot."

Diana returned the smile. "I'm happy to know you are attentive to your duties." Diana walked across the room and retrieved the book from the floor. It was one of her daughter's favorites. "You were reading to Selena?"

"Aye. She woke with a dream and could not fall asleep again. She likes for me to read to her, but in truth, I can't say why. She reads better than I do." He stood and carried the child back to her bed. "I ain't had much schooling, but I like to try."

How kind of him! Diana considered the book in her hand. "I cannot believe you find children's stories very enjoyable."

"They are well enough, I suppose." The big man did not sound very convincing.

"Perhaps you should ask his lordship—" She broke off as the door opened again and Throckmorton lifted the pistol.

"Ask his lordship what?" Vincent stepped into the room and held up his hands as he spied the weapon leveled at him. "Whoa! Hold your horses. It is only I."

"Sorry, me lord." The boxer grinned and lowered the gun. "Already I came near shooting Lady Diana. Mayhap I best lock the door."

"Yes, I would recommend that, even here." Vincent suited the action to the word and turned the key. "Now, what were you to ask his lordship?"

"I was just saying," Diana explained, subduing the burst of fear that had flashed through her when Throckmorton had raised the gun, "that you might have a volume or two in the library that Throckmorton might enjoy reading more than he does the children's books."

"You like to read?" Vincent gazed at his henchman with new interest.

"Well, sir, I do like it, but I ain't too good at it." The battered man actually blushed.

"That's easily remedied with a little practice. Remind me tomorrow and I'll see what I have."

"I'm much obliged, me lord. But was you wanting me for something?"

"No, I just came to look in on you and the children. Apparently all is well?"

"Oh, yes, sir. All right and tight."

"Then I'll say good-night." Vincent started toward the door, only to turn and walk back to the children's bed. He gazed at them for a heartbeat, then straightened the blanket and tucked it under Bytham's chin.

Diana followed him and placed a kiss on each precious face. "I'll come, too. It is time for bed."

They repeated their good-nights to Throckmorton and Vincent unlocked the door. Diana followed him into the hall, her heart sinking as she heard the lock click between her and her children. He offered his arm and escorted her the short distance to her own bedchamber, pausing when they reached it.

He turned her so that he could study her face, placing her in the light of the wall sconce. His fingers brushed across her cheek. "Your injury seems better."

"Y-yes, it is healing now, thanks to Mistress Annie's fomentations." His touch made her breath catch in her throat. "But there will probably be an ugly scar."

"Nothing about you could ever be ugly." He leaned down and touched his lips to the spot.

"I—I…" She could not get the words out. Didn't know what words she wanted.

Gazing into her eyes, he smoothed her hair with his hand—his big hand. Strong. Gentle. "I will not press you, Diana. You need have no fear. But you should lock your door, also. If any alarm occurs, I will be right across the corridor."

"Is that your bedchamber? I thought…"

"No, my chamber is at the end of the hallway, but I will be sleeping here." He opened her door for her. "And, Diana…"

She stopped halfway through the opening. "Yes?"

"*My* door will not be locked."

Sleep had not come easily to Diana. She had lain awake long into the night, achingly aware of the *two* locked doors between her and Selena and Bytham. And of one *unlocked* door across the corridor. How long would her resolution hold? Alone in the night, and lonely, she found it harder and harder to maintain her suspicions of Vincent. Her fear of him had diminished. How could it not? He treated her with respect and kindness. He said he cared for her, and she could see his growing affection for the children.

And feel her own growing affection for him. She needed his comfort so badly.

Her reputation had by now been damaged beyond repair, in any event. If it did not already, the polite world would soon enough know of her unchaperoned journey in his lordship's company, without even a maid to lend her propriety. And now she was sequestered in Vincent's home. The gossips' tongues would flay her alive.

Another thing that hardly mattered if she did not survive.

So why did she lie cold and forlorn in an empty bed?

For how long would she do it?

The following morning Vincent emerged from the door of the stable where he had been reviewing his riding stock. He already owned a dainty dapple-gray mare that would make an excellent riding animal for Diana, but he must have his groom search for two ponies suitable for Selena and Bytham. The lively pair should have the opportunity to learn to ride.

Not that any of them could go very far afield. At least, not yet. But sooner or later their pursuers would reveal their cards, and when they did, Vincent intended to put an end to the pursuit once and for all. And then…

And then, what? Vincent found himself thinking more and more of the future. For most of his life he had not expected to have much future, had not cared how long—or how short—his life might be. Recent events had changed that. The woman he most desired was no longer wed to his best friend. She was here, in his home, under his protection. She needed him.

As did her children. A pang of surprise struck Vincent whenever he thought of Bytham and Selena. Whence had come this longing for fatherhood? For wife and family? And why must it appear now—now when he was engaged in the most dangerous venture of his life? When his association with the surviving Corbys only placed them in further danger?

He could not let that continue. He must bring the matter to a close, find the proof he sought and put a stop to the Bonaparte conspiracy. Then perhaps he would be free to build a life for himself.

And Diana, if she would have him.

Down the lane behind the stable, a figure caught Vincent's attention. A man was strolling toward him, playing a sailor's pipe and avoiding the two small, shaggy terriers that scampered about his feet. He wore a shabby brown coat. Vincent strode to meet him.

"Good day to you," the man hailed as Vincent came into earshot. "You need any rat catching done today, guv'nor?"

"I might—if I can find the rats." Vincent glanced around, and seeing no one else, asked, "Have you been here long?"

The man in the shabby brown coat grinned. "I been ambling about the neighborhood for a few days. Caught a rat or two." He jingled the coins in his pocket. "Figured you'd show your front here by now. Any problems on the road?"

"A few," Vincent admitted. "They were dealt with." They set off walking down the path to the cow byre.

"See you have a new footman." The man nodded past Vincent to the garden, visible in the distance, where Diana and the children played, attended by Nurse and Throckmorton.

Vincent's eyes narrowed. "Aye. You know him?"

"A bit. Used to box. Got too old, I think."

"He isn't that old." Uneasiness stirred in Vincent's chest.

"Nay, mayhap not. Went to work for some lord, I heard."

"Litton?"

"That'd be him, aye."

"Throckmorton ever in any trouble with the law?" Vincent squinted against the sun, trying to get a better view of the group in the garden.

"No more'n most. Left town for a while, but came back in his lordship's employ."

Not very reassuring, but not seriously alarming, either. Vincent bit back frustration. He could never be sure of anyone, it seemed. "You have news for me?"

"A bit. Been watching St. Edmunds and his friends. They meet pretty regular at a certain pub. I keep me listeners open. Ain't been able to get no proof of anything, nor heard no actual plans, but they're scheming, right enough. I've got a list of them for you."

"Bloody hell! I had hoped to become a part of the group, get my hands on some documents perhaps, learn how they intend to affect the escape from Elba, but now…"

"Too late now, me lord. You piking on the beam with the lady mort done put the fat in the fire."

Vincent sighed. "No doubt. I'll have to assign someone else to do it. I'm afraid I'm now compromised beyond repair."

The man shook his head. "I think they was on to you, any case, me lord. Best you should lie low for a spell."

Vincent thought about that. It could be true. "Perhaps it is just as well. Whomever attacked Lady Diana and her children will surely appear here in time. Perhaps I will be able to eliminate some of the conspirators when they do. Any word on Deimos's whereabouts?"

"Nay, guv'nor, not a whisper. You think mayhap he retired? Maybe he don't like the new king."

"I doubt it, but I suppose we may hope so." Vincent stopped, scowling into the distance, his instincts clamoring. "No. I don't like it. I don't like it at all. He is out there somewhere, and wherever it is, he means someone no good—most likely me."

"That's the God's truth. Well, I'll be about if you need me. Where's them rats you want caught?"

Vincent wished he knew.

Two days later Vincent received two more communiqués. One was a note from Litton, penned with characteristic directness.

We are coming.

Before he could decide if that succinct news was welcome or the contrary, hoofbeats coming up the drive caught his attention. He had been sitting on a garden bench, reading his mail and keeping one eye on Diana and the children while she gave them a lesson on nature. He must see about hiring a governess soon.

Throckmorton now held a small box in which resided a number of insects, and the knees of Bytham's britches were distinctly grimy from his search under bushes. Selena's hair blew in the wind and as she pushed it out of her face, he saw a streak of dirt appear on her nose. They were really quite beautiful.

Down the drive Vincent perceived a tall, gray-clad figure cantering toward him on a gray horse. So…it appeared that Diana was about to make the acquaintance of his "terrifying" Uncle Charles. Before Vincent could decide whether or not this second advent was welcome, his visitor reached him and swung down from his saddle.

"Uncle Charles." Vincent bowed, then extended a hand.

"Good to see you, Vincent." Caldbeck handed his reins to the groom who had just run up, and clasped his nephew's hand firmly, his face expressionless. "Adam wrote to tell me that you were expected here shortly. I came to see if I might offer you any assistance."

"Thank you. At present all seems quiet enough. I suppose he told you…" He nodded in Diana's direction.

"Aye. Has further danger to the children manifested itself?" The two men started walking toward the schoolroom party.

"We had some trouble north of London, but escaped unscathed. This has been very difficult for Lady Diana, however, and I fear that the real danger is to her rather than the children."

Caldbeck nodded. "Very likely an accurate assessment."

Hearing a strange voice, Diana looked up from the mysterious creature Bytham had just captured. Oh, dear, a stranger—and with the three of them all windblown and untidy. Vincent's black locks also fluttered in the breeze, but his companion's severely styled silver tresses seemed not to move at all. Dismayed, she hastily wiped her hands on her skirt and ran them over her own tousled mane.

Vincent stopped beside her. "Lady Diana, may I present my uncle, Lord Caldbeck."

Oh, my! The formidable earl himself.

"Charles Randolph, your obedient servant." Caldbeck removed his hat and bowed. "My pleasure, Lady Diana."

Diana could see not a single sign of pleasure in the saturnine countenance. Not a trace of a smile. Every thread of the man's clothing, save his shirt and cravat, was gray and his silver eyes... A little shiver ran up her spine as she offered her hand. "How do you do, Lord Caldbeck?" A tug made her aware of her offspring. "These are my children, Bytham and Selena Corby." Selena curtseyed, and Bytham essayed a bow before hiding again behind a fold of Diana's skirt.

"Ah. Well done." Much to Diana's astonishment, the imposing lord went to one knee, placing his face nearer the level of the children's. His expression softened infinitesimally. "I am happy to know you, Miss Selena. Bytham...what do you have there?" Bytham retreated further into his mother's skirt, but held out a grubby hand. Lord Caldbeck examined it seriously. "I see. A very fine beetle. I trust it will not later appear in your sister's slipper."

"Oh, my lord, do not suggest it!" Diana could not help laughing. Bytham shook his head vigorously and added the beetle to the box.

"My son is much of an age with you. You must make his acquaintance." Caldbeck stood, and Diana signaled Nurse who had just come out of the house.

"I'm sure you have business with Lord Lonsdale, and we are hardly presentable, so if you will excuse us, my lord..."

He inclined his head slightly. Taking this as assent, Diana shooed Bytham and Selena back toward the house.

Vincent watched their retreat thoughtfully for a few moments before turning to his guest. "Come in for some brandy, sir, if you have time."

"Thank you."

They made their way to the library where Vincent poured their drinks before they settled into the comfortable leather chairs. His uncle sipped in silence for a moment, studying Vincent over the rim of his glass. Obviously he had something on his mind. Vincent waited.

At last Caldbeck spoke. "What are your plans with respect to Lady Diana?"

Vincent briefly considered feigning confusion over the question, but gave that up as useless. His uncle had come to take him to task…again. "I don't know."

"I'm sure I need not point out the impropriety of this situation."

"No, sir, you do not." Vincent paused. "And I assure you, I have given it much thought."

"And you have concluded…?" Caldbeck's eyebrows rose a fraction of an inch.

"I have concluded that I would above all things like to offer for Lady Diana's hand."

"So have you?"

"It is not that simple, Uncle Charles." Long practice informed Vincent that the expression—or rather, the lack of it—on his uncle's face indicated doubt. "In the first place, I am not at all sure that she would have me."

Caldbeck's lack of expression indicated further disbelief. "What choice does she have?"

"That, I fear, is the second place." Vincent smiled wryly. "She has none."

"Then I fail to appreciate the problem."

"I do not want her to wed me for that reason. And…you know as well as anyone what I am. I would not press any woman…"

"To accept your unworthy self?"

Vincent frowned, wary of his uncle's penchant for hidden humor. Whether the comment was an example of it remained unclear. "Just so. But in addition to that, I have involved myself in certain matters that might bring further danger to her. I do not want to do to her and the children what Wyn has done to them. Had I a family, I would never have… But I did not, and I have."

"Can you extricate yourself from these arcane matters?"

"Perhaps, in time, if I live long enough."

Caldbeck peered at him over his glass. "Most alarming. What must you do to prevent this impending premature demise?"

"I must identify those who threaten Lady Diana and remove them," Vincent stated firmly. "And I think that will also solve at least a part of *my* problem until I can honorably withdraw."

His uncle steepled his fingers and regarded Vincent across them. "Which returns us to your first problem—the lady herself and your matrimonial prospects. Allow me to impose on you with some advice. You may not be aware that Catherine married me for precisely the same reason. She had no choice. I did not allow that to deter me."

"I… No, I did not know that." Who would have thought it? But what woman would not want the distinguished Lord Caldbeck? "But you, sir, were a man of honor. I, on the other hand…"

"Have you learned nothing of honor in the last four years, Vincent?" His uncle gazed at him intently.

"I would like to think so." Vincent's mouth quirked at the corner. "I have thought about your definition of honor every day since that time."

"Have you indeed?" Caldbeck actually sounded a bit startled.

"Your exact words were, I believe, *'honor is a matter of having courtesy toward others, of treating inferiors kindly, of keeping your word, of paying your debts. Of treating women of all stations well.'*"

Something surprisingly like a chuckle escaped his reticent relative. "I did not remember my own eloquence. Do you tell me that you think of it each day, but do not practice it?"

Vincent's brows drew together. "I do my best."

His uncle inclined his head an inch. "Just so."

Vincent got up and brought back the decanter. He poured again for both of them, and they drank in silence while Vincent attempted to decipher that last cryptic remark. At last, Caldbeck set down his glass and rose. "I must be going. I will bring Catherine and the children to visit Lady Diana. Call on me if you need my aid."

Vincent walked with him to the front door. As he was going out, Caldbeck turned back. "Vincent, all of us can forgive the mistakes of an unhappy boy and a misguided young man—especially when he has put them aside. I suggest you allow yourself to do the same."

God damn the useless bloody bitch to hell! How dare she disobey him this way? The two weeks he had given her to think about her fate had come and gone without a word from her. Apparently she was conquering her fear of him. A great mistake on her part. He would soon administer another dose of it.

And how dare the slut take his coin and give nothing in return? Well, she would learn soon enough that he always collected his debts.

Always.

One way or another.

If she feared only that he would send her to the hangman, she underestimated him. When he established his control over her, she would wish he had.

Chapter Eleven

For the rest of the afternoon, as he rode over the park looking for signs of intruders, Vincent pondered Caldbeck's parting remark. If Charles and Adam and Helen, of all people, could forgive Vincent's past offenses, perhaps Vincent was not as far beyond the pale as he believed. But did four years of amendment pay for twenty-two of spite and affront? It did not seem likely.

And even if it did, it did not mean he could win Diana.

He hoped only for respect.

He did not expect love.

Occupied as he was with these consuming thoughts when he strolled through the front door on his way to dress for dinner, the fact that the door was not locked did not immediately catch his attention. Nor, for a heartbeat, did the unaccustomed stillness. Then he felt his hair lift and his pulse increase. He stopped in his tracks and turned slowly in a circle, one hand feeling for the pistol in his belt.

There was no one in the entry hall, but several large doors opened off it, gaping darkly and ominously. Vincent did not keep a porter stationed there. Largely because he did not invite them, he had too few visitors at Inglewood to bother. But there should have been some sounds of activity from Durbin or a footman somewhere in the area. Someone should have been available to open the door. The small dining room in which he and Diana had been having their meals lay within earshot through a series of salons to his left. Ordinarily at this hour they would be preparing it for dinner.

Vincent eased up to the first opening and, back to the wall, peered around the edge into the room. He could see nothing in the dim light but the shadowy forms of rarely used furniture. When nothing moved, he slipped into the parlor and made his way to the next connecting door, where he repeated the procedure. Hmm. No one there, either.

Perhaps he was imagining things; his nerves were on edge. He stepped into the second room and walked through it quietly, looking behind sofas and chairs. No one. He had just decided that he was becoming daft when a stealthy movement beyond the next door caught his eye. Vincent crouched and froze.

A tall, thin form crept through the door, casting glances left and right as it came. Vincent stood, pistol ready. "Hold where you are!"

The man threw up his hands, revealing a pistol clasped in one of them. "Lonsdale?"

"Who? Sudbury? What the devil are you doing lurking about my house?"

"No, no! Not lurking…not at all." The slender man carefully slid his weapon back into his belt. "Came to call. Knocked. No one answered, but the door was open. Everything seemed too quiet somehow. I thought…" He raked light brown hair back out of his eyes.

"You thought what?" Vincent had not lowered his own pistol.

"Couldn't help but remember that business in the park."

Sudbury sat on the arm of a sofa. "Heard you had brought Lady Diana north, and I feared…"

"Where did you hear that?" Vincent set his jaw.

His prisoner shrugged. "Couldn't say. Where does one hear anything?"

"And how is it I find you in Yorkshire in the first place?"

"Been to my aunt. Expectations, you know, and besides, I quite like the old girl." If Sudbury felt any trepidation with respect to having Vincent's pistol leveled at him, it wasn't evident. "But where is everyone? Couldn't raise a soul."

"I don't know. They should be making the dining parlor ready for dinner, but I don't hear them." What the devil was he to do now? He could not hold his acquaintance at pistol point much longer without deciding that he did, indeed, represent a threat.

But did he?

Suddenly a unmistakably feminine scream rent the air.

"Diana!" Vincent wheeled and bolted for the stairs. The cry had come from above. He pounded up two pair of stairs, barely aware that Justinian Sudbury followed close on his heels. If the man *was* a menace, that should soon become evident. He would deal with him after he discovered what endangered Diana.

They erupted into the corridor at the top of the steps in time to see Throckmorton, pistol in hand, pulling Diana by one arm down the hall toward the children's bedchamber. He thrust her inside and shouted, "Lock the door!"

He was about to race off when Vincent shouted, "Throckmorton! What is it?"

"He went this way, me lord!"

Vincent and Sudbury, who again held his own weapon, pursued the footman into a side corridor and all but crashed into his broad back as they rounded the corner. The big boxer stood stock-still, staring around him, his pistol swinging left and right. "Now where did he go? The bastard coulda hid in any one of these here rooms."

Vincent's heart sank. "These and numerous others. But wait… There is an old service corridor in this hall—hasn't been used in years." He felt along one wall and triggered a hidden catch. A panel swung open, revealing a hallway. Squatting, he studied the marks in the dust on the floor. "*Someone* has been here." He stood and moved back to Throckmorton, murmuring softly, "Stay and keep watch in case he comes out of hiding up here."

Throckmorton nodded and silently backed until he could see both the side corridor and the door to the children's bedchamber. Vincent beckoned to Sudbury and they slipped into the hidden hallway. He could not be sure of the man's intentions, but at least he could keep an eye on him. Leave him this near to Diana and the children, he would not.

They ran along the passage and down steep stairs into another hallway, following it until it came to a sharp bend. Before Vincent could make the turn, Sudbury's hand closed over his shoulder from behind, pulling him back. Vincent slowed. His companion pushed him firmly toward the floor, signaling for quiet with a finger to his lips. Vincent complied with the unspoken suggestion and, crouching low, they squinted around the corner.

A shot rang out and splinters flew from the wall above them.

"Damnation!" Vincent ducked back.

Running footsteps faded into the distance. The two of them again gave chase. They burst out of a door into the pantry. Oddly it, too, was deserted. The outer door stood open. They made for it and plunged into the dying light of day.

There was no one to be seen.

"We will have to search the grounds and the outbuildings." Vincent stood, panting.

Sudbury nodded, also gasping for breath. "But you will need help to both search and guard the house."

"By the time I get it, he will be gone." Vincent stared around him at the vast grounds and considered the resources at his command. "Bloody hell!"

An hour later Vincent was still sorting out what had happened. Sounds from below had led him and Sudbury to the kitchen where they beheld a scene of chaos. Vincent could hardly believe his eyes.

The room was full of bats.

The maids huddled in the corners while Durbin led the broom-wielding footmen on a campaign to rid the room of the agitated trespassers. Bats flapped and squeaked. Girls squealed and ducked. Durbin swung a frying pan. Cook ran to and fro, seizing dishes of prepared food and fleeing with them. Vincent stared in dismay, dodging as a winged missile flew blindly at his head.

Behind him Sudbury spoke. "Appears dinner will be a bit delayed."

Vincent turned to glare at him and shouted to the room at large. "What happened? Where did these creatures come from?"

"From the old flue, my lord." Durbin paused to wipe sweat from his forehead. "All at one time, they just came boiling out with a cloud of smoke." He flailed at a luckless creature as it fluttered by.

"Deal with them!" Casting a look of frustration over his shoulder, Vincent abandoned the battle for possession of the kitchen and ran back up the several flights of stairs to find Diana. The bats were the least of his worries.

He and Sudbury found Throckmorton where they had left him, warily watching the doors of both corridors. He turned to them eagerly. "Did you snabble him, me lord?"

Vincent shook his head. "Nay, he made it out of the house before we could stop him. What happened up here?" Without waiting for an answer, he knocked on the door behind which Diana had disappeared. "Diana, it is I. Open up. Are you all right?"

He heard the key turn in the lock, and Diana looked cautiously through the crack. "Yes, we are all here—Nurse and the children and I."

She pushed the door open and stepped back, her small pistol still in her hand. The men all crowded into the bedchamber and ranged themselves around the walls. Nurse sat on the sofa with a comforting arm around each of the wide-eyed children.

"Now," Vincent said when they had all settled themselves, "will someone please tell me what transpired?"

Diana, looking a bit dazed, sat on the edge of the bed, her arms wrapped around herself. "There was a man. I was on my way to look in on Selena and Bytham before I dressed for dinner. As I came to the top of the stairs, I saw him opening doors and looking into the rooms." She rocked back and forth as if consoling herself, her face white. "At first I thought he belonged here, but he turned toward me and I saw that he was dressed roughly—not one of the footmen." She paused and swallowed. "I—I realized then he was looking for the children. I screamed and ran at him."

"Aye, sir." Throckmorton took up the tale. "I heard her and came out on the run, as you may believe. The blighter gave her a shove and knocked her down and ran past me while I was trying to get to her. By the time I got her into this room, you two were in the hall."

Mindful of his audience, Vincent restrained the urge to

go to Diana and gather her to him. She had been through so much, and now she had sustained yet another physical attack and another threat to her children. He wanted to wrap his arms around her and ward off the pain and terror that surrounded her, that turned her beautiful face drawn and pale. But he could not do that here. He took a breath to steady himself. Sudbury had followed him into the bedchamber and stood with arms folded, his lanky frame propped against the door frame. His pistol had again disappeared. Was it possible that his advent on the scene was pure coincidence? If not, then what was it? Vincent regarded him with narrowed eyes. Sudbury maintained an air of innocent attention.

Vincent pondered the situation. Had he not found the man prowling through the salons with a pistol in his hand, he would think Sudbury's actions had been entirely in the spirit of support. He had done nothing further to arouse suspicion.

In fact, he had had ample opportunity to shoot Vincent in the back as they'd chased the interloper through the service passage. No one else in the house had seen Sudbury except Throckmorton, who did not know him. He might easily have done it and escaped without revealing his identity, possibly even silencing Diana in the process.

So likely he did not pose an immediate threat.

But could he be depended upon for help?

As if reading Vincent's thoughts, Sudbury straightened. "Bad business, this. Happy to offer my assistance."

"Justinian?" Diana appeared to suddenly realize he was in the room. "What are you doing here?"

"Your most obedient servant, Lady Diana." The tall man bowed. "Visiting in the neighborhood. Stopped to call."

"At just the right moment." Vincent kept his voice carefully neutral. Whether it was the right moment for his benefit or that of his opponents still lay open to question. But for now he would accept the man at face value.

And watch him.

Sudbury nodded. "If you don't mind putting me up, I can help keep watch."

Rather like setting the fox to watch the chickens? Well, if Sudbury *was* one of his enemies, then at least he would know where to find him. And he would see to it that he had no chance to play him false.

"Much obliged to you, Sudbury." Inwardly he sighed. Another direction in which he must maintain vigilance. Another person of whom he could not be sure. "Throckmorton, do not let Selena and Bytham out of your sight for an instant. I will send a footman to keep watch in the hall. Lady Diana, this occurrence means that you may no longer move around, even in the house, without an escort. I will take you to your room now and call to take you to the dining parlor later—quite a bit later, I fear. It will take a while to restore order in the kitchen."

Throckmorton gave him a perplexed stare. "I thought the trouble was all up here. What's afoot in the kitchen, me lord?"

"Bats."

Vincent offered his arm to Diana and led her out of the room, leaving Sudbury to follow and his henchman to gaze after him with furrowed brow. Down the hall at her own chamber, he opened the door for her and stepped in to look around. Finding no one in the wardrobe nor under the bed nor behind the screen, he paused before leaving. "Diana, I want to be sure you understand me. Do not open the door for anyone but me."

She nodded. "Very well, I shall not."

Vincent cast a meaningful glance out the door where Sudbury waited in the corridor.

"And, Diana—I mean *no one*."

* * *

When dinner had finally been served, Diana found herself unable to eat more than a few mouthfuls. The stay at Eldritch Manor and the last several days of peace at Inglewood had lulled her into a sense of security. The afternoon's incident had shattered it. Vincent had told her that their arrival at his family home would attract their pursuers, but she had somehow continued to deny the reality.

But reality had again become undeniable.

Those who would harm her had found her. She would no doubt next see the arrival of the Runners to take her away. The time limit Deimos had set for her to betray Vincent was nearing an end. But how could she betray the man who had steadfastly placed himself between her and any number of dangers? The man who had dried her tears, had held her in his strong arms. Had so tenderly made love to her. The man for whom she could sense her own feelings growing.

She would not do it!

At least the children would be with Vincent, and he had told her that Litton and Helen were on their way to Yorkshire. Selena and Bytham would be cared for. They would grieve, but perhaps in time they would forget her.

Suddenly, at that thought, a great anger rose up in Diana. She would not let that fiend win so easily! She would fight him—fight him with the truth, with lies if she must. She would not let him separate her from her family. Not if she could keep breath in her body. Surely, Vincent would help her.

If she dared explain the matter to him.

The strain of the evening had been somewhat relieved by Justinian Sudbury's amiable conversation. He supplied them with the latest *on dits* from London and an entertaining description of his favorite aunt, cheerfully admitting that without her patronage his financial future as the younger son of an impecunious, albeit genteel, family would be gloomy indeed. Could so pleasant and innocuous an individual possibly have been involved in her husband's death?

And why was he here?

Vincent had walked with her to her room and stationed an armed footman in the hallway outside her door before rejoining Justinian downstairs for brandy and cigars. Now Diana lay awake, staring at the plaster design on the ceiling, her ears straining for any sound of disturbance. Suddenly she heard voices—Vincent calling good-night to Sudbury, the sound of doors closing, murmurs right outside her door and footsteps.

And then a light tapping at her door. And a whisper. "Diana?"

She swung her feet out of bed and fumbled in the dark for her wrapper. Padding barefoot to the door, she leaned an ear against it. "Vincent?"

"Yes, it is I. Open the door."

Diana turned the key and carefully looked around the edge of the door. His lordship, without coat or cravat stood just outside, the candlelight from one still-burning sconce striking lustrous sparks from his dark hair. Without asking, he gently pushed her away from the door and entered.

When he had locked the door behind himself, he turned back to her, clasping her upper arm with one hand and gazing at her face in the dim light. "How are you?"

Diana sighed and shook her head. "Frightened. It seems I have been continuously frightened since—" She broke off and blurted out, "Why is Justinian Sudbury here?"

"I don't know. But as long as he is in the house, you will not sleep in here alone. I haven't enough men to watch everywhere, night and day. I have sent a note to Uncle Charles requesting the use of some of his people, but still…"

The wail escaped Diana in spite of herself. "He was there, Vincent! Justinian was there when Wyn was killed." Anguished doubt welled up in her. "And…and…and *so were you!*" Realizing what she had said, Diana clapped a hand over her mouth and stared up into his tense features with tear-filled eyes.

He released her and stood silent for several heartbeats, his arms at his sides. Then he said, very softly, "I did not kill Wyn, Diana."

"I… Forgive me. I don't think… I—I just don't know what is happening, what to believe. Do you think that Justinian…?" Diana bowed her head.

Vincent shrugged. "I cannot say. He did not do it himself. I *was* there, and I do know that. But whether he arranged for it—possibly identified Wyn for the assassin…" He ran his fingers through his hair impatiently. "Like you, I can no longer be sure of anything. *Except that I did not contrive Wyn's death.*"

They stood there, staring at each other in pained silence, his eyes angry. Suddenly, Diana could bear it no longer.

"Oh, Vincent!"

She threw herself against him and his arms closed around her, all but crushing her.

"Ah, Diana." His lips brushed her forehead, sought her damp eyelashes, her cheeks. "Trust me. Please trust me a little longer. Trust me and let me help you."

Diana clung to him and lifted her face. "Hold me, Vincent. Please hold me. I'm so frightened—for my children, for myself."

A rough sound rumbled deep in his chest. His lips came down hard on hers. His tongue probed and she opened her mouth, her body straining against his. He tasted of tobacco and spirits and something else. Something heady… Himself. At last he freed his mouth and gazed into her eyes. "Diana, I have loved you, wanted you for months—often wished Wyn at the devil—but I would never, *never* have harmed him. Please believe me."

God help her, she *did*.

She nodded wordlessly against his shirt and he picked her up and carried her to the bed. Clothing flew in all directions. His boots, her wrapper. His shirt, her nightrail. His britches and stockings. When they both stood naked beside the bed, suddenly he stopped his urgent hands and gazed down at her. "My God, Diana. What am I doing? I am about to fall on you like a falcon." He drew in a long breath. "Forgive me."

Words hung in Diana's throat, her own feelings choking her. She spread her fingers against his chest, stroking the dark hair, crisp and smooth beneath them. Ran her hands down his flanks to his lean hips. Rested them on his waist, her thumbs brushing the squares of muscle on his taut abdomen.

He shuddered and reached around her for her braid, his forearms pressing her against him. He worked the braid loose and thrust his fingers through the heavy mass, pulling her face to his, kissing, tasting, teasing. Diana's knees went weak and she clung to him, arms tight around his waist.

Vincent turned them and he sat on the bed, pressing his face against her breasts as she stood in front of him. He kissed the valley between them, slowly moving outward until his mouth covered one nipple. Diana moaned and clutched his shoulders for support as her knees threatened to buckle. He fastened one arm around her waist, holding her up, and his other hand found her bottom, stroking gently.

She could not breathe. She could only gasp as his hand and mouth stoked a blaze in her such as she had never known. Her gasps became moans and her moans threatened to become cries. Before she could betray them to the rest of the house, Vincent swung her around onto the bed. His body came down on hers, his mouth silencing her as he entered.

He thrust no more than twice before the world fell away under Diana, leaving her in the darkness of the void. Sensation rushed from her toes to her scalp as her body convulsed. She did not know how long she hung there before she again became aware of the motionless heat and weight of his body on her. She looked up into his face.

He smiled his skewed smile and began to move again. Oh, God! Tension built in her again with each slow thrust, with each glance at his rapt expression. Once more he pushed her to the brink and over it, once more muffling her mouth with his own. She soared again, spiraling upward, poised as time stood still, and then drifted back into his arms.

His voice sounded softly in her ear. "Again, Diana."

She tried to tell him she could not, then found, as he thrust again, that was not true. She could, and she did. But now he no longer stilled himself, but moved faster and harder, demanding one more cry of release from her before his own muffled shout erupted against her mouth.

They lay together, exhausted, his body still on hers, his forehead resting against hers. At last he murmured, "Ah, Diana. I have wanted this for so long—have loved you for so long."

She did not know how to answer. Dare she admit her own tormenting desire? But how could he fail to know of it—now after this? She nodded. "I know," she said, and kissed his cheek gently.

He rolled to one side and smoothed the tangled hair away from her face, his expression serious as he gazed at her. "Diana, I have been thinking. This situation is completely unacceptable. I want you to have the protection of both my arm *and* my name. I believe we should marry—as soon as possible. When we have dealt with the present difficulties and I have settled one other matter, I shall conclude my service to the Crown so that it will not bring further danger to you."

"Vincent…" She reached up to touch his face.

He shushed her with a finger against her lips. "Do not answer now in the afterglow of lovemaking and in haste. Consider the proposal with clearer judgment tomorrow. And the next day—for as long as you wish. I do not want you to rush into it out of fear or gratitude or…" He paused for a moment, then continued, "I realize I am offering you a questionable bargain—my past, my nature, my reputation."

"It could hardly be worse than mine at the moment. I thank you, but you are correct. We should both give this more thought. You may, also, wish to reconsider. There are circumstances…"

She could not bring herself to tell him. Not now.

She simply could not tell him about Deimos in this tender moment. Shame froze her tongue. And Diana did not want to think about what lay in store for her. She could not accept Vincent's proposal, of course. If she were destined to hang, she would not bring that disgrace on him. In fact, she could not answer him at all, for unless she told him about her accuser, Vincent would think a refusal meant she did not want *him.* She would not have him believe that.

She was coming to know that was far from true.

Once again he had slipped out of her room and returned to his own before dawn. And once again it was, in all likelihood, an unnecessary discretion. Having spent this much time in an unchaperoned state, no one would believe that they were not lovers. Still… He found himself unwilling to flaunt his conquest to the world. If he did so, and she did not accept his offer of marriage, her situation would be worse than ever.

If that were possible.

She had not refused, and Vincent found himself cautiously optimistic. Her feelings for him might not equal his for her, but he now believed that she at least wanted him. He would put his dependence in patience.

And in ardor.

Vincent could not suppress a grin whenever he thought of her magnificent response to his lovemaking. God! She was every man's dream—beautiful, kind, courageous, and, beneath that quiet exterior, passionate. Having made the decision to wed her, he would not give up. Only one doubt nagged him.

She still kept her secret.

He came into the breakfast parlor to find Justinian Sudbury already eating. Durbin informed him that Emma had carried a tray up to Diana. Smiling inwardly, Vincent hoped that her failure to appear was attributable to her being too tired to come down. After last night she deserved a rest.

"I say." Sudbury spoke around a mouthful of ham. "Been thinking."

Vincent gave him an inquiring glance.

"How did that rascal know about the service passage?"

"An excellent question." Vincent filled his plate and set it on the table. "I have been considering that myself. And how did he know which chimney led to a little-used fireplace in the kitchen?"

Justinian took a large swallow of coffee. "On your staff?"

An icy chill trickled down Vincent's neck at the thought. "I cannot believe it of the present staff. But there are those who have left my employ over the years." Many with good reason. And with good reason to hate him. "It might have been one of them, or someone to whom they gave the information."

"Can you find them?"

Vincent shrugged. "Some of them, perhaps. It would take time to find them all, but it might be worth it. The devil's in it that I cannot go haring off on that kind of hunt right now. I need to ride the grounds this morning."

"Might find a sign. Probably won't." Sudbury poured himself another cup of coffee. "Happy to help you."

"Thank you." Was that offer one of help or hindrance? Vincent sigh silently. He would have to keep his guard up until he could discover which.

Breakfast completed, he and Sudbury strolled together to the main entry where grooms waited with their horses. Cheerful summer sunlight greeted them, seeming to put the lie to the alarms of the evening before. Vincent was just at the point of commenting on the good weather when they heard the thunder of horses' hooves.

He stared openmouthed at the cavalcade pounding up the drive. "My God! It's the Light Horse."

"I say." Sudbury took a step back. "Who is this?"

"My relatives, I believe."

Vincent walked down the steps to greet Caldbeck and Litton, who led the column of riders now milling about at their foot. Half the men rode gray horses and wore the gray livery of Caldbeck. The balance displayed the varied colors of Litton. "Good morning, my lords. What is the occasion for all the cavalry?"

"Charles says you need help." Litton swung down from his mount. "Said someone broke into Inglewood yesterday, apparently looking for Lady Diana's children."

"Aye." Vincent gazed unbelieving at no fewer than twenty extra grooms and footmen. The response stunned him. What had he ever done to deserve such loyalty? "I'm much obliged to both of you. I—I never expected…"

"Helen and I are concerned for the children, as well as you and Lady Diana." Litton shook hands with Vincent and Sudbury. "After we received her—" he broke off with a glance at Sudbury, then continued more cautiously "—her request, we set out immediately. Arrived just last night."

Caldbeck dismounted and joined the group on the steps. "These are all men you may trust. I know from uncomfortable experience how important that is in a such a situation as this. I kept the ones I know less well at Wulfdale."

Litton nodded agreement. "Mine are yours for as long as you need them. How would you like them deployed?"

Suddenly, Vincent found himself the commander of a small army. He took a breath and gathered his thoughts. Never before had anyone come to his aid—certainly never so handsomely. Probably because he abhorred asking for it. Somehow he would find a way to repay them. "I believe we should have those most comfortable on horseback search the grounds, even though I fear the miscreant has long since fled. We can later set up regular patrols."

Caldbeck signaled to a young man astride a tall gray. "Give James Benjamin your orders. He will see to it." The young groom bowed from the saddle and began immediately to gather the other stablemen.

"The others, I believe, I will use in the house." He glanced inquiringly at Litton. "Whom would you suggest…?"

"Use young Feetham. He's clever and well organized. He'll be my butler when his father retires."

The well-built redhead Litton indicated got down from his horse and the other footmen followed suit. James Benjamin set about giving orders and soon the spare horses were under the care of Vincent's grooms and a large mounted party spread out over the Inglewood grounds.

Vincent returned to the house and rang for Durbin, bidding him to instruct Feetham in the configuration of the house. By the time luncheon was served, guards had been posted near all the regularly used rooms and the irregularly used entries, and Vincent had heaved a sigh of relief.

Throckmorton would continue as bodyguard to Selena and Bytham, but there was only one person with whom Vincent would trust Diana's safety.

That was, of course, himself.

Life took on a new rhythm. For the next few days the presence of so large a body of guardians should have relieved Diana's fears and allowed her to relax, but somehow it did not. She could only hold her breath, wondering when the next disaster would befall her and what form it would take. Vincent had not brought up the subject of marriage again, and neither had she.

She did not know what to say. She still could not bring herself to tell him about Deimos and his threats. Surely, Vincent would never believe that she had conspired in Wyn's death in order to seduce him. That accusation was too fair and far off even for Deimos to make believable— except possibly when combined with the allegation she could not deny.

Would that combination cause Vincent to believe the whole fabric of denunciation and innuendo? And what if he learned that she had taken Deimos's money—that hateful gift that had sucked her further into his web of power? Would Vincent turn away from her in disgust?

No, she could not yet allow herself even to think about a safe future as Vincent Ingleton's wife. The dream hov-

ered too far from her reach. Losing it would break her
heart forever. So she would not tell him. She would live in
the moment for as long as she was allowed to do so. She
would sleep in his arms each night in defiance of every
principle of propriety, every opinion of her honor. Would
romp with her babies and hold them close for as long as
heaven permitted.

Since the coming of the extra men, Vincent had made
it a point to be with her almost every moment. This afternoon they strolled through the garden near the drive, avoiding the sheltered but concealed paths and tall hedges of the
mazelike shrubbery walk. Her hand rested properly on his
arm, but she knew anyone observing them would surely
have identified them as lovers.

His dark head bent attentively toward her fair one. When
she glanced into his face, the look that passed between
them sent shivers throughout her frame. He was so darkly
beautiful. So taut, so intense. So fierce of countenance. No
wonder she had feared him. A part of her still did. Perhaps
that explained her reticence with him.

Even though she was falling in love with him.

Why? Why now? Now when she feared her future lost.

She had just looked away from those black eyes when
she spied a figure in a stylish curricle progressing up the
drive at a smart trot. At first she could not discern his features, but as he drew nearer a strange shock of recognition
struck her.

But surely she had never seen the man before. She
looked at Vincent who was gazing intently at the newcomer. "Who is that?"

"I don't know." He turned them back toward the house.
"And until I discover his identity and his business, I want
you out of the way." He beckoned to the footman standing
guard by the front door. The man hurried to meet them.

"Please escort Lady Diana back to her room and stay with her until I return."

"Yes, my lord." The footman stepped behind Diana as she walked to the entrance, shielding her from the drive.

As Vincent strode toward the curricle, she stopped to peer at the man driving. No, she did not know him. So why did she...? Suddenly she understood. He looked much like Vincent, with a face of sharp planes and hair of raven-black. Who could he be? As she watched, Vincent's hand moved to the opening of his coat, where she knew he carried a pistol. The gesture reminded her of her situation.

She hastened into the house.

Vincent approached the open carriage cautiously, his hand on his pistol. He did not relish strangers appearing unannounced. The man looked vaguely familiar, but Vincent could not place him as anyone he had ever met. Endeavoring to keep his expression neutral, he waited until the man's servant had jumped down from his perch and come to the horses's heads.

"Lord Lonsdale?" The man descended from the seat and bowed. "Allow me to introduce myself. I am Henry Delamare, your most obedient servant."

"Mr. Delamare." Vincent nodded. "How may I serve you?"

The man smiled, apparently taking no notice of the lack of an offer of hospitality. "I have a matter I would like to discuss with you. May I do so in private?"

Vincent cast a quick glance over the man's frame. He could see no obvious sign of armament, but that meant little. On the other hand, neither could he see any sign of threat, and his keep was now well defended. He extended an arm toward the house.

"Come in." He led the way into the library, gratified to see that Diana was nowhere in sight. "May I offer you brandy?"

"Thank you." Delamare took the glass from Vincent and sat in the chair he indicated.

Vincent sat behind the desk and studied his visitor. The sense of familiarity hung on the edges of his awareness. "Have we met before, Delamare?"

"Oh, yes." The man's smile did not reach his eyes, even though creases in what appeared to be weathered skin appeared around them. "We have been at many of the same entertainments. I have been in London frequently over the last few years, though my business keeps me away much of the time."

"I see. And what *is* your business?"

"Shipping. I captain my own ship." Delamare sipped his brandy comfortably.

"I regret to say I don't remember you." Vincent narrowed his eyes and looked harder.

His visitor shrugged. "At large affairs, one never sees everyone. But we *have* met before."

Vincent's eyebrows rose. "Where was that?"

"Here." The smile widened.

"Oh?" Vincent scowled. He was losing patience with guessing games.

"I am Henry Ingleton, Vincent. Your brother."

Chapter Twelve

The words momentarily deprived Vincent of speech. For several heartbeats he could only stare in astonishment. Then anger began to grow. "Do not be absurd, Delamare. My brother drowned when he was eight years old."

"And where is his body buried?" The smile lingered on Delamare's lips.

"Obviously you know that it was never found. It was assumed that the tide carried him out."

"Ah. Just so. Assumptions are always so dangerous." Delamare sipped delicately.

Vincent glared across the desk. "Enough, Delamare—or whoever you are. What do you want?"

"That should also be obvious. After years of exile, I desire to return to the home of my fathers." The man's expression became serious as he set his brandy aside and leaned forward. "Forgive me, Vincent, for enjoying your surprise. I have for years pictured the reaction my return might create—a dream I have lately decided to bring into reality."

"I suppose you have an explanation for your return from the dead?" Vincent leaned back in his chair and crossed his arms.

"Actually, you see, I have never been quite dead." Delamare smiled again. "Only absent."

Vincent raised an eyebrow and waited.

"I made the mistake that young boys so often make—that the world beyond my horizons must be wonderfully large and exciting and adventure-bestowing." He got up and refilled his own glass. "I wanted to see it." He returned to his chair while Vincent watched with narrowed eyes as he continued.

"When Papa took me with him to see the ship in which he had invested, I took advantage of a moment's inattention while he visited with the captain on the dock. I slipped away and hid, working my way down the dock." Delamare sat silent for a moment, as though staring into the past. "I remember that the day was warm. I took off my jacket and left it near the water somewhere along the way."

To be found by Vincent's father. Vincent well recalled the time of the panicked search, the dragging of the harbor, his mother's heartbroken sobs. Even his father's tears.

His own inability to comfort them.

But the man's assertion remained outrageous. He refused to dignify it with a response.

Undeterred, his visitor went on. "I made my way onto a French ship—although I did not know its nationality at the time—and found a place to hide. They did not find me until we reached Calais. By then I had become homesick and wanted to return, but I could not make them understand me. By the time my French improved enough to explain, no one believed that the cabin boy was in fact the son of an English earl. I quit saying it after the captain lost patience and had me beaten. But I did not forget who I am."

"Very affecting." Vincent could not keep the cynical tone out of his voice.

Delamare's expression hardened. "I am not asking for your pity, my lord."

"What *are* you asking for?"

"Only the opportunity to be here again. To get to know you. To perhaps convince you that I am, indeed, your brother."

"It is not I you will have to convince of this Banbury tale." Vincent stood. The implications were becoming clear to him. Henry had been his *older* brother. "If you wish to displace me as Earl of Lonsdale, Delamare, it is Parliament you will have to persuade."

"But I have not said that I wish to do that."

"Then why are you here?"

"Vincent, I simply want to come home."

At least the man had not asked to stay at Inglewood. He had taken himself off, back to the Blue Boar in the village, asking only that he be received again the next day.

"And you allowed him?" Diana asked in amazement later that night after Vincent had slipped into her room. "I would have thought that you would speedily send him to the right about."

"I may do so yet." It had been all he could do to sit through dinner in the presence of Justinian Sudbury and say nothing to Diana of his visitor's presumptuous announcement. Sharing his thoughts with her had become a habit. "But there were several things he said—things about Inglewood and our childhood together…" He fell silent and stared into space.

"Could someone have told him those things?" Diana propped the pillows against the headboard behind her and leaned back, watching as he sat on the bed and divested himself of his clothes.

"Some of them, probably. But, Diana…" He stopped with one boot in his hands, still looking thoughtful. "He apologized for the time he locked me in the schoolroom cupboard. I didn't think anyone knew about that prank—not even Nurse. Henry made me promise not to tell."

"Hmm. That does give one pause." Her brows drew together thoughtfully. "But you cannot be sure she didn't know—or perhaps your tutor did. Where is he?"

"He died of a fever a few years after Henry drowned." He pulled off the other boot and tossed it aside.

"So he is no source of information. What else did Mr. Delamare say?"

Vincent tugged his shirt over his head. "He said he wanted to see the spring again—the one at the foot of the park where we used to wade. Of course, anyone who was here then might have told him that." He moved nearer to Diana and turned to look into her face. "But I have the strangest feeling…"

"What is that?" She reached up to move a strand of hair away from his forehead.

"That I know him." Vincent sighed and leaned forward to kiss her forehead.

"How could you? Even if the man *is* Henry, he would be too much changed for you to recognize him." Her lips touched his chin.

"Very likely. Still…"

"What will you do?" She moved her hand to his chest, stroking the curve of the muscle.

A thrill of desire shot through Vincent. He allowed a moment for it to subside before he answered. "I will be very cautious. I knew coming here would reveal our enemies, but I never thought there would be so many candidates—nor a ploy so completely unpredictable. I thought I would easily recognize them." He clasped her hand and brought it to his lips. "Is Delamare one of the plot to free Bonaparte, Diana? Or simply a soldier of fortune seeking to take my place? Or…" He drew a long breath. "Is he truly my brother?"

"He may be all those things." Her thumb traced his lips.

"Egad! What a thought!" Vincent grimaced. "But you are correct. How am I to know?"

"You cannot yet know."

"No. Again, you are correct. So, as with Justinian, I must give him time—time to either prove himself or prove himself false." He reached out and gathered her to him. "Which, if he intends it, will also give him time to betray me."

Even as Diana's arms fastened around his neck, he could not shut out the thought. Secrets. So many secrets.

Her secrets.

Might they also betray him?

The taste of her lips wiped the thought from his mind.

Vincent sat by the spring alone. He needed time to think.

To think about secrets and betrayal.

About trust and honor.

He had begun to realize that he could no longer say that he trusted no one. To his surprise, he had been obliged to acknowledge that he held not one shred of doubt about the motives of his stepfather and stepuncle. Neither Charles nor Adam would ever play him false. They were both too firmly rooted in honor. His lips curled ruefully at his next thought.

They might beat him with a riding crop if they deemed it a need, but they would not betray him.

He fervently prayed he would never again require their chastisement. Not because of its severity. Three licks on his backside that he barely felt when he was drunk...? Hardly. His fear was that he might disappoint them again. Might somehow once more fail in honor. They would not give him another chance.

Vincent plucked a blade of grass and chewed on it absentmindedly, scarcely noticing the green taste of it. Had he already failed in honor with respect to Diana? Had he taken advantage of her fear and despair to bring her into his arms? God knew he intended her no harm. If she would have him, he would happily make her his wife. Assuming he could bring this present affair to a conclusion with both of them still living.

Which brought him back to secrets and betrayal. What mystery did she harbor? Why would she not tell him? In the beginning, of course, she did not trust him enough to take him into her confidence. He understood that. But now…now she seemed willing to rely on him. So why did she remain so stubbornly silent?

Might she possibly betray him?

He could not imagine it. She was herself very firmly rooted in honor, in duty and responsibility. She did not have it in her character to lie. But perhaps keeping the secret obviated the necessity to lie. And, intentional or otherwise, not having the information she held might just as well bring about his downfall. He would scarcely be the first agent to have been brought low by his desire for a woman.

Vincent sighed and lay back on the grass, studying the clouds. And now he had two more unknowns to deal with—Justinian Sudbury and Henry Delamare, a man who wished to see the spot where Vincent now reclined. He trusted neither of them at all. Did coincidence alone bring them to Inglewood within days of one another? Vincent did not like the concept of coincidence. Either or both of them might be in league with St. Edmunds. In all likelihood he should send them both packing. But if he did, he would not know where they were or what they were up to.

If anything.

Why was he even considering Delamare's assertion? The story was absurd. Yet if there were even a chance that it were true… Could he turn his only brother away? If his visitor was, in fact, Henry Ingleton, then Vincent was not, by rights, the Earl of Lonsdale. Inglewood and its income did not rightfully belong to him. What did honor demand of him in this situation? Certainly that he attempt to discover the merits of the claim. And just as certainly that he not naively turn his heritage over to an imposter.

If that could be done at all. What Parliament and the Crown would do regarding such a claim, he had no idea. Errors had been corrected in the past. In all probability it would take the whole of their lifetimes to resolve the matter legally.

But what was his moral responsibility?

Not for the first time, Vincent wished his father were still alive. Perhaps he would be able to discern the truth, to look into the man's eyes and see him for who he was. Papa had always wanted his older son back. Had never ceased to grieve, had never ceased to search for him.

Vincent never felt that he had been enough for his father.

But that was neither here nor there. He must make a decision regarding Henry, must plumb the truth of the tale. He must give the man enough rope either to hang himself or to pull himself to shore out of the dark ocean of the past. Vincent smiled.

He would kill the fatted calf.

Diana could hardly believe that she was actually dressing for a dinner party. And that she actually owned something suitable to wear. The lovely silver satin dinner gown she had inherited from Helen would be perfect. Never mind that it was no longer the height of fashion or that the donor of the gown would be one of the guests. It looked very well on her. The color reflected her eyes and brought out some pink in her wan cheeks.

It had been so long since she had socialized, she feared

she would not know how to behave. But what a welcome distraction from her present troubles. Emma sounded as excited as Diana felt. "His lordship ain't never had guests for dinner before—not since I worked here."

Diana pondered what Vincent had told her about his former "entertainments." "How long have you been here?"

"Three years. I started work in the scullery, but Mrs. Buckden, she liked my work so she moved me up." Diana could hear the pride in the girl's voice. "I helped her with her hair once, and she liked how I dressed it, so she sent me to you."

So young Emma had been spared Vincent's earlier excesses. Very likely the stolid Claugh would not have allowed his daughter to be employed in such a situation, in any event.

"And," Emma continued, "Lord Caldbeck and Lord Litton and their ladies are to be with us until tomorrow."

An interesting ploy on Vincent's part, Diana reflected. In fact, the whole affair showed his cleverness. Rather than vigorously denying Henry Delamare's assertions—or accepting them—Vincent had invited him to meet his family. Had offered him the chance to convince them of his claim.

Or be discredited.

Caldbeck and Litton would remember the boy Henry Ingleton. Possibly they would be able to discern some clue about the man Henry Delamare. And the more people in the house, the more difficult it would be for an enemy to act undetected.

A knock at the door signaled the arrival of her escort. As she opened the door, Diana realized she had never before seen Vincent in proper evening attire. It became him. He had chosen to wear all black, the somber color reflecting his sable hair and setting his dark eyes to glittering. And the glitter revealed something else.

Tonight he was on the hunt.

Tonight Vincent would stalk the truth through the maze of danger and deceit that surrounded him. His onyx gaze rested on her and for a moment Diana felt utterly naked. He knew. He knew she harbored secrets. And he would find them. Sooner or later, he would find her out in her shame and dishonor. A flash of the fear of him she had formerly felt washed over her.

What would he think of her?

What would he do?

But now, this evening, he bowed, and the sense of menace retreated. He offered his arm. "Come, beautiful lady, our guests await us."

Our guests. As though they were already married. As though she were his hostess. She was not, of course. Helen, as his only female relative, would perform that function in his home tonight. Diana would probably never do so. Another tormenting reminder of what could not be.

She managed to smile and, followed by a vigilant footman, walked with him to the drawing room. There, as he had predicted, were Justinian Sudbury, Lords Litton and Caldbeck, Helen, and a young, flame-haired lady Diana did not know. The gentlemen stood and bowed, and Diana hurried to Helen where she sat with the other woman near the fire.

"Lady Litton! Helen…how happy I am to see you again." Somewhat to her own surprise, Diana discovered how true her words rang. She *was* glad to see the lady who had treated her so kindly. The one who would very likely have the rearing of her children.

Helen, clad in a glowing royal purple that set off her fair skin and dark hair, stood and embraced her, pressing a soft cheek to hers. "Diana, I am so relieved to find you well. And Selena and Bytham?"

"Well, also, thanks to Vincent and Throckmorton. They love being in the country."

"Oh, yes, the country is so much better for youngsters." Helen extended a hand toward the red-haired lady who displayed an exquisite sapphire necklace and was gowned in a matching blue. "Catherine, may I present Lady Diana Corby? Diana, this is Lady Caldbeck, Catherine Randolph."

A warm smile lit the woman's sparkling blue eyes. "How do you do, Lady Diana? I am happy to know you."

"And I, you, Lady Caldbeck." Diana clasped the hand she offered. "I met Lord Caldbeck just a few days ago."

"Yes, he told me. But please, I am Catherine." Lady Caldbeck turned to Vincent. "So, my lord, where is this mysterious gentleman whom we are to examine?"

"I expect him at any moment, my lady. He is putting up at the Blue Boar."

"Very odd thing, this." Justinian took a sip of sherry. "I mean, your inviting him here. You really believe he is your brother?"

"Not yet." Vincent shrugged. "He knows that I do not accept his tale—that he is here pending probation. I made that clear to him. Perhaps one of you will discern something about him that I have not—either for or against his allegations. Are you acquainted with Delamare, Sudbury?"

"I've met him. Don't like him above half. Uh…" Justinian flushed. "Sorry. I mean, if he *is* your brother…"

"Then you will like him no better." Vincent's oblique smile flashed.

"Ha!" A crack of laughter burst from Litton. "Whether he is or not, very likely none of us will like him."

"Hush, Adam." Helen's gentle voice broke in. "I hear footsteps."

Durbin appeared in the doorway. "Mr. Delamare," he announced importantly.

Delamare stood for a moment framed in the doorway, body erect, head held high, light from the sconces in the hall haloing his dark hair. Vincent stepped forward and Diana heard an intake of breath from the assembled company. When seen together, the resemblance between the two men could not be missed.

However, if Delamare were indeed Henry Ingleton, then time had not been kind to him. He looked older than the two years between Henry and Vincent would have made him. Perhaps the result of his years on the sea. He bowed, first to Vincent and then to the company. Litton and Caldbeck stepped forward, flanking Vincent.

"My lords, may I present Henry Delamare?" Vincent extended a hand in his direction, and Delamare bowed again. "Lord Caldbeck and Lord Litton."

Both of these gentlemen offered their hand and Delamare grasped each in turn. Vincent scanned the eyes of all three. None of them revealed the least bit of emotion—no recognition, no hostility, no anxiety. Only the most formal courtesy. He made a note not to gamble with the lot of them.

He gestured toward the room. "Please come in. Let me make you known to the ladies." Delamare followed him to where the women stood watching, curiosity writ large on their faces. Vincent stopped before Lady Catherine, the ranking lady of the party. "Lady Caldbeck, this is Henry Delamare." He indicated Diana. "Lady Diana Corby." Henry bowed to each of them.

An imp of amusement stirred in Vincent. He was looking forward to the last introduction. "Lady Litton, may I present your stepson?"

He had the satisfaction of seeing Delamare's urbanity crack. He cast a startled glance at Vincent. "My…my *stepmother?*"

Helen chuckled. "Had you been with us at the time, yes."

"Forgive me if I call you not *Maman*." The man made a fast recover, kissing the hand she held out to him. "It would be…quite impossible." For the first time Vincent detected the hint of a French accent. Had he at last succeeded in damaging the man's composure?

Composure or brass-faced gall.

Durbin again arrived in the drawing room, addressing Helen. "Dinner is served, my lady."

Vincent flicked a glance at Diana, then bethought himself of his duty to the Countess of Caldbeck and turned to her, offering his arm. No need to draw any more speculation to his relationship with Diana than necessary by altering precedence. He was moving to the door when, from the corner of his eye, he saw Delamare bow to Diana. Vincent checked for a heartbeat as he watched her smile up at the newcomer and accept his escort. Quelling a pang of jealousy, he led the countess into the dining salon and seated her properly to the right of his own place at the end of the table.

With five men and but three women in the party, correct seating was out of the question—a matter that was hardly of burning importance to Vincent, in any event. However, he found himself less than pleased when Delamare positioned himself in the place of honor to Helen's right at the far end of the board as though he was, in fact, a ranking earl. He placed Diana on his other side, thus establishing her as his dinner partner and putting an intervening place between her and Vincent.

Vincent wondered if he caught just an instant of amused challenge in the glance his alleged brother sent his way as he took his chair between Diana and Helen.

Presumptuous rascal.

To Vincent's relief, Litton took the chair between himself and Diana. Otherwise she would have been trapped between Sudbury and Delamare, both possibly among his enemies. He shuddered inwardly. Bad enough to have her within the reach of the debatable Henry—and out of his own.

Should trouble arise, he would have to put his dependence in Litton to get her out of its way. He had made sure that both Litton and Caldbeck knew to suspect Sudbury, as well, and he knew they would react. That they both carried pistols.

He had asked for help once again.

Throughout dinner the informal conversation centered on Delamare. Everyone had questions for him, all worded with the utmost courtesy, all designed to fathom the truth of his story. Henry dealt with the questions gracefully, spinning tales of his life and his rise from cabin boy to ship's master, entertaining them with anecdotes of his adventures and mishaps.

Never explaining his appearance on the English social scene.

Vincent pondered that. Appearing from nowhere, how had he been accepted even into the fringes of the ton? And where had he come by his own ship? Unfortunately these were not inquiries that could be phrased politely. But Vincent would ask them—soon or late, politely or otherwise.

As he filed away details of Delamare's narrative for further verification, Vincent struggled to smother his annoyance at the small attentions his avowed relative bestowed on Diana. Seeing to it that her glass was filled. Suggesting tidbits. Addressing his remarks to her. Looking into her eyes as he smiled. He didn't have to be that attentive.

The perfect dinner partner.

Damn his eyes!

Diana sighed with relief as she followed Helen and Lady Caldbeck back into the drawing room and found a place with them near the fire while the gentlemen drank their port in the dining salon. Delamare's proximity at table had disturbed her.

In spite of his impeccable manners, she had felt crowded by him. It seemed that his shoulder too frequently touched hers, that his elbow inevitably brushed hers when he moved, that whenever she glanced his way, she found his gaze waiting to engage hers.

And, uncomfortable, she would quickly look away.

Helen spoke first. "I pity Mr. Delamare, undergoing the scrutiny of those three over his port. So, what did you think?"

Catherine thoughtfully rested her chin on one hand. "Very gentleman-like. Very persuasive."

"Perhaps too much so." Helen stretched a slippered toe toward the fire. "I found myself believing everything he said until I recollected the unlikeliness of it. What do you say, Diana?"

"I don't know." Diana tried to separate her personal response to him from the possible truth of his claim. "As you say, it all seemed perfectly reasonable when he said it. But, of course, I never knew Henry Ingleton as a boy."

"Nor did I." Catherine's brow puckered. "But I have the feeling that the man is just a bit too eloquent—that he could convince one of anything. Although that does not mean he is lying."

Diana considered that idea. "No, of course it does not. He might be trying to persuade us of the truth. Helen, was Vincent's brother a sly child?"

"Perhaps. He was just a little too young for us to be play-mates, but I have the impression that he might have been."

"Does Delamare look like Henry?" Catherine asked.

"I am trying to remember." Helen closed her eyes for a moment. "I can picture his face, but whether it would grow into the face we see tonight…" She opened her eyes and shrugged.

"He looks very much like Vincent," Catherine observed.

Did he? Diana saw the similarity, but… "He does, but somehow he also seems very different. His *nature* seems different."

Both the other women looked at her. Oh, dear. Had her feelings for Vincent betrayed themselves in her words?

Finally, Helen said, "Yes. But Vincent's nature is very much changed in recent years. Still, you are correct. Vincent has never been persuasive."

Catherine laughed. "He has never wasted time with it."

Diana felt herself flushing. What they said was true. Vincent had never attempted to convince her to do what he wanted. He just did it and pulled her along with him.

Except when he asked her to trust him.

Then his heart was in his eyes.

Chapter Thirteen

With so many potential observers of his activities in the house, Vincent dawdled in his own room until he was confident everyone else was safely tucked away before gliding down the hall on stocking-clad feet to Diana's. But with yet another questionable presence in residence, he had no intention of allowing Diana to sleep in her room alone. Propriety be damned.

As much as he might have wished it, Vincent found himself unwilling to be so discourteous as to turn a guest out to travel to his inn in the dark. The vexatious Henry had been assigned a bedchamber on another floor, in fact, the chamber Henry had occupied as a boy. Had Vincent given in to his inclinations, he would be housed in the farthest corner of the building from Diana, but that would create too much work for the staff.

And it would be rather obvious. Vincent chuckled. If he truly had his way, the man would be in some far corner of the universe.

As for confirming Delamare's story, the evening had proved inconclusive. Vincent had no opportunity to talk privately with Litton and Caldbeck. If their suspicions had been increased—or decreased—he would have to wait until the morrow to hear it. In spite of the man's convincing performance, Vincent's own dislike of him had hardened.

No mystery about that. Delamare's gallantry toward Diana had awakened a demon of possessiveness in Vincent that he did not know he had. Vincent had never cared so much for any other woman, had never allowed anyone else to become important to him. All of his relations with the opposite sex had been casual, in fact, usually professional in nature. He did not allow strings.

Until now.

He could hardly bear seeing Diana on Delamare's arm. The possibility existed, of course, that Delamare did not know that he and Diana were lovers. But Vincent did not believe that for a moment. The blackguard looked so damned proprietary. So bloody smug. No, his assurances to the contrary notwithstanding, the man was subtly setting himself as Vincent's rival in every area.

As Henry always did.

Damnation!

He tapped quietly on Diana's door and waited impatiently for her to unlock it. He wanted to see her face, to feel her body beneath his hands. Barely waiting for the door the open, he squeezed past her and wrapped his arms around her waist from behind while she made the door fast.

"God, I have wanted you alone." He lowered his head to brush kisses across the nape of her neck. "At dinner I was ready to kill Delamare where he sat." He lifted a hand to cup her breast.

She covered it with one of hers, leaning her head back against his shoulder. "He made me very uncomfortable, but he had no way of knowing that you and I…" A flush crept up her neck. "Well, that we…"

"Of course he knows." Vincent moved his lips to a point

just below her ear and she shivered in his arms. He pressed his rapidly growing erection against her soft bottom, gratified at her response to him. She was his, and by God, tonight he intended to see that she knew it.

She sighed and rubbed her cheek against his. "I suppose everyone is aware of it by now."

"Yes, but that is of no consequence." He covered her other breast with his free hand. "When we are married, these weeks will be forgotten." He began to gently press her nipples between thumb and forefinger through the thin fabric of her gown.

She slumped against him, her breathing quick and shallow. "Vincent… About marriage… I…"

He gave her no opportunity to argue. He moved one hand slowly across her belly, letting it come to rest at the juncture of her legs. She gasped as he circled his fingers against her swollen nub. He put his mouth against her ear. "I will not take no for an answer, Diana. I will not give you up."

He increased the pressure between her legs and scarcely had time to cover her mouth with his other hand before she cried out. When she hung limply against him, he scooped her up and carried her to the tall bed. He laid her unresisting body down on the edge, facing him, and stepped between her legs while yanking at the buttons of his britches.

The moment he had the flap undone, he grasped her thighs and thrust into her. She lay, eyes closed, arms flung over her head, moaning softly. He stilled himself, waiting to regain control. Then he used slow thrusts and the pressure of his thumb to shatter her again. He wanted more, wanted to see her beautiful face in the throes of release again and yet again, but the sound of her breathy cries, the wild response of her body around his, sent him soaring over the edge. He bit his lip to silence himself, pumping his essence into her.

Making her his in the way of men and women since time began.

* * *

This could not go on. She could not allow him to continue thinking that marriage to her was inevitable. Diana lay watching the sun creep over the edge of the world and slip its arms through her window, its fingers stroking the warm lights in Vincent's hair where it lay against her pillow.

She had not slept for thinking that she should tell him.

She rolled toward him and found his gaze on her. The ardor in his eyes brought tears to her own. He wiped them away with a gentle hand. "What is it, Diana? Why are you weeping?"

A sob came up into her throat, shutting off the words. He pulled her into his arms, tucking her head under his chin. "Don't cry. We are safer now than we have been since this affair began."

She nodded, choking back her sniffles. "I…I know. It is not that."

"What then?" Vincent rose on one elbow to look down at her.

"It is… It is about… I cannot marry you." The sobs broke through again. Even with her eyes closed, she could feel him becoming very still, wary. She took a breath and tried again. "You don't understand, Vincent. I want to become your wife more than I can say. I have fallen in love with you—in spite of myself. But there are things…"

"Things?" She could feel the tension in his body like a drawn bow.

"Things you don't know about me." There…she had said it.

"I know that, Diana."

Her heart almost stopped. "You…you know?"

"I know you are keeping a secret from me." He sat up and looked down at her, the covers dropping to his waist.

His brow was furrowed, but he did not look angry. "You have done so since we left London. What is it?"

"I cannot tell you." It came out as a wail.

"And why not?" He reached down to straighten her tangled hair.

"You will despise me." She rolled away and buried her face in the pillow.

A firm hand on her shoulder rolled her back. "Look at me, Diana." Reluctantly she met his gaze. "I cannot imagine anything that you could tell me that would make me despise you. However, if this secret affects your safety— or mine—I want you to tell me at once."

"I don't think it does. It has nothing to do with anything that Wyn told me. I truly do not understand why anyone thinks I have any sort of information that would harm them. It is… It is something that happened…a long time ago."

He waited patiently, but she could not go on. Finally he said, "I have loved you for a long time, Diana. I cannot imagine your doing anything so awful that I would not wish to marry you, would cease to love you."

"But sooner or later, I would bring a terrible disgrace to you, and you would come to hate me." Her resolve firmed. "I will not do that."

"Hmm." He leaned back against the bedframe and studied her. "Very well. If it does not affect our present situation, you do not have to tell me. But know this, Diana." He rolled forward, leaning over her with a hand on either side of her face. "I *will* find out."

He rose and began to put on his clothes, looking back at her when he finished and reached for the door. "And it will make no difference to me."

Early that afternoon, his guests all departed, Vincent sat his horse under the shade of the spreading beech by the side of the lane and waited, the dappled sunlight and soft bird-song a stark contrast to his dark thoughts. What the devil had Diana done that she considered so disgraceful?

It sounded rather as though she had consorted with another man at some time during her marriage to Corby. Vincent could hardly blame her if she had, considering her husband's neglect of her. But it rankled that, if she needed comfort, the hypothetical comforter had not been he. He would have loved to provide that anytime these past two years.

But he was getting far ahead of himself. He had no reason to believe any such thing of her, and that sort of behavior seemed so far out of her character… Besides, he would have known. He had spent a great deal of time in the Corby home. Vincent's experience suggested that this great secret concerned something seen as contemptible only by Diana. Something for which no one would condemn her—except herself.

Very likely he could ferret out the mystery if he wished. Discovering secrets was his business, after all. But he would not do that. Vincent wanted Diana to tell him herself. If he caught her in it, he would not feel able to trust her. He would wait for the answer. One thing he had learned in the intelligence trade was patience. Another was that secrets always came out. Always.

But what in thunder could Diana's be?

These musings were interrupted by the cheerful sound of the sailor's pipe. A glance down the road revealed the man in the shabby brown coat, his little dogs scampering along beside him. Vincent swung down from his saddle and waited until the man drew even with him.

"Good afternoon to ye, me lord." The ratcatcher tipped his battered hat. "I trust I find you well."

"Well enough. And yourself?"

"Aye, guv'nor, right as rain."

One of the terriers put his paws on Vincent's knee and Vincent bent down to scratch the thick fur behind the ears. The ratter wagged the whole rear half of his body in ecstasy. "Have you been to London?"

The man nodded. "Aye, rode the mail there and back. The news ain't good."

Vincent sighed. "Somehow I did not expect it to be."

"That's a fact, guv'nor. Ain't nothing about this business gone right. St. Edmunds ain't been seen by none of our lads in the last week."

"Damnation! He's missing, too?"

"Aye, sir. Seems so."

"And Deimos?"

The ratcatcher shook his head dolefully. "No sign of him, neither."

"Bloody hell!" Vincent kicked a stone across the road. Took several steps up the road and paced back down.

The man in the shabby brown coat awaited events, unperturbed. "Told you it wasn't good."

"Aye. And you were correct." Vincent took a long breath and contained his temper. "Well, they will surface eventually."

He had no doubt of that. Deimos had promised to kill him. Vincent had disrupted his plans one time too many. Once would have been enough for the ruthless assassin. But Vincent had made a similar vow with respect to Deimos when he had found what was left of one of his best men.

He changed the subject. "Caught any rats at the Blue Boar?"

"Aye, inn stables are good hunting."

"There is one rat in particular staying there that I would like to catch. I need to know if he does anything suspicious—meets anyone who isn't local."

"I'll keep me daylights peeled. What's his name?"

"Calls himself Henry Delamare. Looks a lot like me."

"Oh, that cove. I've seen him. Has a rum-looking cully with him. They say he's his valet, but he don't look like no valet to me."

"That so? What does he look like?"

"Like a ship rat in fancy clothes. I'll cap downright he's good with a shiv." The man whistled to his dogs. "I'll keep him in my eye. What's this Delamare say he's doing here?"

"He says he's my brother."

That, of course, had required an explanation. By the time Vincent had made it and sent the ratcatcher on his way, it was getting late. He had been away too long. Spurring his horse to a fast canter, he headed back to Inglewood. He had left good men to watch over Diana, and she was in all likelihood with Throckmorton and the children, but his absence made him nervous.

Besides, he had hoped to spend some time with her and Selena and Bytham. He still did not have much skill in playing with the youngsters, but he was learning. He watched Throckmorton with them enviously. The big boxer seemed to know instinctively how to handle them.

It was at that moment that Vincent had a revelation.

He trusted Throckmorton.

Vincent did not know when it happened, but sometime over the last weeks, his wariness of the man had dissipated. He had ceased to worry about the man's proximity to the children. The realization both shocked and relieved him. Of course, he had no guarantee of Throckmorton's credibility. One never did. With people, there were no guarantees. But occasionally one could take another on faith.

And he had been taking the man on faith for weeks.

As he rode up the drive of Inglewood he overtook one of his grooms ambling along aboard a chestnut hack.

"Good afternoon, m'lord." The young man turned in his saddle to greet him. "I've been to get the post."

Vincent drew up beside him and held out his hand. "Thank you. You may as well give it to me now."

The groom passed over a handful of letters. Vincent nodded his thanks and cantered away up the drive, glancing at them as he went. There seemed to be nothing of importance—a message from his man of business, a brace of bills directed to the housekeeper—except for one thin note addressed to Diana.

This one had not been forwarded, but sent to her directly at Inglewood. He turned it over in his hand, debating whether he should investigate its contents. Perhaps it contained a clue to her supposedly shameful secret. But he was not ready to do that. She would tell him. Eventually she would tell him herself.

As he came in sight of the house he saw that Nurse and Throckmorton had already taken the children in for supper, but Diana still sat on a garden bench in the fading light, reading. Two footmen loitered a short distance away. Vincent gave his horse to the care of a groom and strode to join her. She smiled tiredly at him as he stopped beside her, telltale circles under her eyes betraying her lack of sleep.

"I have brought the post." He handed her the letter and stood looking at her intently.

Diana turned it over and examined the address closely. To her relief, the hand was not Deimos's. She did not recognize it, and there was no return address. Vincent still watched her sharply. She knew he wanted her to open the letter, to perhaps provide a clue to her secret. But this letter would not do that. She smiled sadly to herself and broke the seal.

She unfolded the paper. There was nothing at all written on it. But lying in the crease was a lock of hair. A lock of hair so pale gold it was almost silver. She knew only two people who had hair that color.

"Selena!" She flung the paper to the ground and jumped up, running for the house. After only a moment Vincent caught and passed her, the letter clutched in his hand. The footmen raced along behind her without knowing why. She reached the top of the steps as Vincent was pounding on the door of the children's room. By the time it opened she was beside him, gasping for breath.

"Selena! Bytham!" Diana pushed past him and ran into the room. Both children, Nurse and Throckmorton looked at her in wide-eyed astonishment. She ran and knelt by Selena and began to run her fingers through her silky hair, looking for signs that a strand had been cut out.

"Mama!" Selena tossed her head impatiently and tried to pull away. "What are you doing?"

"Be still, Selena." Diana glanced at Vincent, her heart thumping hard in her chest. With a deep breath she calmed her frantic activity. She didn't want to infect her daughter with her own panic. "I don't see anything cut."

"What's afoot?" Throckmorton frowned at Vincent.

Vincent held out the message. "This came in the post."

Throckmorton peered at the lock. "That looks like Miss Selena's hair—or her ladyship's."

"Aye," Vincent responded grimly. "That it does."

At this point Nurse left off buttoning Bytham's shirt and hurried across the room. She looked at the shining hair, gasped and clapped both hands to her mouth.

Vincent grasped her elbow. "What is it?"

The old woman just shook her head, her face pale.

Diana stood and came to her, gently placing a hand on her arm. "Nurse? Do you know something about this?"

Nurse wound her hands in her apron, crumpling the starched, white fabric. "Someone took it. Someone took her hair."

"Yes." Vincent slid an arm around her bony shoulders. "Do you know how that happened?"

"But I buried it. I always bury it, Lord Vincent." She began to rock herself, arms crossed over her chest.

"Buried her hair?" Vincent's eyebrows drew together in puzzlement.

"Like I always do." Nurse took on a stubborn expression. "Like I did yours and your brother's."

"Ah." Enlightenment. Diana nodded encouragingly. "You trimmed Selena's hair recently?"

Nurse turned to her. "Aye, my lady. It had got too long on the sides, so I evened it up a bit. But I buried it."

Diana turned to Vincent. "My nurse always did that, too."

"But why?" Vincent looked no less puzzled.

"So no one will get it." Nurse frowned at him, as if addressing a slow student.

Vincent looked questioningly at Diana. Relieved, she smiled. "They say that having a part of someone's body gives you power over them."

"Nay, then. It's no matter to laugh at." Nurse's scowl increased. "They can bring harm to the child."

In spite of herself Diana shivered. She herself, having nowhere to bury them, had always burned hair trimmings. Relief that no stranger had touched her daughter and an unreasoning superstitious fear warred in her breast.

"Show me where you put it." Vincent ushered the old woman toward the door. Diana followed them out, catching a glimpse of Throckmorton shaking his head skeptically as he closed the door.

The two footmen who had been guarding Diana had

taken up positions outside the bedchamber door. They added themselves to the entourage and the five of them trooped out, past the garden and into the park. Diana found herself almost running to keep up with Nurse's spry steps.

The sun now drifted toward the dark, sending fingers of shadow across the grass and fingers of color across the sky. Farther into the park the pond frogs were tuning up for the evening and Nurse led the way in that direction, over the hill toward the spring. When she came to an elder tree near the stream, she knelt and began to feel around near the roots.

"It's gone," she wailed, rocking back on her heels. "I wrapped it in a handkerchief and put it right here. They took it."

Vincent bent down and put his hand into the hole. "You are sure this is the place?"

"Aye, m'lord." Nurse gave him an annoyed glance. "Of course, I'm sure."

He placated her with a smile. "Of course. You saw no one while you were digging?"

Nurse shook her head. "No, but it was dark. I always wait until it is dark. I don't want them to see."

"Well, someone saw." He stood. "At least we know how the hair was obtained."

Diana nodded and sighed. "Yes. That is a relief. I could not believe that with Throckmorton there anyone could have entered, and I know he would never allow anyone to harm the children, but…"

"No." Vincent took her arm and started back to the house. "I am now confident of that. For a moment I thought perhaps…but, no. It was not Throckmorton. But this, again, means that someone is watching the house. Damnation!" He slapped his thigh angrily. "With all the patrols we have, how could they go undetected?"

"This is a big place, my lord." Diana patted his arm soothingly. "One person might easily hide in the grounds."

"I know. Especially if they were familiar with them." Vincent's expression became grim. "It is time to discover who that is."

Nurse moved up to Diana's other side, still distressed. "But, my lady, they have her hair. What are we to do?"

Diana gazed at her for a moment, thinking, then flicked a glance at Vincent. He was giving orders to the footmen.

She turned back to the old woman and said quietly, "I'm sure you know what to do better than I, Nurse. Tonight I will help you."

Vincent propped his boots on his library desk and leaned back in his chair. "Come in, Throckmorton."

"You wanted to see me, me lord?" The big man ambled into the room and stood in front of the desk.

"Aye." Vincent pushed two small books across the desk to him. "I think you might enjoy these more than nursery tales. They are written for adults, but the going is not too difficult." He indicated a chair. "Have a seat."

Throckmorton took the books and eased himself into a chair. "Thank you, me lord. I try to read to pass the time when Miss Selena and Master Bytham are asleep, but I *have* grown a bit weary of *Tales from Times Past...*" He grimaced. "*With Morals.* What's in your mind?"

Vincent put his hands together and tapped his lips with his fingers thoughtfully. "We have a problem."

The boxer grinned. "I'll warrant we do, me lord. A whole gaggle of 'em."

"But one in particular." Vincent thought for another moment. "Someone who knows Inglewood is spying on us— someone who knows where to hide in the grounds, where the flues are, the service passage. It is time to find them."

Throckmorton frowned. "You think it's someone in the house, me lord. I wouldn't a thought…"

"Nay. No one here now. But unfortunately there is a large supply of those who once worked here and left me in anger."

"You, me lord? Now why would they do that?"

Vincent smiled ruefully. "Suffice it to say, they had reason."

"So what's the lay?"

"How long has it been since you had an evening off, Throckmorton?"

The big man scratched his head. "I dunno, me lord. Since before we left London, I'd hazard."

"Perhaps we can kill two birds with the proverbial single stone." Vincent took his feet off the desk and leaned his elbows on it. "I think you should spend a little time at the Blue Boar."

"Oh, I think I could do that all right and tight. Wouldn't mind at all." Throckmorton grinned. "I might even complain a bit over a heavy wet."

"Definitely complain." Vincent reflected his grin. "You don't get enough time off. You have to play nursemaid to a pair of brats. Even sleep in the room with them."

"Aye, it's a dirty shame." A chuckle erupted. "Barely have time to go to the privy. But who's to watch over the little ones while I'm gone, me lord? I couldn't bear…"

"I will when you are away. And young Feetham and the others. We cannot let down our guard. Even though we found the source, sending that lock of Selena's hair to us was a threat. Someone still means to frighten Lady Diana into silence."

"The blackguards! And her such a kind lady." Throckmorton shook his fist. "If I could but get me fambles on 'em, I'd send 'em to grass. They best not make a try at the wee ones while I'm on watch."

"I know." Vincent looked into the big man's eyes. "And I thank you."

Diana let Emma brush out her hair and tie it back with a ribbon, but she did not undress. She sent the girl to bed and sat down by the window to wait. Vincent was still downstairs. He had a conference with Throckmorton earlier, but the big boxer had returned to his duties in the next chamber. Apparently, Vincent was now playing billiards with Justinian Sudbury who still graced them with his presence.

Why was he still here? Did that amiable gentleman represent a threat or a friend? Diana never knew whether to be open with him or wary. He certainly had a way of turning up at suspicious moments. She wished he would go away.

And that Vincent would come up to bed soon.

What would he say when he learned her plans for tonight? She smiled, thinking of the to-do that was likely. But she knew she would prevail. Nurse must be calmed. And so must she. Diana did not believe for a heartbeat that her enemies wished to put a spell on her child, but still… She would welcome a bit of metaphysical protection for her.

No, the intention of whomever had sent the lock of hair had been to make another threat against her daughter, to frighten Diana again. And they had succeeded. For one horrible moment as she flew up the stairs, even though she had just seen her minutes before, she had expected to find her daughter missing. Or to find evidence that someone close to them was in league with their opponents. With so many people in the house, how could they ever be sure?

A light tap on the door broke into her thoughts. She placed her ear against it. "Who is there?"

"I, m'lady." Nurse's voice.

"Are you alone?"

"Aye."

Diana unlocked the door and Nurse slipped into the room. Just as Diana was closing it, Vincent's voice sounded down the hallway.

"Diana, what are you doing?" He came hurrying toward them, frowning. "I don't want you to open your door for *anyone* but me."

"It is only Nurse." Diana stepped back so that he could enter.

"But someone might be watching and overpower you."

"Vincent, I cannot remain a prisoner in my own room every night. Feetham is just outside in the corridor."

"True enough, I suppose." His frown eased. "But still... What are the two of you doing?"

Diana braced herself for the explosion. "We need to take the children outside."

Vincent didn't disappoint her. "What! Out in the dark? Have you run mad? Were you going to do this without me?"

"Oh, no! We were waiting for you."

"Got to be done." Nurse folded her arms across her gray-clad bosom.

"Why?" Vincent turned his scowl on her. "What has to be done?"

"Miss Selena must be protected."

"Protected? She is quite adequately protected where she is." Vincent propped himself against the wall and folded his own arms. "Diana, what is this foolishness?"

"It is the hair."

"Damnation! You don't believe they would bother with some kind of sorcery? Or that they could harm Selena with it if they did?"

Diana hesitated. "Not really, but Nurse does. And, truthfully, I would feel better if…"

"Can't you do whatever it is you want to do here, in the house?" He glared at both of them.

"The moon's light has got to fall on her," Nurse stated firmly.

Vincent rolled his eyes toward the ceiling in an expression that spoke louder than words. *Women!* He turned to Nurse, unable to keep the sarcasm out of his voice. "What are you going to do? Pray to the moon?"

Nurse favored him with a look that clearly indicated that, had she still the power to do so, his mouth would soon be washed out with soap. In icy tones she pronounced, "That would be unChristian."

He raised his hands in surrender. Obviously he was not going to win this argument. Logic was not going to apply. If he did not help them, he could see that they would find a way to do it without him. Best to get over heavy ground as light as you can. "Very well. Let's get the nonsense behind us. What must be done?"

"Bring the children to the courtyard. It's safe enough. I'll do what's necessary." Nurse opened the door and moved to the children's room.

With a snort of disgust, Vincent followed, Diana on his heels. Throckmorton looked at him in disbelief when he announced that they would carry the sleeping Selena and Bytham out to the courtyard. Vincent shrugged. "Some blather the women are about. You take Selena." He picked Bytham up out of the bed and beckoned to Feetham. "Best come with us."

They descended the stairs as quietly as they could. Vincent didn't want Sudbury to wake and follow them. Not only did he not want him near the children and Diana in the dark, the last thing he wanted was to have to explain this absurdity to anyone. He felt foolish enough as it was.

Vincent had Feetham scout the dark courtyard before they ventured out, hating the feeling of vulnerability. If their spy were lurking about... But, then again, how likely was it that anyone would be expecting this lunacy?

No one appeared to be in the area. Nurse led them to a seat in the center of a circular paved area surrounded by flower beds and hedges. A pile of branches lay beside it.

"Here, m'lady. You sit down and hold Miss Selena. Lord Vincent, you keep Bytham with you for now." Nurse made shooing motions. "No, no. Over there."

Vincent shifted Bytham to a more comfortable angle in his arms and stepped back into the shadows, signaling Throckmorton and Feetham to do the same. The light of the full moon cast everything into contrasting light and the blackest shadows. Damnation! He could not see anything except the stone bench. A brigade could be hidden in the hedges.

Diana sat, and Throckmorton carefully placed Selena in her lap before taking up a position in the darkness opposite Vincent. Feetham moved into a different quadrant farther from the building. The girl muttered sleepily and rested her head on her mother's shoulder. Diana smoothed her hair and whispered reassurances. Nurse picked up a branch from the pile at her feet.

"Elder," she muttered. Rummaging under the bench, she lifted up a bottle and poured something on to the leaves. Then she bowed her head and appeared to be praying.

But not to the moon, Vincent grumbled to himself. *That would be unChristian.*

Her prayer apparently complete, the old woman began to walk clockwise around the bench, shaking the branch toward Diana and Selena and muttering. The hair on the back of Vincent's neck rose. Seeing the three of them in the eerie light—Selena, Diana with the child in her arms and her hair streaming down her back, and Nurse wielding an elder tree branch—reminded him of a carving he had seen at a Roman ruin. Something to do with the Roman triple goddess—the Maiden, the Mother and the Crone. Perhaps the veneer of Christianity lay much thinner over England than he had always imagined.

Nurse completed three circuits around Diana and Selena, then, standing before them, began to strip leaves from the branch. She tossed a handful in each of the cardinal directions, then broke the branch into three pieces and tossed it into the hedge.

A sudden puff of air ruffled his hair and far out in the park an owl hooted. In spite of himself, Vincent shivered.

"There." Nurse dusted off her hands. "Miss Selena will be safe. Now we must see to Master Bytham." She felt under the bench again, coming out with a long-handled pot. A puff of smoke rose from it when she lifted the lid. Thrusting another branch into it, she stirred it about until the leaves began to smolder. She carried the small torch to where Vincent stood holding Bytham and repeated her previous ritual of circuits around them.

When she had finished, she tossed the branch at Vincent's feet. "Stamp it out," she instructed.

He did so hastily, uncomfortable with even that small amount of light, then looked up quickly as a dog howled somewhere off toward the stables. "Are we finished?"

Nurse nodded. "Aye, we're done."

Vincent gestured to Throckmorton and the big man took Selena from Diana. The whole escort moved back toward the house. As they approached it, a movement in the doorway caught his eye. He instantly handed Bytham to Diana, loosening his pistol from his belt.

Justinian Sudbury stepped out of the shadows. He wore no coat or boots, and Vincent could barely see the outline of the gun stuck in his waistband.

"All's well?" Sudbury glanced over the group and back at Vincent.

"Yes." Be damned if he was going to explain the reason for the gathering. "Some of Nurse and Lady Diana's doing."

Sudbury nodded sagely before turning back into the manor. "Women."

Chapter Fourteen

He would never look at his old nurse quite the same way again. Vincent had known her literally all of his life, but hitherto only as the comforter of skinned knees, the washer of faces and, on one occasion, the administrator of a soapy mouth. He grimaced. He could still taste the soap. But the lesson had been learned. He'd never said *that* again.

But now… The image of her in the moonlight presiding over elder, fire and water would never leave him. Nor would the moment of seeing Diana in her mystical role as Mother. Now that he thought about it, all women seemed to have something otherworldly about them, something elusive that men rarely glimpsed.

And never understood.

This morning, on the front steps in the light of the sun, the whole episode seemed unreal. And all *too* real. A chill ran up his back. Perhaps he should adopt Sudbury's laconic attitude.

Women.

As if the thought brought him into being, Sudbury appeared at his side, yawning. "Riding this morning?"

"Yes. Did you not sleep well?"

"Well enough. Not partial to mornings." He yawned a second time. "Mind if I ride with you?"

"Not at all." Vincent wondered if that were the truth. Sudbury was good company, but why was he still at Inglewood? He had originally offered to stay and help keep watch, but now Vincent had an abundance of watchers at his disposal, and he had never asked Justinian to help, in any event.

The possibility existed that Sudbury needed a place to stay. If he were under the hatches, he might find it convenient to enjoy Vincent's hospitality until quarter day.

Or he might find it convenient to watch Vincent for someone.

The under groom brought Vincent's muscular black stallion up to the steps and Vincent sent him back for Sudbury's mount. Just as the man turned back to the stable, Vincent caught sight of another rider coming up the drive. Delamare. He called the groom back. "Please tell Murton that I will need him this morning."

Vincent seldom rode out with a groom in attendance, but he decided that this morning should be an exception. He had little doubt that Delamare would also offer to ride with him, and he had no desire to become isolated in the company of those two. If he could locate James Benjamin somewhere on the grounds, he would attach him, too, on the pretext of inspecting the patrols.

Someone had to watch his back.

"Good morning, gentlemen." Delamare reined in his tall bay by the steps, but did not dismount, instead bowing to them from the saddle.

"Delamare." Vincent squinted up at him where he sat against the brilliant sky. Trust the man to make them crane their necks to see him.

"Servant, Delamare." Sudbury sketched a bow. "Fine morning."

"Yes, indeed." Delamare glanced Sudbury's sturdy chestnut being led from the stable. "May I join you?"

"Certainly." Vincent vaulted into his saddle and Sudbury followed suit. "Through the park?"

"I'd like to see the spring, if I may." Delamare fell in alongside Vincent as they started down the drive.

Vincent nodded. "This way."

Sudbury came up on his other side and Vincent's groom, Murton, brought up the rear. They left the drive at the first convenient spot and cantered through the park in the direction of the stream.

"I meant to ask you yesterday." Delamare moved his horse a bit closer to Vincent's. "Do you remember that old service corridor—the one we used to play in?"

Vincent's whole body tensed and he cast an inquiring glance at his visitor. Was the man baiting him, letting him know he had access to the house? Had he sent that intruder? Or had Sudbury simply mentioned something about the occurrence to him? On the other hand, Delamare might simply be tossing out evidence of the relationship he claimed.

"What about it?"

"I tried to find it when I stayed there night before last, to test my memory of the place, but I could not. I remember that it comes out in the pantry, but I could not find the end in the upstairs corridor."

The possible implications of a stranger searching for that passage shook Vincent for a moment. Then he put the subject aside for later contemplation. "You were searching on the wrong floor."

"Indeed?" Delamare stroked his chin thoughtfully. "I thought it was on the same floor where we slept." He glanced at Vincent inquiringly. "That was my old bedchamber, was it not?"

"Aye." So…he had remembered. Or guessed. Vincent decided he had no more to say about that.

They rode over the rise that separated the house from the wooded borders of the small stream. Delamare looked up and down the brook and turned unerringly toward the spring. When they reached it, he dismounted and stepped up to the banks. Bending down, he trailed his fingers through the water, his eyes unfocused, as if staring into the past.

He touched his fingers to his lips. "Now I recollect the smell." He pointed downstream. "And we fished there, in that pool." He stood. "That is where I got the fishhook in my ear."

He touched his left ear and all of them looked at it. A white scar ran from the center of the lobe to the edge.

Before he thought, Vincent said, "And you screeched like the very devil."

Delamare frowned and said, testily, "Well, it hurt. And it was *your* hook. The farrier had to cut the barb off to get it out."

Vincent nodded, deciding once again he had said too much. The scar looked old, but it was altogether possible that Delamare had been talking with someone who had been at Inglewood in those days, and scars could be created. He turned in his saddle and directed a look at Murton. He had been with them for decades. Murton shrugged. Never mind. Vincent would ask him about it later.

As they jumped a narrow spot above the spring and continued up the next hill, Vincent found himself with a great deal to think about.

Diana had come to dread seeing the post lying on the entry table. Each day when she passed, she looked to see if there was anything directed to her, then hurried by as though to avoid a reptile. Perhaps she *was* avoiding a reptile—one of the two-legged variety. But happily, since they had come to Inglewood, there had been nothing from Deimos.

Had he actually gone to the authorities? Diana doubted it. It had become clear that getting what he wanted from her was more important to him than seeing justice done. That must always be true of blackmailers. She began to wonder if her fears had been foolish. But no matter what he did, she would not tell him one word about Vincent. She could not imagine why the fiend wanted to know about him, but whatever it was, it could bode Vincent no good.

Suddenly another thought struck Diana. When she had told Vincent that her secret did not involve their safety, she had been thinking only of whomever had tried to take the children—most likely Bonaparte's supporters. They had been uppermost in her mind for so long that she had not thought about how much threat to Vincent might be involved in Deimos's order. When he made the demand, Diana had not known that Vincent was involved in espionage.

All at once the threat loomed large. She must tell him. She could not risk putting him in danger.

As though the idea brought about the reality, today when Diana peered at the assortment of letters, one addressed to her in that hated hand lurked among them. She reached for it hesitantly, loathe to touch it. As she lifted it, it slithered out of her fingers and fell to the floor.

Quickly, before one of the footmen could retrieve it, Diana bent and picked it up. As she stood, she heard a commotion at the front door. Looking toward it, she beheld the riding party coming in, Delamare in the lead followed by Sudbury with Vincent ushering his guests through the door. She crammed the message into her pocket and forced a smile.

"Good afternoon, Lady Diana, your most obedient servant." Delamare stopped beside Diana, bowed and gazed down at her. "You look especially lovely today."

The gallantry meant nothing, but Diana saw something in his eyes—the same kind of intensity that she often saw in Vincent's—that made her want to step back. She did so. "Mr. Delamare. I hope I find you well, sir."

For a moment she thought he would take another step toward her and she retreated again, fetching up against the hall table. What he would actually have done, she was never to learn. Vincent saw her at that moment. "Hello, my lady. We have come in search of a glass of wine. If you can tolerate us in all our dirt, will you join us?"

"Why, thank you." Diana surreptitiously touched the paper in her pocket, gently so as not to betray its presence with a crackle. She would have much preferred to go upstairs and read it. What a horror to have hanging over her head while she made polite conversation. But something told her that Vincent wanted her to come with them. "I would enjoy that."

As they started toward the stairs, Henry Delamare, one step ahead of Vincent, offered her his arm. She could see no way to politely avoid him, so she accepted it and climbed the steps with him.

"Which chair would you like, my lady?" he asked solicitously as he led her into the drawing room.

"I like the one there—with the footstool." Diana indicated a seat with no other immediately adjacent to it. At least he would not be able to sit beside her.

He did, however, make a point of bringing her a glass of sherry, of asking if she wanted it refilled, and of addressing most of his remarks to her. Vincent made no obvious objection, but Diana could sense that he was not pleased. She carefully avoided answering Delamare's invitations to flirt. The last thing she wanted was to appear disloyal to Vincent.

After several yawns Justinian Sudbury excused himself

and went in search of a nap. Delamare stayed the proper half hour, and took himself off, stopping before Diana's chair to kiss her hand. As soon as Vincent had seen him out and returned, Diana would tell him about Deimos. She would show him the letter.

But just as Vincent came back into the drawing room, Durbin intercepted him to say that Rugerton, his steward, wanted a word with him. "Forgive me, Diana. I wanted to speak with you, but I suppose that can wait. I best see what's needed."

He followed the butler away down the hall, and Diana sat for a moment in thought. Then she stood and made for her bedchamber, her bodyguard trailing behind her.

The letter was by far the worst yet. This time Deimos did not include even spurious courtesy. He was raging.

Lady Diana, my worthless whore—
I hope you have enjoyed your interlude in Lons-
dale's bed, for it will soon come to an end. No one—
no one—my beautiful strumpet, accepts my favors
without returning them. I always take what is due to
me. You have accepted my silence, yet refused to pro-
vide the simple service I have requested. But I will
have use of you, nevertheless. You have taken my
gold, and I will have the worth of it.
    Do not fear the Runners. I will not send them. I
am coming for you myself. And when you feel my heel
on your neck, you will wish I had sent the hangman.
Fear me, my lovely whore.
Fear me.
Deimos

Diana crumpled the message in her hand and shook. She stood, shaking for a long time. Then she put the paper in the cold fireplace and reached for the flint. She could not show *that* to Vincent. She would tell him, but she would not let him read those lying words. The monster made it sound as though she had been his bedmate for the sake of money. She had never sunk that low.

Nor would she—ever.

But would Vincent believe that?

Having made the decision to tell Vincent the whole truth, Diana could scarcely wait until bedtime. His business with the steward took up the whole afternoon while she paced about in her bedchamber. She dined with him and Justinian and later drank tea with them in the drawing room, fidgeting internally all the while. Later, the two men played chess while she watched, admiring Vincent's elegant profile while pretending to read. He had become so beautiful in her eyes.

When she told him, would she still be beautiful in his?

She left them to their game and their brandy and went up to change for bed. She was again pacing the room when Vincent knocked on the door. He had barely shut it behind him and turned the lock when he came to her and took her in his arms. Diana had opened her mouth to speak, but he silenced her with a long kiss.

When he released her, he started talking immediately. "Diana, I need to discuss the matter of Delamare with you." He sat of the edge of the bed and began to pull off his boots.

Oh, dear. He was annoyed by the man's flirting with her. "Vincent, I…"

But he continued, apparently without hearing her. "He said several things today that I must seriously consider."

Ah. Not the gallantry. She went to sit beside him on the bed. "What sort of thing?"

"Details that he remembered about Inglewood." He shrugged out of his shirt. Diana's gazed drifted to the dark curls covering his hard chest, then back to his face. Vincent went on. "He asked if the room in which he slept had not been his bedchamber as a boy. It was, of course. I wondered if he would recognize it." He removed his britches and leaned back against the headboard, pulling Diana into his lap.

"And he did." She snuggled her head against his shoulder. So comforting. She did not want to tell him, to risk that comfort.

"I suppose." Vincent stared at the far wall for a moment. "The possibility also exists that he predicted that I would do exactly what I did—test him with it—and thus hazarded the guess."

"I imagine he is shrewd enough to do that. He would have had nothing to lose in trying it." Diana fingered the crisp, black hair tickling her chin. "Had he been wrong, he could simply say that he must have forgotten."

"He can say that about anything—anything that we ask. It has been twenty years." He began to stroke her thigh absently. "But there were other things. He knew exactly how to find the spring."

"Perhaps he has been on the grounds before."

"Aye, he may have reconnoitered before ever approaching me. Were I planning such a deception, I certainly would. We know someone is prowling about."

"Do you think it might be he? That he is giving the information to our enemies?" A frightening thought. She sat up a little straighter in his arms and looked at him.

He pulled her close again, reassuring her with a touch. "He knew about that concealed passage—asked me about it, in fact. I wondered if he were taunting me, daring me to unmask him." He paused, thinking. "But no. I don't think he would have known about the chimneys—unless he really *is* Henry, but probably not at all. It would have to be someone who worked in the kitchen or who did maintenance. If he is not Henry, it is more likely that someone is giving the information to *him*. But then there is the matter of the fishhook."

Diana chuckled. "The fishhook?"

He smiled down at her and dropped a kiss on her forehead. "Yes. The tale of a childhood accident he related. I remember it well. He has a scar in the right place and seemed to be still annoyed that it was my hook."

"Oh, my. That does sound authentic." She turned her face up.

"And very much like Henry. He always blamed me for everything—and wanted everything I had." He lowered his face to hers and brushed a kiss across her mouth. "Even you. He is making it plain that he wants you."

"If this man is Henry."

"Whoever he is." He kissed her again, harder this time, holding her tighter. She could feel his erection growing under her. "But he will not have you. I used to give my toys to Henry, but I never had anything in my life that I value as I do you."

"Oh, Vincent." Diana wound her arms around his neck and held him close.

He moved his lips to her throat, one hand coming to her breast. "Ah, Diana. I want you. All I must do is touch you, smell you, hear your voice, and I am consumed with desire."

He let her body drop back across his arm and lifted her, covering her nipple with his mouth, wetting the thin fabric that covered it. Diana moaned and arched upward as sensation coursed through her. His hand found the hem of her gown and slid slowly up one leg, coming to rest between them.

His fingers began to work their magic—circling, pressing, entering—while his tongue and lips on her breast drove every thought out of her head. Diana could only press up against his hand, writhe against it, gasp for breath, vaguely aware of the words he whispered.

"Yes. Yes, Diana. Come to me, beautiful lady. Come to me."

And she did, in shattering completion. He covered her shriek with his mouth while everything went dark, and she could only convulse in his arms. And just as the feelings began to subside, he rolled over and thrust into her.

And it all began again.

Diana could never have said how long they lay entwined, how many times he brought her to release. She only knew that sometime later—much later—she became aware of him pounding against her, smothering his own shout against her neck.

They lay there together, exhausted, dozing. After a while, the chill began to nip at them and they found their way under the covers and slipped into slumber, wrapped in one another's arms.

She hadn't told him. The thought surfaced for a moment before sleep claimed her. Another night's reprieve. But she must. Soon.

Dear God, why was it so hard to do?

The next morning a knock at his library door heralded Throckmorton's approach. Vincent had left Diana sleeping. He interrupted fond memories of the night before to call, "Enter."

The big footman opened the door and took the chair Vincent indicated with a wave of his hand. "I think we have us a nibble, me lord."

"Aha." Vincent leaned back and stacked his heels on the desk. "That did not take long."

"Nay, sir. That it didn't. Only spent a brace of hours in the tap room, neighboring with the tapper. Talked to anyone who came around. Drank enough to let them think I was addled." He grinned slyly. "That would take a lot of ale."

Vincent could believe that. Big men often had amazing capacity. "So, what did you learn?"

Throckmorton's brows drew together. "That someone, God rot 'em, still wants a way to Miss Selena and Master Bytham."

"Go on." Vincent's eyes narrowed.

"When I started home, I hadn't been on the road for more'n five minutes when this cull comes outta the bushes with a lantern. Not a boy exactly, but not a man grown, neither. Young. Says he knows someone who wants to have some words with me."

"Ah. What did this young'un look like?"

Throckmorton stared into the upper corner of the room for a heartbeat. "Light brown hair." He closed his eyes for a moment, then opened them. "Not as tall as you. Skinny. Bad skin."

"Hmm. Was he missing a tooth—one a bit to the side?"

"Aye, now that you say it. You know him?"

"I think so. Tobias Hawkins. Damnation! I have done my best to make amends to that family, but that rascal wants to blame his own bad behavior on his anger at me." Vincent dropped his feet to the floor and crossed his arms. "Go on. What else?"

"Well, he said there was a cove what wanted to meet up with me, wanted to set a time." The boxer smiled. "I figured you might want me to do just that, so I told him tonight—that I'd slip out sneaking-like and come meet them. Asked him first if there was any brass in it for me."

"I suppose he said there was." Vincent smiled wryly.

"Oh, yes." Throckmorton scowled. "I made it plain that

there would have to be brass. Can't be betraying my trust for nothing."

Throckmorton's contempt for treachery was clear in his voice. Vincent sighed. If only there were more men like him. "Very well. Where are you to meet?"

"The cully said there's a beech tree by the lane—a big one. I marked it as I came on back. Says there is a clearing right behind it."

"Yes, I know it." A good meeting place. Vincent would have to stop using it. "What time?"

"Right after moonrise."

"Then I best be there well before. Better a long wait than being seen." Damn. This errand would take up his time with Diana, even dinner. He would have to think up an excuse for Sudbury. "Do not be concerned that you do not see me when you come. I do not intend to be seen."

"Aye, sir. And I'll show up with the moon."

"Very well. I'll arrange for Feetham to stay with the children. Good work, Throckmorton."

Vincent stood. "Tonight we hunt."

Chapter Fifteen

Vincent watched him from the branches of the tree. Tobias Hawkins it was, indeed, searching the clearing and the woods around it. Vincent smiled grimly. *Too late, Tobias. I have been here for several hours.* People rarely thought to look up—at least not amateur schemers like young Hawkins. Clothed in black britches and shirt, soot on his face, and screened by leaves and ivy, Vincent sat motionless well up in the beech, comfortable in a large fork. Even if the searcher looked his way, it was unlikely that he would see him.

The question now was, where was Hawkins's confederate, the person to whom he was providing information? And who was he? With luck they would soon discover the answer. Vincent resisted the impulse to peer through the foliage in an attempt to locate him. He would not risk being discovered. Most likely Tobias's ally had not yet arrived, in any event, using Hawkins to do the scouting for him.

Eventually the boy left and Vincent settled in for the wait. Two days past the full, the moon would not rise until it began to get dark. He watched the sun set, warm colors filtering through the leaves gradually cooling to the lavender of dusk. The balmy dark wrapped around him. Looking up, he could see the stars peeping down at him through the spaces. At last he saw glimpses of the silver disk climbing above the horizon. He sharpened his watch.

Down the lane a tuneless whistling could be heard approaching. Throckmorton. Silently, Vincent eased himself farther down in the tree. The moon's light had not yet reached into the clearing. He felt safe enough in finding a spot where he could see the men on the ground.

The whistling stopped as Throckmorton moved into the clearing, surveying the area warily. He then leaned against the trunk of the beech and folded his arms across his massive chest. Vincent held his breath and listened. A faint rustling in the surrounding brush alerted them both to the coming of Hawkins.

Throckmorton straightened and stepped away from the tree. "Who's there?"

"It's me, guv'nor." Tobias came out of the woods.

"Where's the cove I'm to meet up with?"

"Nay then, he'll be here." The boy sounded surly. "Hold your horses."

"Who is this cull? He local here?" Throckmorton edged away from the tree a bit.

"Nay, he come from London."

"What's he doing here then?"

"Fell things. His master is a lord." Tobias now sounded very pleased with himself. "A great lord."

"He got a name?"

Silence.

The big man took a threatening step forward. "Look, boy, I like to know who I'm doing business with. What's this lord's name?"

Suddenly there was a disturbance in the brush. Vincent and Throckmorton both focused on it. Abruptly the boxer jumped forward, shoving Hawkins away from him.

"'Ware!"

A pistol cracked. The muzzle flash flared across the clearing. Throckmorton shouted and stumbled into Hawkins. They both went to the ground as Vincent came hurtling down through the branches of the tree. He swung to the ground and rolled as he landed. The crashing of a body running through the underbrush told him that the assailant was in retreat. At the point of giving chase, Vincent realized that Throckmorton still lay on the ground.

As Hawkins tried to find his feet, Vincent seized him by the arm. "Oh, no, you don't!" He took Throckmorton, who was attempting to rise, by one shoulder and pushed Hawkins to his other side. "Get him into the woods!"

The boy obeyed unthinkingly. Together they half dragged the boxer to the edge of the trees and dived out of sight. Vincent knelt by Throckmorton where he sat gasping for breath. "How bad are you hurt? Do you have the ball?"

"I don't think so, me lord. Just seems like the wind got knocked out of me." He slipped his hand inside his coat. "Hmm. Well, maybe…" He held the hand out for Vincent to see. It shone wetly.

"You have it, all right." Vincent turned to the boy who crouched beside him, looking stunned. "You see what kind of friends you have? Your partner tried to shoot you—would have, had Throckmorton not saved your worthless neck."

"Must have thought you was going to tell me a name." The big footman got to one knee.

"But I don't know no name!" Tobias blurted.

"You were answering too many questions, nonetheless." Vincent stood and put a hand under Throckmorton's arm. "Can you stand?"

"Aye, me lord. It only smarts a little." He came to his feet.

Vincent turned on Hawkins. "How many are there?"

"I never saw but just the one, me lord." Tobias began sidling away.

Vincent grabbed him again. "Come back here. You are going to help me get him home." He shook the boy angrily. "You young scoundrel, I gave you a chance, but no. You rather quit your position and act on a grudge."

"Nay, then. Weren't much position." The boy scowled. "Naught but scrubbing pots and chasing swallows out of the flues. Besides, you came near burning my sister alive."

"Not by design. And if you want honest work—which clearly you don't—you have to start somewhere. Now… shut up and take his other arm."

Young Hawkins complied sullenly and the three of them made their way back to Inglewood. All the while Vincent was seething with anger and worry. He took them in a side door with his key and escorted Throckmorton up the stairs to the room across from Diana's. By then the footman was moving under his own power, but Vincent insisted he sit on the bed.

Vincent pushed Tobias into a chair, shaking his forefinger at him. "Don't you move." The guards stationed in the corridor looked in curiously. "Watch him," Vincent instructed.

He went to the bedchamber Nurse occupied next to the children's and knocked. She came to the door, nightcap askew, buttoning her wrapper.

"Throckmorton needs you." She followed him without a word. By the time they reached the room where he had left the boxer, Diana had emerged from the door across the hall. "Go back inside," he told her. He did not want her anywhere near Tobias Hawkins.

"No, my lord," she said firmly. "If Throckmorton is hurt, I will come to his aid." She tossed her shining braid over her shoulder and marched across the hall.

Vincent shrugged. He had no time to argue with her. He

went to the bed where Nurse was helping Throckmorton out of his coat. "How bad is it?"

"Don't know yet." Nurse handed him the coat.

Vincent held it up and looked for a hole while she pulled the man's shirt over his head.

"Well, I'll be damned!" Vincent held the coat out for them to inspect. "He had a book in his inside pocket."

"Aye, that I did." Throckmorton leaned forward and took the coat, putting his finger into the hole. "A book what's got a hole in it now." He smiled ruefully. "Now I'll never know what happened to old Robinson Crusoe."

"I'll get you another copy. I'm just grateful it was between you and that pistol."

"Oh, yes. Thank God for that." Diana moved to help Nurse examine the wound. "It isn't deep. I see the ball just under the skin. The book saved you." Gently she spread the opening in the skin and fastened her fingernails around the bullet. Throckmorton grimaced, but sat motionless while she coaxed it out of the wound.

Nurse went to the door. "I'll go for a bandage."

Vincent turned to the nearest footman. "There is some brandy in my room. Fetch it, if you please."

The man turned to go and almost collided with Justinian Sudbury.

"What's the commotion?" Sudbury yawned. He was tying the belt of a dressing gown hastily donned over a pair of buckskin britches. He had on no shoes and his light brown hair stood on end. "What's that black on your face?"

Vincent had forgotten his sooty face. He rubbed a hasty hand over it. Then for a moment, before Sudbury pulled the robe together, Vincent thought he caught a glimpse of mud on the knee of the trousers. He glanced at Tobias, but saw no sign of recognition. Still, he found himself loathe to make explanations. "It's a long story."

"Throckmorton's hurt?" Sudbury peered at Throckmorton's chest.

"Nay, sir, just a scratch." Throckmorton blotted the blood away with his shirt. "And a Godamighty bruise."

"Oh, my." Diana sank down into a chair. "I'm so sorry, Throckmorton. This is all for my sake—mine and the children's."

"Nay then, me lady. I've had worst in the ring dunnamany times. Ain't nothing I wouldn't do for Master Bytham and Miss Selena."

"I know." Tears slid down her face. "I know."

"Ah, Lady Diana." The boxer looked as though he might cry himself. "Don't go napping your bib on my account."

Vincent went and put a hand on her shoulder. "He'll be all right and tight with a little brandy on the outside and a bit more on the inside. Go back to bed, now. You, too, Justinian. I'll stay with him tonight, to be sure." He pointed a finger at Tobias Hawkins and nodded at the footmen. "Take him downstairs and lock him up somewhere. I'll decide what to do with him later."

And that would be a difficult decision to make.

Guilt made decisions difficult.

Diana did not see Vincent until breakfast the next morning, and she had no opportunity to speak with him privately then. Justinian Sudbury came in just as Vincent was holding her chair for her to be seated.

Sudbury took his plate to the buffet. "That youngster you had under guard last night the one providing information to someone?"

Vincent nodded, speaking around a mouthful of ham. "I believe so."

"Should have told me." Sudbury gave him a reproachful glance. "Be of more use to you."

"Thank you, but last night's situation required stealth rather than force." Vincent took another bite and Justinian followed suit, grunting something unintelligible.

"Who was the boy, Vincent?" Diana buttered a scone and took a bite.

"His name is Tobias Hawkins. He worked in the house for a while. And he does have a grudge against me."

Both Diana and Justinian looked at him inquiringly.

Vincent sighed. "From my evil days. I was the cause of his sister almost being severely burned."

"Good God!" Justinian reached for the jam. "What happened?"

Vincent smiled crookedly. "I was in my cups, as usual in those days. She was serving at a tavern a few miles from here. I accidentally knocked her down onto the hearth trying to…" He glanced at Diana. "Uh, take liberties. Her long hair caught fire. I didn't even realize that. I just could not get to my feet until someone pulled me off of her."

He paused and gazed into the distance, his eyes deep pools of regret. "It was later that I was deliberately cruel. I continued to harass her until she quit working for the inn—and her family needed the brass. Her father was dead."

He went back to his breakfast and, for a moment, Diana thought he would not continue. "But what about Tobias?"

"Later I tried to make up for my stupidity. I compensated her family and, even though they were not my tenants, made sure they were not in want. I think the girl forgave me, eventually, but about two years later the mother came to me about Tobias. He was keeping bad company, and she could not control him. So I offered him a position."

"Didn't want a position, I'll warrant." Sudbury went back to the buffet.

"Hardly." Vincent joined him and they both refilled their plates while Diana watched in awe at the amount of food they ladled out. Both of them were trim and Justinian was actually thin. Would Bytham one day eat that way? "He had no skills and so was assigned to the scullery. But he might have improved himself. Instead he remained surly with me, impudent to Durbin, and disobedient to Cook."

"So you were forced to dismiss him." Diana pushed her plate away and sipped her coffee.

"Not exactly. Eventually he ran away and went back to his home." Again a look of sorrow filled Vincent's face. "He was using his anger at me as an excuse for bad behavior. I, of all people, understood that, but—" He broke off and shook his head.

"More fool he." Sudbury picked up the coffeepot and offered to pour for Diana. "Did what you could."

Diana held out her cup and Justinian filled it. "What will you do with him?"

Vincent rubbed the back of his neck thoughtfully. "That's where the devil's in it. I don't know."

"Send him to the magistrate." Justinian blew gently on his fresh cup of coffee.

"I could, I suppose." Vincent stared out the window. "But that would entail more explaining than I wish to do. And…"

"And you still feel guilty." Diana glanced at him in sudden understanding. "You wanted to do for him what your uncle did for you."

"He needs someone." Vincent's sad face turned toward her. "But no, I don't feel guilty. I am sorry for what I did, but I have done all I can do to make it right. I just don't want to make more trouble for his mother."

"Not you doing it."

Vincent looked at Sudbury. "That's true. Tobias must take responsibility for his actions, just as I had to do. But I am also afraid, that if I let him go, the person to whom he has been reporting will not miss his next shot."

Sudbury's eyes narrowed in thought. "You have the right of that."

"So you had best keep him here." Diana rose and the two men quickly came to their feet. "If you gentlemen will excuse me, I must go up to the children and also look in on Throckmorton. He is insisting that he is fit for duty, but…"

"I'm sure he is." Vincent escorted her to the door. "He seems to be a very durable individual."

"I suppose." They stepped into the hall. Diana peeked back into the breakfast parlor. Justinian had gone back to his coffee. "Vincent, I need to speak with you privately…when you get the opportunity."

"This afternoon, after I deal with young Hawkins. You are correct. He must stay here for a while, like it or not." He glanced around quickly and, seeing no one in the vicinity, dropped a quick kiss on her lips. He lowered his voice. "I missed you last night, my love. Let us hope that we will have no further alarms this evening."

Diana smiled up into his face. "Surely we will not."

If any more unwanted guests appeared on his doorstep, where would he put them? Perhaps he should lock Tobias Hawkins, Justinian Sudbury and Henry Delamare all up together until he had sorted them out. Vincent had wanted his enemies to show themselves, but he had hoped for better definitions as to who they were.

He had spent the morning glowering at Tobias, questioning him about his recent employment. Being the target of a bullet definitely had a salutary effect on one's attitude, Vincent reflected. While still sullen, young Hawkins was clearly reconsidering the wisdom of his loyalties. Unfortunately he had little of value to impart and he imparted that reluctantly.

His description of the man who had approached him for

information did not sound like anyone of Vincent's acquaintance, and other than the fact that the man's master was a "prime lord," Tobias knew nothing about him. He admitted to helping create the invasion of the bats. In fact, he sounded rather proud of that accomplishment. Vincent wanted to shake him until his teeth rattled.

Or take a riding crop to him.

In the end, Vincent had Hawkins taken to a servant's room on the top floor and locked in where he could make no more mischief for a while—or get himself killed. Of course, if he tried to escape by the window, he would very likely break his neck. *Which will save me the trouble,* Vincent thought grimly as he made his way back to the drawing room. The young rascal had cost him far too much time and trouble.

Just when Diana wanted to speak privately.

The thought that she might be ready to take him into her confidence lightened both Vincent's mood and his step as he made his way up the stairs from the storeroom where Tobias had spent the night, but a wave of disappointment washed over him as he entered the sitting room. Delamare sat on the sofa beside Diana, his knee touching hers, regaling her with an exciting tale of a sea adventure in which he seemed to figure as the hero.

Vincent stood in the doorway for several heartbeats and listened. Damn the man! Somehow he told the story without ever sounding like the braggart he, in fact, was. Still, he subtly wove his own role into it in a way that would surely stir any lady's heart.

Or loins.

Vincent clenched his teeth.

It proved to be one of the more frustrating afternoons of Vincent's life. No sooner than he had arrived at the drawing room than Durbin announced that a nuncheon was being served. They had little choice but to invite Delamare to partake, and of course, Justinian Sudbury also joined the party. The only private communication he had with Diana was a shrug and a glance that reflected his own exasperation.

Unfortunately, if he wanted to learn the truth about Henry Delamare, Vincent had to tolerate his presence. But he didn't want to do it when he needed to have some time with Diana. The truth, of course, was that he didn't want to do it at all. Whether or not the man was who he said he was, Vincent knew him for an enemy—someone who wished to deprive him of his position.

And, apparently, his woman.

Brother or no brother, he would soon have a word with Mr. Delamare.

As they were finishing their meal, a footman appeared with a message for Diana from Nurse, asking for her to come up.

"I hope you will excuse me." Diana rose and laid her napkin aside. "I best go and see if something is amiss with the youngsters."

She had only been gone for a few minutes when, as the gentlemen sat savoring their wine, Nurse herself came to the door of the dining parlor. "May I speak with you, m'lord?"

Vincent excused himself and stepped out into the hallway. "What is it? Are the children ill? I though perhaps Bytham was coming down with the sniffles yesterday. Is he…?"

Nurse waved a hand. "No, no. Bytham is right as rain. Their mother is with them—and Throckmorton, bandage and all. I just thought mayhap… If you think it fitting, that I might have a bit of a chat with Mr. Delamare. If he is not who he says, I will know."

Now why hadn't *he* thought of that? He had too much on his mind of late. Of course Nurse would be the most likely living person to recognize his brother—or to unmask an impostor. "That is well thought of, Nurse. Why don't I suggest a walk in the garden? I'll go with you and hear what he has to say."

He turned back into the dining parlor. "Delamare, Nurse Marshaw would like to renew acquaintance with you. Are you available this afternoon?"

"Certainly." Delamare came to the door, winked at Vincent, and dropped a kiss onto Nurse's wrinkled cheek. "I have been looking forward to the opportunity."

"Don't mind me." Sudbury stretched. "I'm for a nap."

He headed up the stairs, and Vincent, Nurse and Delamare made their way out of doors. They strolled together for much of the afternoon, exchanging stories of the boys' youth, laughing at most of them. A few of the incidents Nurse related, Delamare said he did not remember. Most of them he professed that he did and even provided occasional details. Vincent did not know what to think.

He didn't remember all of those occurrences himself.

Diana wanted to scream with frustration. Every time she tried to speak with Vincent, someone or something interrupted. She could not discuss something so potentially disruptive in a few stolen minutes. Tonight, after he had come up to bed, she would tell him about Deimos if she had to stuff a stocking in his mouth to keep him from kissing her. If he kissed her, Diana knew she would lose her resolution again.

Dear God, she only hoped that he would still want to kiss her later.

They enjoyed a quiet dinner in the small dining salon with Justinian providing most of the conversation. Delamare had gone back to the Blue Boar after his walk in the garden with Nurse. Vincent seemed preoccupied, but managed to send her an intimate glance now and again. She was certain that his fingers brushing her shoulders as he held her chair had been no accident. She smiled back at him, her heart aching with love and heavy with dread.

Just as the last course was being served, a footman came into the room from the kitchen. "My lord, James Benjamin is asking for you. He says it is important."

"Very well. If you will excuse me, Diana…"

Oh, no! Not another complication. Diana laid down her fork as Vincent stood. What little appetite she had, fled. Vincent did not wait for an answer, but hastened out of the room behind the footman. Justinian, apparently unperturbed, continued to eat.

Only a few minutes passed before Vincent reappeared. "Forgive me. I am going to have to go. I don't know when I shall be back."

"Trouble?" Justinian was on his feet.

"Possibly. But don't disrupt your meal."

"Don't mind." Sudbury followed close on Vincent's heels as he hurried out of the room.

Oh, dear! Something else had happened. In all likelihood something dangerous to Vincent. And Justinian? Would he harm Vincent? In the next heartbeat Diana's breath almost stopped as another idea struck her.

This might be another distraction. They might again be trying to reach the children. Throckmorton was hurt and…

She leapt out of her chair and dashed up the stairs.

Vincent and Sudbury joined James Benjamin at the stable. He was kneeling, examining a small dog. He looked up when they entered. "I think this is one of the ratcatcher's dogs, m'lord, and he's got blood on him. A lot of it."

"Rat blood?" Sudbury peered down at the terrier.

"Nay then, mighty big rat, to bleed this much." James

Benjamin ran his hands through the fur. "And I don't think this little fellow is hurt."

Vincent got down on one knee. "Aye, he's soaked." A cold lumped formed in his stomach. His man was hurt. They had to find him. But of course, he could not say that. Instead he said, "It may be his master needs help."

"Think he will take us to him?" Sudbury stared speculatively at the dog.

Vincent thought for a moment. If only he could be sure of Justinian, he could certainly use his help. But where had he been all afternoon? He could represent a threat to the man Vincent wanted to save.

He would have to chance it. Considering the amount of blood, they might have little time. "It's worth a try." Vincent stood. "We'll have to go on foot. James Benjamin, call another man or two and bring horses. We may need them." He walked to the stable door, turned back to the terrier and snapped his fingers. "Come on, lad."

The little dog came to him, wagging its tail. Vincent took another step and murmured coaxingly, "Come on. Take us to him."

As if he suddenly understood, the ratter ran past him and into the twilight. Vincent and Sudbury took off in pursuit. James Benjamin shouted at a pair of grooms and ran for his horse. For a moment Vincent lost the little terrier in the gloom, but then he spied him waiting a short distance away. The three of them dashed off again in the direction of the lane.

Every time Vincent thought that the dog had outdistanced them, the creature would coming running back, impatiently darting off again when they came into view.

"By Jove." Sudbury puffed. "I think he knows."

"He seems to," Vincent agreed.

At that moment they again lost sight of their quarry. They paused to catch their breaths and heard barking a short distance away. They followed the sound off the path, across the ditch and into a small copse of trees. Both terriers sniffed at a dark shape on the ground. Vincent ran to it and knelt. Oh, God. It was as he feared. A man lay on one side, a knife protruding from the vicinity of his shoulder blade. Blood soaked his shabby brown coat.

Vincent touched his arm and the man moaned but did not move. Relief flooded Vincent. "He's alive."

"Won't be for long." Sudbury touched the bloody sleeve of the coat. "Bleeding too much."

Vincent reached toward the knife, but Sudbury caught his wrist, stopping him. Vincent stiffened, but Sudbury said, "Leave it. You pull it out, it will gush. Get him to the house."

Acknowledging the wisdom of this advice, Vincent shouted for James Benjamin. He and the other grooms with their horses had waited on the path, but at the hail, James Benjamin jumped the ditch and guided his mount into the copse. He dismounted, bending down to the man on the ground.

"You want him across the saddle, m'lord?"

Vincent hesitated, glancing at Sudbury. "What do you think? That would put him head downward. I'm afraid he might bleed more."

Sudbury nodded. "Better hold him up."

Vincent climbed into the saddle. "See if you can pass him up. I'll pull."

With some difficulty the three of them managed to get the dead weight of the injured man onto the horse. Vincent held him tightly with one arm, but the man slumped forward, his head resting against the horse's mane. He had not made another sound.

"Come on, hurry. Ride double." Vincent carefully walked the horse across the ditch rather than jump it. "One of you ride ahead and get Nurse Marshaw. Tell her to make ready the room we had Throckmorton in. I'll come as fast, but as easy as I can."

If the man survived, Vincent wanted him to be where they could guard him without spreading his men too thin. Damnation! If his forces took any more casualties, he would have to install an infirmary. The horse carrying James Benjamin and another groom galloped off into the dusk.

Sudbury, riding with the third groom, came up beside Vincent, and Sudbury extended a hand to steady Vincent's burden. It made for awkward going, but it helped hold him still. An eternity later they reached the building. Several men waited with a hurdle and Vincent eased the man down to them.

"Should I ride for Dr. Dalton, m'lord?"

"Aye. And as fast as you can." Vincent nodded at the groom and followed the men carrying his friend up the stairs—a friend he could not even acknowledge. Vincent's heart ached.

Both Nurse and Diana, with their full contingent of guards, were waiting for him at the bedchamber. They worked the limp figure onto the bed and rolled him to his side. More blood leaked around the blade.

Diana looked at Nurse. "We must stop the bleeding."

The old woman nodded, but frowned. "Can't with the knife in him." She turned to a footman. "Get my scissors."

He ran to obey, but Sudbury pulled a heavy blade out from under his coat. Vincent's every sense came to full alert.

Sudbury met his gaze for a heartbeat, then handed him the weapon. "Better to cut his coat off."

Vincent took the knife and began slicing away the heavy fabric. When Nurse's scissors arrived, she attacked the thinner material of the shirt and together they laid bare the man's back.

Vincent glanced at her inquiringly. "Can we wait for the doctor?"

She shook her head. Vincent sighed and looked at Sudbury.

"Tricky." Justinian rubbed his chin thoughtfully. "No choice." He reached across the bed and grasped the man's shoulder firmly. Diana stood by with an armful of towels. Vincent breathed a prayer and took hold of the knife. *God, let this be the right thing to do.*

He pulled.

The knife hung in the bone for a second, then came free. Vincent took a sudden step back before catching his balance. True to Sudbury's prediction, blood gushed from the wound. Diana moved in with the towels and pressed them against the gash. They began to turn red.

"Harder." Vincent moved her hands aside and leaned against the towels with his own. Sudbury braced the shoulder from the other side. Nurse folded more towels into a pad and slid it into position. Vincent pressed harder. Gradually the flow seemed to subside.

"Don't let up," Nurse said beside him. "Not until the doctor comes and sews it together."

Vincent glanced at Justinian and they both nodded grimly.

Chapter Sixteen

It had been a long night. Dr. Dalton had finally arrived and done the necessary needlework. He complimented their efforts in stopping the bleeding and tried to send them all away, but met with resistance from Vincent. The doctor scowled at him. "I'll sit with him, my lord. No need for you to exhaust yourself further."

Diana also offered to keep watch with the doctor to relieve Vincent, but he had stubbornly refused, and surprisingly, so had Justinian. At last the three men settled into the sickroom and Diana gave it up and went to bed. Another night in which she would have no opportunity to speak with Vincent.

Would this never end?

And today she was expecting a visit from Lord and Lady Caldbeck and their children. She had been looking forward to it. She liked Catherine, and Bytham would especially enjoy having another little boy to play with. Like all little girls, Selena was fascinated with babies. Perhaps Catherine would let her hold her infant daughter. It would have been a treat for all of them had Diana been less tired and worried.

She did not know how Vincent could keep going. He had been without sleep for most of two nights, although this morning he had gone to his own room for a nap. The rat-catcher had roused with the dawn and Dr. Dalton had ordered that he be fed beef soup and red wine.

"We must replace and strengthen his blood," he explained when Diana had looked in on the patient.

Whoever the patient might be.

Diana had been told that he was a ratcatcher, but she had her doubts. Vincent was plainly frantic with worry. The man had some other importance to him. Perhaps, if she ever got the chance to speak with him, Vincent would explain his true relationship to the man.

Vincent did not emerge from his bedchamber until just before the arrival of Caldbeck's family. The adults partook of a nuncheon and then had tea in the drawing room while Nurse—under the watchful eye of Throckmorton—presided over the nursery and naps in the children's room. At midafternoon Nurse sent word that she and the Caldbeck nurse were taking the youngsters out for an airing.

Vincent stirred restlessly and glanced at his uncle, who nodded. Both of them stood.

"I believe I need some air, as well." Vincent moved toward the door, followed by his uncle.

Diana turned to Catherine. "Shall we join them?"

They all strolled out to the gardens. Diana and Catherine found a comfortable spot on the lawn, sitting on a rustic seat shaded by a huge, old oak. Sunlight streamed through the branches and brightly illuminated the masses of flowers divided by the brick walks of the garden. A soft breeze ruffled their hair and Diana could hear bird calls in the shrubbery walk that lay just the other side of the flower borders. Caldbeck and Vincent sauntered on to where Nurse Marshaw and Caldbeck's nurse supervised the children.

As they approached the little group, Vincent scanned the area warily. Having Selena and Bytham out of doors made him nervous, especially with all the hostile activity they had been experiencing. But he could hardly keep them mewed up in the house forever. Besides, the garden teemed with protection. In addition to himself and Charles, Vincent could see three footmen ranged around the edges with Throckmorton stationed at the far end.

The two of them paused for a moment where Selena sat beside Caldbeck's nurse, admiring little Sarah. Charles touched his baby daughter's hand with one finger and she promptly closed her tiny fist around it. As usual, Vincent could see no flicker of emotion on Charles's face, but the gesture spoke volumes. He became aware of an ache in his throat.

Would a child of his own ever clutch his finger in that trusting way?

Selena broke into his reverie. "See how pretty she is, Papa. Can we have a baby, too?"

His uncle gave him a look which clearly said, *Papa?*

Vincent felt his neck turning red. The name always caused a moment of uneasiness, followed by one of longing. He shrugged at Charles and patted Selena on the shoulder. "You had best ask your mother that question."

As they continued their tacitly agreed-upon patrol, he thought he actually saw a twinkle in Charles's eye.

Bytham and young Edward, only a few months his junior, had launched a game of hide-and-seek in the knot garden. One head of straight black hair and one of golden curls bobbed up and down behind various plantings, and fits of giggles drifted to them on the wind. Vincent had just begun to relax and enjoy the comforting domestic scene when he saw Delamare riding up the drive.

His pleasant mood evaporated.

One way or another, the man was trouble. Delamare dismounted at the steps and handed his reins to a groom. He then set off toward the ladies and stood smiling down at Diana. Vincent scowled. Yes, he would soon have a chat with this potential brother.

He and Charles completed their circuit of the garden and moved back toward the trio under the tree. As they approached, Diana abruptly stood and called, "Bytham, that is far enough. Come back now."

Vincent turned to see the little figure with the sun-drenched curls leave the knot garden, heading for the hidden paths of the shrubbery.

"Oh, dear. He knows he is not supposed to go there. He will get lost." Diana started toward her son.

"I'll get him." Vincent signaled to Throckmorton and trotted off after the escapee. The boxer nodded and moved on an interception course.

"Charles." Catherine stood and nodded at their son who had started in pursuit of Bytham. His lordship nodded and made for his heir, calling his name. Edward paused, then started reluctantly back toward his father.

A bad feeling came over Vincent. He picked up his pace. "Bytham, come back at once."

Bytham laughed and waved. Drat! The little rascal was still playing least-in-sight. Vincent broke into a run. By this time the various footmen had also converged on the sheltered paths. Bytham ran into the shadows through a gap in the hedges and disappeared.

A very small gap.

Vincent and Throckmorton arrived at the spot at the same time, but neither of them could get through. Vincent pointed. Throckmorton nodded and dashed off, searching for the far entrance. Vincent went the other way. He knew exactly how to get into the walks, but by the time he did so, the fugitive was nowhere to be seen.

"Bytham!" No answer. Not even a giggle.

Real fear began to battle with annoyance. Vincent ran down one path and up another. No one. His next circuit brought him in sight of two of the footmen, but they both shook their heads when he hailed them. Maybe the boy had gone back to the garden. Vincent found a break in the hedge large enough to wriggle through and emerged into the sunlight.

Diana was hurrying toward him. "You didn't find him?"

"No. I think he is hiding. He believes we are playing the game with him and Edward."

"Let me look." Diana started toward the entrance to the leafy maze.

"No! You may not be safe." Vincent grasped her arm, alarm shooting through him. "Go back to Catherine and Charles." Even as he spoke, Caldbeck handed his son over to his nurse and came toward them. "Stay with Charles."

Diana turned back, reluctance in every line of her body. Out of the corner of his eye, Vincent saw Delamare step toward her. Did the man pose a threat to her? For a moment he was torn between finding Bytham and guarding Diana. But Charles would watch Delamare and Feetham kept his post near her as he had been instructed. Good man.

Throckmorton put his head out of the hedge, pointed and called, "I think I saw something that way, me lord. I'm going after him."

As he ducked back into the bushes, Vincent realized that the path he indicated led back toward the lane. He ran for Delamare's horse. Jerking the reins away from the groom, he vaulted into the saddle and cantered off down the drive. He peered into the trees and bushes along the side where he hoped Bytham would come out. Then, up ahead, around a bend in the lane, he heard the crackle of twigs breaking. He spurred forward.

And came to a rearing stop.

In the center of the road, astride a tall chestnut horse, sat Lord St. Edmunds.

He had Bytham in his arms.

Vincent's heart went to his boots. St. Edmunds was not overtly threatening the boy, but he had one hand resting almost casually against Bytham's chin and the other on his shoulder. One quick jerk would break his neck. St. Edmunds could do it before Vincent could draw the pistol from his belt. Vincent took a long, steadying breath. He could not make a mistake here.

"Good afternoon, St. Edmunds. I see you have found my ward."

St. Edmunds smiled coldly. "Yes, it does seem so at last, does it not?"

Vincent nudged his mount forward. "I'm much obliged. I'll take him."

"Not yet." St. Edmunds backed his horse a step. "I would like first to speak with his mother—privately."

Not a chance. Vincent knew it was Diana that the conspirator wanted. Her son was only a means to that end. He considered possibilities. How could he arrange…

At that moment Throckmorton stepped out into the road from behind a tree. He had his pistol in his hand. St. Edmunds cast him a startled glance and tightened his hold on Bytham. Bytham whimpered. Throckmorton didn't move, but held his weapon steady. St. Edmunds spoke to Vincent. "Tell him…"

Hoofbeats sounded a bit farther down the lane, behind St. Edmunds. He turned cautiously and looked over his shoulder. Vincent followed his gaze. Justinian Sudbury rode around a curve and drew rein, the gun in his saddle holster clearly visible. He nodded amiably. "Servant, St. Edmunds."

Who would Sudbury support? Vincent held his breath. St. Edmunds studied each of the three of them in turn. Then he slowly eased Bytham to the ground.

Vincent breathed again. Throckmorton stepped forward and, taking Bytham into his arms, quickly disappeared into the shrubbery. St. Edmunds looked at Vincent with raised eyebrows.

Vincent smiled grimly, his hand on his pistol. "I believe, my lord, that you should come up to Inglewood with me for a bit of conversation."

Diana let out a sigh of relief as Throckmorton, surrounded by the other footmen, came through the hedge. Bytham was safe in the big man's strong arms.

At her elbow Delamare said, "The little brat deserves a good hiding."

Diana frowned. "I do not beat my children, sir. He must learn to obey, yes, but he is very young yet."

Delamare shrugged. "He caused you a great deal of anxiety."

"Children do that all too often." She relented and smiled at him. Perhaps she had become a bit too defensive of her children. "It is the cost of parenthood."

He reflected the smile. "Something about which I know very little." He looked back toward the drive. "At least my horse is being returned. But who is that with Vincent and Sudbury?"

Diana followed his gaze. "Dear God! St. Edmunds."

"Is it, indeed?" Delamare squinted. "Yes, I do believe you are correct. What is he doing here?"

Panic gripped Diana. "Throckmorton," she called. "Take the children into the house at once."

But Throckmorton was not waiting to be told. He had reached Nurse and Selena, and was shooing them inside.

Caldbeck had already sent his family back to the drawing room, but he cast a quick glance at the doorway, as if to be sure they were safe, and another at the shrubbery. "I believe we should all go in immediately."

The hair rose on Diana's neck. She took one running step toward her children before the sound of a shot split the air. A shower of bark from the tree beside her spattered her face. She jerked away from it, and Delamare grabbed her elbow, spinning her in front of him, away from the hedges.

Caldbeck took her other arm, and they ran, taking her along with them. Feetham pounded along behind her, thus surrounding her with bodies. Her feet barely touched the ground. Their momentum lifted her up the stairs and they all four stumbled into the entryway.

Behind her she heard galloping horses, but Diana could not spare them any attention. She ran for Bytham and Selena. "Get the children upstairs!"

She followed them up, fumbling for the small pistol in her pocket. They all reached the bedchamber door at the same time, and Diana crowded in with Nurse and Throckmorton. She turned the key in the lock and pointed the gun at the door, her knuckles white.

Behind her, Throckmorton's big hand settled on her shoulder. "All's well for now, me lady. There is no one there. They are safe."

Diana's knees buckled and she sank to the floor.

Vincent had abandoned any pretense of courtesy. He hustled St. Edmunds into his library at pistol point and left Sudbury to watch him while Vincent conferred with Charles and went upstairs to reassure himself of everyone's safety.

Only to find blood once more on Diana's white face.

Vincent's anger boiled. He left Nurse ministering to the injury and stomped back down the stairs to the library. He did not like to picture himself shooting a man in cold blood, but he would have a battle with himself not to put a bullet through St. Edmunds on the spot.

. He had been certain when the shot sounded that St. Edmunds would bolt while everyone sought cover, but he had not. Instead he had galloped up to the door with Vincent and Sudbury and dashed into the house with them— as though he feared for his own hide. Well, if he did not before, he should certainly fear for it now. Vincent stalked into the library and slammed the door.

And remembered Sudbury. He could not discuss the matters he intended to discuss in front of him. Sudbury was proving himself as a friend, but Vincent was loathe to involve him in the espionage. Vincent turned to him. "Much obliged for your assistance, Sudbury. We need to speak later. But now, if you don't mind, I need a word alone with Lord St. Edmunds."

Sudbury nodded toward St. Edmunds. "His coat."

Of course! What was he thinking? The stocky lord almost certainly carried a weapon. "My lord, would you be so good as to remove your coat?"

St. Edmunds did so without comment and handed the garment to Sudbury. Sudbury patted the pocket, walked around St. Edmunds and pulled a knife from the back of his waistband. Then he nodded again and left the room.

Vincent motioned St. Edmunds to a chair and sat behind his desk. They watched one another silently until, at last, Vincent sighed. "I believe, my lord, that we are both checked, if not mated."

St. Edmunds inclined his head and compressed his lips. "Just so."

"I cannot prove that you are planning the escape of Bonaparte, but I *can* render you ineffective." Vincent leaned back in his chair and steepled his fingers. "I have already written to my superiors about your involvement in the scheme. You will be watched too closely to continue. In fact, a list of your associates has also been forwarded to them. Napoleon will have to put his dependence on some other group."

"Which he will do. Never doubt it, Lonsdale. Bonaparte will return. Mark my words. The Bourbon king cannot rule France." St. Edmunds thought for a heartbeat. "I'll allow that your people have baulked mine. But your usefulness to the Foreign Office is also at an end. You are known. I have seen to that." He crossed his legs and flicked a crumb of dirt from his boot. "I had grown suspicious of you. When you absconded with Lady Diana, I was certain."

Vincent crossed his arms, his brows drawn together. He spoke between gritted teeth. "Apparently, having failed to control her, you have decided to kill her."

St. Edmunds put up a hand. "No, no. Not I. But there are those… I did all I could to avoid it. I admire Lady Diana, but I could not allow her to communicate our plans."

"What plans? She tells me she knows nothing. Do you really think Corby told her anything that he did not tell the whole world?"

"I do not know what Corby told her, or even exactly how much he knew about our arrangements. What I absolutely could not allow was for her to tell any of it to Deimos."

"Deimos!" Vincent jumped to his feet and leaned his fists on the desk. "What does Deimos have to do with Lady Diana?"

"So you do not know." St. Edmunds smiled faintly with satisfaction at his reaction. "I do not know exactly myself. I came into her sitting room one day in time to see her hastily toss a paper into the fire. She left then to fetch Corby, and I was able to pluck the note out of the flames. Most of it had been consumed, but the signature was plain."

"Does he now serve the Bourbon king?" Vincent sat down and covered his mouth with one hand, pondering this revelation. Deimos. Of all men. What in the world had Diana to do with *him?*

St. Edmunds shook his head. "I don't know who he serves at present. One can never tell with Deimos. My people cannot find him. I suggest you ask Lady Diana."

By God he would do *that!* How could she have been keeping such a thing secret from him? That must be what she had been wanting to speak with him about. He prayed that it was.

But now he had another problem to solve. "And what am I to do with you? I can prove nothing against you, yet I have no doubt you are still a danger to Lady Diana and her children."

St. Edmunds smiled a half smile. "I doubt that I will be for long. Why do you think I came here instead of taking to my heels when that shot sounded?"

Vincent gazed at him with narrowed eyes. "Tell me."

"I have failed to control her. Or kill her. I should have done so immediately, but I wanted…" He shrugged. "I am known. My plans are known. You think you are acquainted with all of my associates, but you are not. You do not know who fired that shot today." He stared at the books for a space. "But *I* do."

"Will you tell me?"

St. Edmunds shook his head silently.

"Not even to save your life?"

More silence.

"I will not keep you here."

"I do not expect it." St. Edmunds got to his feet and walked to the door. "Good day to you, Lonsdale."

As Vincent watched him close the door, he heard a sound at the window. He turned to see Sudbury standing outside.

Sudbury saluted and walked away.

Bloody hell.

Deimos?

The rest of the afternoon had been very confused. Diana refused to leave Selena and Bytham, but Catherine came up to inquire as to her welfare and to tell her that Caldbeck was insisting that she and the children go home immediately. He would see them safe and return.

"I would not think of abandoning you except that I must consider Edward and Sarah." She embraced Diana warmly, a tear in her eye. "I know myself how hard it is not to be frightened, but I'm sure Vincent will keep you safe. Be brave, and be very careful."

Diana thanked her with a catch in her own throat.

Shortly thereafter, a footmen brought Diana a message from Delamare asking after her and saying the he would remain at Inglewood as long as she might be in danger. In answer to her question, the footman told her that St. Edmunds had ridden away.

What did that mean? Why did Vincent let him go? And why had he not come up?

No sooner than she asked the question, another tap at the door announced Vincent's presence. He came in looking very grim.

Diana barely restrained herself from falling into his arms. "What has happened? Where has St. Edmunds gone? Oh, Vincent! I simply *must* speak with you."

"Let us go to your bedchamber." He opened the door and followed her out into the hall. When they were safely in her room, she turned and stood by the bed. "Vincent,

there is something you must know. Something I should
have told you before, but until recently I did not think—"

She broke off at his dark expression. He crossed his
arms and leaned against the door.

"Tell me about Deimos."

Chapter Seventeen

Diana sat down on the bed with a thump, both hands flying to her mouth. "You knew?"

"I do now."

She frowned. "But…how?"

"St. Edmunds told me."

"What? St. Edmunds knows?" Dear God, how could *he* know what she had done?

"What have you been telling Deimos, Diana?" Vincent came to stand directly in front of her, scowling down at her.

She shrank back. "I have told him nothing…nothing at all."

Vincent raised a skeptical eyebrow.

She sat up straighter, groping for calm, and said firmly, "Indeed…I have not." Dear God, he had to believe her. "He threatened me, but he did not ask for anything until…"

"Wait. He threatened you? How?"

Diana looked at him in puzzlement for a moment before understanding dawned.

Then she said, "You *don't* know."

"I know you were corresponding with him."

"No." Diana shook her head. "I never answered him, but he…he was attempting to blackmail me."

Now he looked puzzled. "Blackmail? You? What have you ever done to be blackmailed?"

This was the moment, the moment she must say it out loud. But she could not look at him. Diana covered her face with her hands.

"I killed someone."

Vincent sounded positively dumbstruck. He took a step back. "You killed…? When? Why?"

"It was an accident. I didn't even realize I had done it…"

"You didn't realize you killed someone? Diana…how could you not… Hold a minute." He sat beside her on the bed and gazed intently into her face. "Who did you kill?"

"Roger Goodnight. It was before I stopped going socially—at a ball at Lady Holland's."

Vincent frowned. "Goodnight broke his neck in a drunken fall—before more than a hundred people, including me."

"But I pushed him. Someone saw me—this person who calls himself Deimos."

"No. I saw Goodnight fall myself. No one pushed him over that rail. He leaned over to look at someone below. This does not make sense." He leaned back against the headboard, shaking his head. "You better start at the beginning."

Diana took a deep breath. At last she could tell the story that had been corroding her heart since the first letter from Deimos had arrived. "I had been to the room designated for ladies. It was near the top of the stairs that led down to the ballroom. When I came out, Roger approached me—he was very drunk—and he began to…to…"

"I understand. Go on."

"He was putting his hands on me." Diana studied her

slippers. "So I pushed him as hard as I could and ran back into the room. When I came out again, everyone was gathered around him on the floor below. I still did not realize I had caused that fall...until I got the first letter."

Vincent now looked very thoughtful. "What did it say?"

"That he had seen me push Roger over the railing, had heard me say angrily that I would kill him." She looked up at him. "I did not say that, Vincent, but I *did* push him...and Deimos made it sound so convincing. I feared he could persuade the authorities that I had done it deliberately. But he said...he said he didn't want to see me...hang. He assured me that he would keep silent, but only if I did. That one day I would repay him."

The cold fear rose in her again and Diana turned toward Vincent, drew her legs up onto the bed and wrapped her arms around them, resting her head on her knees. "Oh, Vincent, if I were executed or even imprisoned, what would happen to Selena and Bytham?"

Vincent was beginning to see just a crack of light. The man was a master of manipulation. "Did you tell Wyn?"

She lifted her head and looked at him. "No, Deimos warned me not to, or he would report me. And...and... Oh, God, this is the worst of it. You will utterly despise me." She covered her face with her hands again. "I—I took money from him. I could not tell Wyn that."

The light again became murky. "Deimos sent *you* money? Blackmail usually works the other way about."

"I know. But I had no money, and then he began to write vile, insulting things—as though I were a..." Around her hands Vincent could see the blood suffuse her face. "I thought... I feared...that someday he would try to make me do something... You know."

"Hmm." Not much doubt what that meant. "What did you do with the money?"

She lifted her head and glared at him defiantly. "I bought food with it! And clothes for the children…"

Vincent held up a restraining hand. "I understand." He pondered this information for a moment. "So he held a two-edged sword over you. A threat on the one side and obligation on the other."

Diana sighed. "Precisely. I did not know what to do. I could not give the money back."

"You never saw him?" He watched her closely, but she gazed at him openly.

"No, never. Everything arrived through the post." Vincent nodded. He knew of no one who had ever laid eyes on Deimos—and lived.

"So when did he make his demand?"

"When we were at Eldritch Manor. I received two letters from him—both of them forwarded by Helen. He must have known I stayed with them, but he did not seem to know where we went when we left them. But he said he would find me—no matter where I went." She tightened her arms around her knees and her face paled. "And he accused me of killing Wyn, too, so that I might…seduce you." She ducked her forehead against her knees again. "Oh, he just twisted everything and made me sound like the most wicked, shameless schemer alive. He almost made me believe it. I knew his diabolical tongue could, in fact, have me hung."

"Little wonder you were terrified." Vincent stifled the impulse to take her in his arms and comfort her. He could not let himself be swayed by emotion in making sense of this bizarre tale. "What did he want?"

"Information about you. Details. Anything out of the ordinary. But I would not do it. At the time I was not sure of your motives, either, but I knew I could not betray you. You had taken such good care of us. So I did not respond."

Thank God for that. "And the second letter?"

"He was very angry." She looked up at Vincent again, her face drawn and her eyes hollow. "He gave me two weeks before he took his information—the whole parcel of lies—to the magistrate. That was the night I asked you to care for Selena and Bytham if anything happened to me."

"I see." At least he hoped he did. Vincent stared at the ceiling for a heartbeat. He wanted to believe her so badly.

"But I had no idea he was associated with St. Edmunds."

"He is not. St. Edmunds retrieved one of his notes to you from your fireplace. That is why he feared you—that you knew his plans and were selling them to Deimos."

"Dear God! What a tangle. I knew nothing about St. Edmunds or his friends or Bonaparte or…" She leaned back against the bedpost. "But who *is* Deimos?"

"Deimos is a highly secretive assassin and purveyor of information."

"A spy?"

"More aptly a criminal. His loyalties tend to shift toward the highest bidder. He is utterly vicious." A cold knot of dread coiled in Vincent's belly. The animal had been pursuing his Diana all this while and he hadn't even known it. As farfetched as the story sounded, Vincent believed every word of it—in part because he knew the way the blackguard worked. But he knew now that was only a small part.

He believed Diana because he knew her nature.

He trusted her.

Almost before he knew what he was doing, he lunged across the bed and seized her, crushing her to him. "Good God, Diana. He is a greater danger than St. Edmunds ever was, and he hates me. If I do not stop him, he would destroy you just to injure me."

She clutched him tightly, shivering. "In his last letter—

just four days ago—he said he was coming for me. That I would wish he had sent the hangman instead."

"Very good." Vincent spoke quite softly. "I shall have the opportunity to kill him."

She had clung to Vincent, unable to speak, while he rocked her in his arms until dusk settled outside the windows. Diana had not let herself realize how much Deimos's last letter had terrified her. She had been required to function, to think of the children, to care for the injured. There was no time to be frightened.

But as she spoke the words to Vincent, the horror had washed over her. Suddenly she was too afraid even to weep, to think, to hear or feel. But as he held her she at last began to feel his hands smoothing her back and hair, hear his murmured words of comfort. The fear began to recede.

Finally she was able to sit up and look at him. "Is it all too much to believe, my lord?"

He brushed her tousled hair away from her face. "Had I no understanding of the man—or of you—it might very well be. But this is just the sort of thing he would do—abuse and harass a woman in order to bend her to his will."

"I am starting to think that I have been very stupid. *I* knew I had not intentionally pushed poor Roger to his death. I would have gone to the authorities myself, except that he threatened to bear witness against me. I see now that he would probably never have done so. He wished to make use of me. But then…" She glanced at him apprehensively. "The money truly did put me in his pay, and I didn't want you to know I had taken payment from a man." She covered her face once more with her hands. "I feel so ashamed. Stupid and ashamed."

"As he intended. He makes use of the feelings that decent people have to manipulate them and pull them into his web." Vincent's warm fingers clasped hers. "The shame of the money accrues to Wyn, Diana. Had he taken proper care of you, you would have told him the whole immediately."

"Yes." She stared into the distance thoughtfully. "Yes, I think I would. I felt so alone."

"Damn him." A small muscle jumped in his jaw as his expression hardened. "But you are not alone any longer, and I believe that St. Edmunds is no longer a threat, although his confederates may be."

"What happened to him? Why did you let him go?"

"I no longer had a reason to keep him." He related the afternoon's conversation with the lord.

Diana listened intently. "Do you mean that his own people will kill him?"

"Very likely. He spent too long talking with me, for one thing, but I think he believes his days are numbered. He can no longer be of use to them, and he knows too much."

Diana shuddered. "What awful people."

"Conspiracy is an awful game, Diana." Vincent gazed into her face. "But it is part of who I, also, now am. I sent him to his death. I want you to think about that before you agree to become my wife."

Diana nodded silently. What a complex person she had fallen in love with. A spy. She would not ask him if he had killed. She did not want to hear the answer.

Another question occurred to her. "How did you come to be my champion? I was afraid of St. Edmunds from the beginning. He was so determined to carry me away, I feared he would succeed."

Vincent glanced at her ruefully. She would not be happy with the answer to *that* question. He cleared his throat. "We, er, we cast dice for the privilege."

"What?" She jumped off the bed and glared at him, arms akimbo. "How…how…insulting!"

"Now, Diana." He reached for her, but she stepped away. "I could not allow him to take you."

"But what if he had won?" She folded her arms across her breasts.

"I knew he would not. Neither of us could afford an honest game, so I insisted that we exchange dice. He gave me the opportunity by challenging my honesty. With Sudbury listening, he could not refuse. I expected his dice would deliver an eleven or twelve—a win in a game of hazard—but he surprised me. The ones he produced were loaded for six, a main." He glanced at her puzzled face. "One must first roll a main to control the dice."

"Oh. But you still won."

He nodded, grinning. "My dice were loaded to lose."

"To lose? Why would you want to lose at dice?"

"It is a convenient way to let money change hands with no one the wiser. I used them often with my informants." He sobered. "But I never, even in my worst days, used loaded dice to win."

"So…in addition to the other indignities I have suffered, I am the prize in a dishonest dice game." Her chin rose.

She would not be mollified. He could see that. His only choice was direct action. In one lightning motion, Vincent seized her and flipped her onto her back on the bed. Before she could protest, he covered her mouth with his own. At first she resisted, her body tense under his, but at last he felt her soften. When they had to breathe, he lifted his head and looked down at her.

"I would never have let him have you, Diana. Never."

What they would have done next, they never learned. They were interrupted by a peremptory knock on the door.

Vincent opened it to find Durbin, his brushy eyebrows all but meeting across the bridge of his nose. "We have house guests, my lord."

"I am aware of that, Durbin."

The butler became very formal, addressing his next remark to the far end of the hall. "Cook cannot keep the food hot forever."

Vincent grinned. "I am duly chastised, Durbin. We shall be there directly." Durbin bowed stiffly and departed. Vincent turned back to Diana. "I believe we are in disgrace."

"As we should be." Diana hastily stood and went to the wardrobe. "Quickly. Help me with my buttons."

Vincent complied, but that did not prove to be a very efficient plan. Eventually they managed to concentrate on the task at hand sufficiently for Diana to change to a dinner gown. She then shooed Vincent out to change his own clothes while she restored her hair to its accustomed chignon.

As tired as she was, Diana felt as though a hundred years and a thousand pounds had fallen from her. She had told him. Vincent knew the whole of her foolishness and duplicity, and he believed her. More than that, he still wanted her. That a fiend still stalked her paled to insignificance beside that fact.

She reached the drawing room with her entourage of bodyguards shortly before Vincent. Sudbury and Delamare were drinking sherry together, patiently waiting. They both stood and Delamare hastened to provide her with a glass of wine. Diana had the uncomfortable impression that his sharp, black gaze cynically appraised the faint but telltale signs of her brief dalliance with Vincent—a red mark on the fair skin of her throat, her slightly swollen lips. In spite of herself, she blushed.

Delamare smiled his sardonic smile, then sobered. "I have sent for my valet and my baggage. As long as I am not perfectly sure of your safety, I shall stay here to lend what aid I can. I could not bear to think of your being injured."

"Thank you, sir. I am much obliged to you." Diana spoke the polite words without enthusiasm. She had rather not have to endure his flirting, but perhaps another man would be of help to Vincent.

She managed to avoid him until after dinner when she could excuse herself, pleading fatigue. In fact, exhaustion had finally threatened to put her to sleep where she sat. Emma appeared to help her brush and braid her hair and don her nightrail. Diana hoped that Vincent would not be long in coming. He must be as tired as she was. She lay down on the bed to wait.

Sometime later, knocking at the door waked her. She slid out of bed, and went to the door.

"Vincent?" At the sound of his voice answering, she turned the key. He went straight to sit on the bed and commenced to remove his clothes. Diana followed. "Where have you been? It must be quite late."

He yawned and stretched. "It is. I have been talking to the ratcatcher and to Nurse."

"The ratcatcher… Is he truly…?"

"Aye—one of my couriers. I hoped he would know who knifed him, but he says the blade came out of the dark." He tossed his stockings aside. "I had set him to watch Delamare and his valet. I thought perhaps… But he says that he left them at the inn."

"Speaking of Mr. Delamare and his valet, he says they are moving here." Diana helped tug the shirt over his head.

"So I heard." He laid it on a chair, grinning. "Perhaps he will generously share the valet with me. I left mine in London."

"I wondered. You have not sent for him?" Diana climbed into the bed while Vincent unbuttoned his britches.

"No. He performs certain…tasks for me there."

She sighed. "More subterfuge."

"My life is rife with it." He got into bed beside her. "But when I have settled the matter of Deimos, I will resign my post and put that behind me." He pulled her close against his side. "But now I fear I have another dilemma."

"Oh, no."

"I have been talking to Nurse about the conversation she had with Delamare and me. I told you that I did not remember all the incidents she related."

"Yes. But that is not surprising. You were only six—Selena's age."

He rose on one elbow and looked down at her. "I find I am coming to a very different understanding of my faithful nurse."

"How so?"

"She made those stories up from whole cloth!"

Diana had to laugh at the astonishment in his voice. "How devious!"

"Just so." He lay back and drew her to him again. "But she says that Delamare passed every test. I am beginning to be very much afraid that he *is* Henry. So now I must make a serious decision. If he is, do I acknowledge him, knowing that—as my father's true heir—he may apply to the Crown to take my title, much of my fortune, my home? Or do I deny him and make that much more difficult?"

"Can he do that?"

"I do not know. Parliament would have to decide. But, Diana…" He looked down into her face. "What is the *honorable* thing?"

"It all comes down to honor for you, doesn't it?"

"It is my anchor in a sea of deceit, my salvation from the vile creature I once made of myself."

"That creature is far behind you now." How differently she had come to see him in the last weeks.

Vincent sighed. "I pray that it remains so. But I yet have many wrongs to right, Diana."

She nodded in understanding. "Which is why you serve the Crown as you do—to right the wrongs of the world."

Vincent lay silent for a long moment. At last he said, "Yes, I wanted to make up for the evil I caused. And in so doing, I have involved myself in further evil. But, God willing, that is now coming to an end. I must now learn to be an ordinary, but virtuous, man."

"You have already become a virtuous man."

She thought him virtuous. Vincent considered that fact with overwhelming relief. He had truly tried. He wanted virtue and honor and respect more than anything in his life—except Diana. She had not yet agreed to marry him, but Vincent knew now that it was her own past, not his, that had held her back. While they had not resolved the matter, a comforting understanding now existed between them.

But what if Delamare—Henry—succeeded in establishing his claim to the earldom? What would Vincent have to offer her?

He was still pondering that question when his growing household assembled for a light noon repast. He watched with growing annoyance as Delamare paid court to Diana. She responded no more than courteously, but Vincent had had enough. The time for a discussion was at hand.

As they adjourned to the drawing room for tea, Vincent stopped Delamare. "Could I trouble you to come into the library for a moment, Delamare? I wish to speak with you."

Delamare nodded, bowed to Diana and followed Vincent into his study. "Of course I am always eager to serve you, my lord. How may I do so?"

Vincent ignored the mocking smile and waved him toward a chair. He took his usual place behind the desk. "I believe it is time to clarify a situation for you. From the amount of attention you bestow on Lady Diana, it appears that you do not realize that there is an understanding between her and me."

Delamare grinned derisively. "How could I not be aware of that? You sleep in her room every night. What troubles you, little brother? Are you afraid of losing your mistress?"

A red haze fell across Vincent's vision. He was on his feet before he even realized he had moved. He forced the fury back and leaned across the desk. "Lady Diana is... not...my...mistress."

"Indeed?" Delamare continued to smirk. "I fail to see in what way she differs from that."

A difficult statement to refute. But the man was baiting him. Vincent took a long breath and subsided into his chair. "She is my affianced wife." Almost. He calmed himself and sent Delamare a level look. "Sir, I hesitate to quarrel with a guest in my home, but I think you should realize that, at this time, *you are only a guest.*"

"Ah, but I have the potential for becoming so much more, do I not? You know who I am, whether you are prepared to admit it or not. I wonder how your *understanding* with the lady might change if *I* were declared the Earl of Lonsdale."

"You always wanted anything I had." The words slipped out past Vincent's guard.

"You see?" The man across the desk continued to smile. "You have accepted me as your elder brother. Can Parliament do less?"

"Parliament will do as it sees fit. I still reserve judgment."

"But in the end you will support my claim." Delamare's smile suddenly became a snarl. "Because you are so *honorable.* You were always the favorite, the good son, currying favor with my father, and I hated you for it. I told you that. Do you remember? The day I ran away. I told you I would make him regret it. It was your fault I left, and now I will take back what is mine."

Delamare rose and stalked out of the room.

Vincent sat in stunned silence, every word of the long-ago childish tantrum returning to him. Henry in a snit that day because their father had corrected him, blaming Vincent, pouting until he was allowed to go to the docks. Their father had been very indulgent with both of them. But Henry… Henry had never been satisfied, had always resented Vincent, and in a jealous rage he had run away.

Vincent no longer doubted.

His brother had come home.

That afternoon while Bytham and Selena napped, Diana carried her needlework into the morning room for a few moments of solitude—if one could describe having two footmen outside the door as solitude. Vincent had declared that neither she nor the children could go out of doors until they had apprehended the person who had shot at her. Diana sighed. It might become a long, difficult summer.

Both Lord Caldbeck and Lord Litton had ridden in a short while ago, and Vincent had closeted himself in the library with them. Discussing strategy, no doubt. Dear heaven! What were they to do? How would they find Deimos? And whoever had shot at her?

Diana could not see the end of it.

As she was pondering these discouraging thoughts, the sound of footsteps signaled the end of the little privacy she had. Henry Delamare sauntered into the room. Oh, drat! She did not have the patience today to avoid his gallantry.

She rose. "Good afternoon, sir. I was just going to look in on my children."

He stopped in front of her, almost crowding her back into the chair. "Please do not go just yet. I wish to speak with you." He lifted the sewing out of her hand and set it aside. "I have just been talking with my brother."

Diana raised an eyebrow.

Delamare smiled. "Yes, I believe I may now call him that."

"I don't understand, sir." She tried to step back, but encountered the chair from which she had just risen.

"He and I have had a most enlightening conversation." He took both of her hands in his, clasping them firmly. "I think sufficient doubt has now been raised as to whether he is, in fact, the rightful Earl of Lonsdale."

"Sir, I…" Diana tugged on her hands, but he did not release them.

"I just want you to know that whatever Parliament decides in the matter, that you have the opportunity to become the Countess of Lonsdale. Do not make a hasty decision."

He stepped back and Diana gazed at him in astonishment. He said nothing more, but narrowed his eyes as he watched her for a moment.

Then he turned and walked out of the room.

Vincent made his way up to bed in a decisive frame of mind. He could no longer question the identity of Henry Delamare. He was exactly who he said he was—Henry Ingleton. Vincent felt honor-bound to recognized him as such. Let the House of Lords decide whatever they might.

Whatever it cost him, Vincent would take the honest course.

Tonight he wanted a firm decision from Diana. For so much of his life his only associates had been more interested in what he had than who he was. He did not believe that Diana held that sort of values, but she had endured so much want. Financial security must certainly be paramount to her.

And what else was he offering her? A man with bloody hands, a despised past, a brusque demeanor. Perhaps he should withdraw his offer of marriage. That might be more fair to her.

But by God, he would not do that.

Vincent had struggled for half of his adult life to overcome his past mistakes. He had paid reparations to former victims. He had humbled himself to beg pardon. He had risked his life in the service of his country. What more could he do? Charles had said that he had been forgiven by others, that he should forgive himself. Perhaps now was the time to do that.

The time to leave the past behind and move into the future.

As a child, he had given Henry his toys in a futile attempt to please him, to gain his love. Now he might be required by the law to give him his position, his very home.

But he would fight him for Diana.

Vincent gazed long and hard into her face when she opened the bedchamber door, trying to read her thoughts. As usual he could see only the tranquil exterior she maintained in all but the most distressing circumstances. He folded her in his arms for a long moment. Then he moved to the chairs by the hearth, leading her by the hand. She looked at him in puzzlement as he nudged her into one chair and took the other himself, then sat looking at her for several heartbeats.

At last he said, "I must write to the Lord Chancellor tomorrow. I no longer harbor any doubt that Delamare is, in fact, Henry."

"What happened? He spoke to me today in a…very odd way."

Vincent related his conversation with Henry. "No one would remember that but the two of us, and… And, toward me, he is still just as he was then. He has grown older, but has given up nothing of the past. He still hates me. I would know him from that, if nothing else."

"How sad." Diana nodded and, apparently sensing that he had not finished, waited.

"Aye, it is sad, and it may change my situation entirely. I have asked you to be my wife, and I want that more than I want my next breath. I had thought that I would be offering you a respected title, an historic home, an impressive fortune—but now… My circumstances may change. You should know that."

"But, Vincent, my own circumstances…"

He held up his hand, palm out. "Your situation is not what you have believed it to be. I, myself, can bear witness to Goodnight's death. You had nothing to do with it, and Deimos will never come forward to present his lies. He will not make himself known. You are in no danger of the gallows."

Diana leaned one elbow on the arm of the chair and rested her forehead on her hand. "All these many months…all the fear. And it was all for nothing. I feel a very idiot. How could I have been so stupid as to fall prey to Deimos's manipulation? How could I have been stupid enough to marry Wyn in the first place? To choose such a poor father for my children?"

"Not stupid. You were very young when you married, and you are certainly no match for a schemer of Deimos's caliber. Even if you were…" He thought about his uncle's words again. "All you can do now is learn from the experience and forgive yourself."

"Forgive myself." She sat silent for a moment. "Yes, I suppose that is what I must do. I cannot undo the past. At least I did not succumb to Deimos's threats."

"No, you did not, and that was very courageous of you." Vincent slid out of her chair and knelt beside her, taking hold of her hands. "Diana, I still want you to be my wife. I may not continue as the Earl of Lonsdale, but I will not be penniless. My father had set aside a portion for me as a younger son. That will always be mine, and I have invested it well."

She smiled down at him. "We could go to Eldritch Manor. In spite of the circumstances, I felt almost happy there."

A great rush of feeling rose in Vincent's chest.

Relief.

He had come to know that she loved him, but still… "So will you be my bride, no matter what happens with Henry?"

Diana put a hand on either side of his face. "With all my heart."

His arms reached out of their own accord and pulled her closer. She leaned her head against his, her fingers tangling in his hair. "Oh, Vincent. I love you so."

He heard a catch in her voice and became aware of the warm tears on his own face. He pulled her out of the chair and stretched out beside her on the floor in front of the hearth.

"Diana. Oh, God. My love." He kissed her tears, her eyelids, her hair. The faint scar on her cheek. One knee came up across her body and he found her mouth with his. As he moved his lips down her throat, she melted under him, her hands still in his hair. He untied the tapes of her nightgown and let his lips and tongue trail over her breasts, pause for a moment over her nipples. He was hard and throbbing, but he only wanted to taste her, smell her, to worship her.

His wife.

The mother of his children.

He lifted the gown and kissed her navel, then moved his mouth around the curve of her belly. One day, one day soon, it would grow sweetly, sheltering his child. He moved his head lower, drawing in her scent. He kissed the inside of each thigh. She opened them for him.

Vincent tore the flap of his britches open and rolled over her. She pressed her hips upward and he slipped into her. Their mouths met again, open, seeking. Tongues traced lips, touched, tasted, moved in the primordial rhythm of love. Their bodies followed, hers circling, his thrusting.

When the cry burst from her throat, for the first time he did not stifle it. Let the whole world hear! She was his, and he was hers. For all time.

And then he was falling over the edge, swirling away in a cataract of sensation. He shouted in triumph. She was his.

For all time.

Chapter Eighteen

Aside from a short visit with Diana and the children, sharing a nuncheon and allowing Bytham to wreck his cravat, Vincent had spent the next day in his study composing the letter that must be written acknowledging his brother's return. It proved an arduous task. He wrote and rewrote, scratched out and started over. He had never realized how much Lonsdale meant to him until a threat to his possession of it arose. It had been his home all his life. It had grown into his very bones. Leaving it would break his heart.

But he would still have Diana. And Bytham. And Selena. That thought made the duty bearable.

Henry had regarded him with smug satisfaction throughout dinner. Mercifully, he somewhat abated his pursuit of Diana. A good thing, that. Otherwise, Vincent might have done violence to his newfound only living relative. Obviously the man was not a complete fool. Vincent had told him what he was doing. Henry would not jeopardize his success at this critical juncture.

Vincent excused himself from drinking port with the men and returned to his study to complete a fair copy of the letter. He had just signed his name when Henry entered the room without knocking.

He crossed to the desk and laid a paper on it. "I have also written to the Lord Chancellor, explaining my situation and making my request for recognition. Perhaps you will be good enough to enclose it with yours."

"Of course." Vincent picked up the sheet. He glanced over it, his gaze finally falling on the signature.

Henry David Rufus Ingleton, also known as Henry Delamare.

Vincent stared at the names, something about them catching his attention. Now what was it? What about them looked familiar?

Suddenly he knew.

A boulder of ice dropped into his stomach. He stilled himself carefully. When he looked up, Henry was watching him closely, a feral gleam in his eye. Vincent refused to allow himself to react. He nodded and calmly folded all the papers into a packet. He franked it and placed it in the desk drawer. "I will post these tomorrow."

Henry smiled wryly, bowed and left the library. Vincent sat staring at the door for a long time after he departed. Great God in heaven, what must he do now?

With a living and already patented incumbent holding the title of Earl of Lonsdale, inertia alone would very likely prevent Parliament from forcing a change. But if the title were open... If Vincent had already acknowledged Henry as his older brother... If Vincent were dead...

He had just signed his own death warrant.

Henry Ingleton would not hesitate for a moment to remove the small obstacle of a brother in his path. Vincent had once captured a note written by Deimos. He had memorized every line of it—the handwriting, those flourishing capital *D*s.

His brother and his most-hated enemy were one and the same.

* * *

He did not know how long he had been sitting there, considering the problem. Somehow Vincent must *prove* that Henry Ingleton was a vicious assassin, and he must stay alive while doing it. If he killed Deimos out of hand as he had vowed to do, it would seem that *Vincent* wished to remove a competitor for his position.

And he would be killing his own brother.

How could Henry have done this? Why had he done it? Why could he never simply be the big brother that Vincent wanted, might have loved? With whom he would willingly share. An urgent rap sounded on the study door. Vincent looked up. "Enter."

James Benjamin came into the room, breathless. "M'lord, someone is skulking about in the park. My lads are chasing him now. He might be the cove what shot at Lady Diana."

Vincent jumped up. "I will be right there. Leave my horse at the steps. Don't let that man escape."

James Benjamin darted out of the room and out into the night. Vincent followed, but instead ran up the stairs toward the drawing room. He could not leave Diana and the children unprotected in the house with Henry.

With Deimos. His blood ran cold at the thought.

On the other hand, Diana would not be safe until he apprehended the man who'd shot at her. In fact, that person was of more immediate danger to her than his brother. Henry wanted Diana for himself. He was unlikely to kill her. Perhaps he should tell her, but Vincent feared she would not be able to conceal her knowledge. If Henry learned that Vincent realized he was Deimos, none of them would be safe for another minute.

As he ran, Vincent came to a decision. He could not be in three places at once. He must enlist help.

He must put his trust in Justinian Sudbury.

When he reached the top of the steps, he slowed and pro-
ceeded with stealth. He stopped just outside the door and
peered furtively around the edge. He could not see Henry
or Diana, nor could they see him, but Sudbury sat in his usual
place opposite the door. He glanced up and met Vincent's
eye. Vincent put a finger to his lips, then pointed at Justinian, then in the direction of Henry and Diana. He repeated
the gesture, praying the man would take his meaning.

Sudbury yawned, stretched lazily and looked at Vincent
again, nodding almost imperceptibly.

Vincent turned and went to ensure that his most dangerous enemy would not lay hands on his children.

When Henry left the drawing room, Diana hoped that
he had gone to bed for the night. She had wanted to have
Vincent with her, but he seemed to be busy in his study, so
Diana enjoyed Justinian's droll observations while they
drank tea. But fate was not to favor her. After half an hour,
Henry returned. This evening he did not monopolize the
conversation as he was wont to do, or pay her unwanted
attention, but sat regarding her with disconcerting intensity.

She soon had enough of that. She finished her tea and,
excusing herself, went to her bedchamber. Justinian declared himself to be ready for bed and accompanied her upstairs. Feetham followed her faithfully, but to her surprise
there was no footman on duty in the corridor. Perhaps he
had gone on an errand for Nurse.

As soon as Emma helped her make ready for bed, Diana
dismissed her and went to sit by the window. She thought
she could hear shouting far out in the park. What could be
happening? Had Vincent been called out?

A knock rattled her door. "Vincent?"

"No, my lady. It is I." Feetham's voice. Diana opened the door and he handed her a small package. "The downstairs footman brought this up to you."

"Thank you, Feetham." She closed the door and looked cautiously at the bundle. What now? She untied the string and lifted out a small white garment.

Selena's ruffled underskirt.

The ruffles were still stained with that night's cherry pie, red as blood. Diana's heart began to hammer in her chest as she knelt to pick up a slip of paper that had fluttered to the floor. She looked at the writing, and her worst horror leaped up in her.

Now, my faithless slut—
   Now at last you will obey me. Come at once to the summerhouse at the end of the shrubbery. Alone.
   Fail at your daughter's peril.
Deimos

Oh, dear God. He was here.

Selena!

Diana forced herself not to move—to take time to think. She had been deceived once before by the lock of hair. She must be sure. She struggled into a black walking dress, fumbling to get at least a part of the buttons fastened, then tossed her braid to the back and went to the door. Taking a deep breath, she forced herself to smile at Feetham and walked to the children's room. She opened the door and stepped inside, closing it behind her.

There was no one in the room.

No one.

Not Nurse, not Throckmorton. Not Bytham and not Selena.

Diana's knees buckled and she grasped the door facing to keep her feet. Dear God in heaven! Somehow he had taken them. He had them. Deimos had her children.

She fought to strengthen her knees. She could not be weak now. They needed her. She must find them, which meant that she must go to him. But if that fiend thought she would go meekly, the lamb to the slaughter, he would soon learn his mistake. A rage such as she had never felt swelled in Diana.

She buttressed her resolution and went back to her room, nodding pleasantly at her bodyguard. Once inside she checked the priming of her pistol and put it in her pocket. Then she quickly wrote a note, which she gave to Feetham. "Please take this to his lordship. I believe he is still in the library."

"But, my lady…" Clearly the loyal Feetham did not wish to leave his post.

"It will be all right." She hated her false smile. "I will lock my door." He left with a frown and a backward glance.

Diana pinned a black veil over her light-colored hair and waited only until she heard Feetham's steps going down the stairs before slipping out of her bedchamber and down the hall in the other direction. She had no idea where Vincent might actually be. If he was in the study, then he would come to her aid. If not, sending her guard on the errand would give her time to get to the summerhouse alone.

She flew silently down the back stairs and out a side door. Diana decided she would not go directly to the summerhouse. Coming in from the back of the maze, she might have the opportunity to ambush him. The moon was just rising, throwing very little light as yet into the garden, but she left the paths and worked her way from shadow to shadow, her pistol in her hand.

Diana reached the far side of the shrubbery and crept

along, one hand against the hedges guiding her. There was an entrance on this side not far from the summerhouse, but she did not want to use it. He might be watching for her there. Yet she felt certain that Deimos would underestimate her. He had worked diligently to make her terrified and subservient. That misconception could be made to serve her.

She was no longer terrified—she was furious.

But she must also be clever. Above all else, she must discover where her children were held. Diana slipped the gun back into her pocket. Perhaps he would not know she had it. Aha. Her fingers encountered a thin spot in the hedge and she wriggled into it. The branches scratched her poor abused face and snatched at the veil.

Diana wormed her way on through the hedge, but did not step onto the interior path. She stood still as stone and listened. Someone was coming. She pulled back and watched. A man moved stealthily along the walk. Drawing the dark veil across her pale face, Diana squinted for a better look. Medium height. Sturdily built. Light hair. She had never seen him before.

Deimos.

As he continued toward the summerhouse, Diana slid out of the niche in the hedge. The veil hung in the branches. She tried to disentangle it, but could not see well enough to do so and decided to leave it. She followed the man silently into the dark.

Vincent stamped up the steps to the front door cursing imaginatively. They had lost him. Whoever the lurker in the grounds had been, he had cleanly escaped Vincent's forces. But the search had not been completely fruitless. It had led them past a spinney of small trees where one of his riders had spotted a boot lying on the ground. The boot had proved to contain the leg of Lord St. Edmunds.

Still connected to the rest of his corpse.

His lordship had been correct in his assessment of his own life expectancy. At least one opponent had ceased to plague him.

Just as Vincent approached the library door, a footman called to him. "My lord, I have a note for you. Feetham brought it down from Lady Diana. He didn't like to wait."

Vincent took the message and perused it. Bloody hell! She had gone in pursuit of Deimos! And she still did not know that her tormentor was, in truth, Henry. Diana would walk right up to him, never knowing. Damnation. At least she did not know where Nurse and Throckmorton had hidden the children. Deimos would not be able to force that knowledge out of her. Vincent did not know himself.

He sprinted down the hallway toward the side entrance.

Diana trod quietly in her light slippers, following her quarry down the path toward the summerhouse. But where was Selena? She must be somewhere nearby. Perhaps Deimos would lead Diana to her.

Without warning, something closed around her braid and yanked her backward. A rough hand covered her mouth and she was pulled back against a hard body. She twisted her head and looked up into a familiar face, indistinct in the starlight. Vincent? No…

Henry.

She tugged at the hand covering her mouth and gestured frantically down the walk. He leaned to place his ear beside her mouth, loosening his grip on her face. "Help me, Henry. That man is an assassin, and he has taken Bytham and Selena. I must find them and stop him."

His eyebrows rose and he seemed startled. Then he smiled slowly. He spoke into her ear. "Indeed? Then let us pursue him."

Henry took a firm hold on her arm and pulled a gun from his belt. They hurried down the path. It made a shallow turn and opened into a small grassy lawn fronting a low-arched stone structure. The stranger stood surveying the building. Diana slipped her hand into her pocket, closed it around her weapon and shouted, "Deimos! Stop!"

The man jumped and spun around, bringing up a double-barreled pistol. He pointed it straight at her. Henry shoved her into the hedge and dropped away in the other direction. A shot cracked and the muzzle of the stranger's gun flared.

Diana righted herself and lifted her hand, bringing up the pistol still inside her skirt. She pulled the trigger. The sound of her shot deafened her, and the smell of singed cloth mingled with that of burned powder. The man's pistol dropped to the ground and he fell forward, sprawling face-first across it.

For a heartbeat Diana stood stunned. She had not expected Deimos to simply shoot her. His threats had suggested much worse retribution. But where were Bytham and Selena? She ran forward and knelt beside him, tugging at his shoulder. Perhaps he was not dead. Perhaps he could still tell her.

Henry came up beside her, thrust his weapon into his belt and bent down. He spoke cooly. "How astonishing. I was not expecting *him,* whoever he may be." He looked at Diana with narrowed eyes. "Nor was I expecting *you* to be concealing a pistol. I must be more careful." He stood and pulled her to her feet. "But his presence will prove very useful when I remove my encroaching brother. I shall blame the tragedy on this intruder."

Alarm flashed through Diana. She jerked her arm and tried to step back. "What? What do you mean?"

His grip on her arm tightened punishingly and he caught

her chin in his other hand, digging his fingers into her flesh. His lips curled slowly, grimly. "Do you not know me? I told you I would come for you."

Breath failed Diana. She could only stare at him in disbelief. Finally she gasped, "You? You told me…" The truth struck her like a blow. "*You* are Deimos?"

"As I promised, sweet slut." He released her chin and, gripping her braid with one hand and her arm with the other, began to tow her across the lawn to the summer house. "But now we must await my brother. When he finds you missing, he will come in search. Did you leave him a note?" She refused to answer and he laughed. "Of course you did. You should have obeyed me and come alone."

Oh, dear God! If only she had not already discharged her pistol. But if she had not, she would already be dead. But most important… "Where are Selena and Bytham?"

"I will tell you that when I have made your situation clear to you." They had reached the summerhouse and he turned them so that it sheltered his back. "I must dispose of dear Vincent to ensure that I will be recognized as the Earl of Lonsdale. And you, my brother's whore, will be *my* countess, not his." He leered down at her, twisting her braid around his hand. "I told you I would get my money's worth out of you. I will even allow you to keep your children as long as you obey me. If you do not, I have acquaintances who will make profitable use of them. They are both beauties."

"You will not! I will not let you touch them." Her rage flooded Diana. She swung her free fist at him with all her strength.

Her knuckles connected with his chin. A bolt of pain shot through her hand and up her arm. Startled, Henry grunted and stepped back. Diana grabbed for the pistol in his belt. Forcing her aching hand to close around it, she jerked it out, but could not control it. It fell to the ground and she reached for it.

"Shrew!" His open hand came out of the dark, striking her across the face.

Lightning flashed through Diana's brain. Throwing herself forward, she went down atop the gun, dazed, but still scrabbling for it. She had one thought in her mind. If she could get her hands on it, she would kill him where he stood. He grasped her braid and hauled upward, pulling her head up so that she could no longer see the ground. Her scalp screamed in pain as he lifted her, but she continued to fumble for the weapon.

There. There! She almost had it.

"You bloody bitch!" He kicked the gun hard and it sailed out of her reach, somewhere off into the dark. Diana sobbed in frustration. He dropped her and drew his foot back again. She rolled desperately away from him. His boot struck her between the shoulder blades. The air rushed out of her. She tried to roll again, but her body would not obey.

She could not breathe!

"Henry!" Vincent's voice. Somewhere past the roaring in her ears.

Henry's hands clutched at her, trying to pull her limp form up in front of him. Before he could get her off the grass, a shot thundered. He cursed and dropped her, springing sideways.

From out of the hedge, Vincent launched himself, flying over her and knocking Henry to the ground. The two of them rolled and twisted, kicking and punching. Hands clawed, groped for throats, for eyes. Teeth gritted and snapped.

Breath finally returned to Diana and she crawled away from the grappling men. The pistol. She must find Henry's pistol. She groped blindly in the shadow of the hedge. Where? Where had it landed? Oh, God, she could not find it.

Diana struggled to her feet. She would have to do something else to help Vincent. Perhaps she could use her empty weapon as a club. She fumbled it out of her pocket, took it by the barrel, and peered through the dim shadow-striped light. Two men still fought on the grassy lawn.

But which one was Vincent?

He and Henry looked much alike at any time, but now, in this light… Dear heaven! Which was which? Both wore black coats and boots. Disheveled black hair shaded both their angular faces, obscuring the features. Diana stood uncertainly.

In the next moment three things happened so fast Diana could hardly perceive them. One of the wrestling forms was thrown back and away from the other. Both of them came to their knees. A silver blur streaked out of the shrubbery across the lawn.

Diana heard a *thunk*.

And another shot. Someone fell out of the far hedge.

One of the dark figures crumpled to the ground.

"Vincent!" Diana raced to where the man lay and bent over him. Oh, heaven. Was it Vincent? Was he dead?

Suddenly she was tackled and pulled away, tangled with another hard body.

"Don't touch him, Diana!" Vincent's voice.

Oh, God. Thank God. Vincent's voice. Vincent's arms.

The man on the grassy earth lifted himself on one elbow, allowing the moonlight to fall on the knife protruding from his chest. He coughed. "Clever, little brother." He tugged weakly at the handle of the blade. "You know I would not let you have her."

The knife came free and, with one last burst of energy, Henry threw it at Diana.

The effort proved more than he could do. Vincent easily moved her aside and the blade fell harmlessly beside them. Henry dropped onto his back, blood now spurting from his chest and pouring from his mouth. His voice gurgled as he spoke.

"Damn you. God damn you, Vincent. I should have won."

He did not move again and Diana knew that Henry Ingleton, the man known as Deimos, had spoken his last words.

Vincent, still kneeling, covered his eyes for a second. Finally he shook his head and laid his hand on his brother's shoulder. "Why did it have to be this way, Henry? Why?"

Of course, there was no answer.

There never would be.

Diana became aware of Justinian Sudbury walking toward them, a pistol in his hand. "He done for?"

"Aye." Vincent stood and helped Diana to her feet. "Much obliged to you, Sudbury. Who threw the knife?"

"Valet." Sudbury gestured at the figure that had fallen out of the hedge.

"You shot him?"

"Aye." Justinian nodded. "Been following him."

"But who did *I* shoot?" None of the night was making sense to Diana.

Vincent walked across and gazed down at the third casualty of the melee. "I am not certain, but I believe that Tobias will tell us that this is the confederate of St. Edmunds that enlisted him."

"I thought he was Deimos, but I would not have shot him except that he fired at me first." Diana wrapped her arms around herself. What a nightmare!

"And not for the first time, I'll warrant. He almost certainly shot at you yesterday." Vincent pulled her close. "But I think that has come to an end." He looked at Justinian. "The Office send you?"

Justinian grinned. "Aye. And you have a hard back to

watch." He looked at Diana's wide eyes and spoke to Vincent. "Take her back to the house. I'll tidy up."

"No!" Diana baulked. "The children! He said he had them."

"He lied, Diana. Again." Vincent put his arm around her waist and guided her through the maze. "The children are safe. Nurse and Throckmorton have hidden them."

"Thank God. Oh, thank God." Diana laid her head on his shoulder. "But now I really have killed someone." She sniffled.

"Do you regret it? He would have killed you, taken you from Selena and Bytham."

"I know. I would do the same again, but…" She broke into sobs.

"My only regret is that it was not I who killed those who were hounding you." Vincent stroked her back and held her close. He let her finish weeping before gently lifting her face and kissing her. "My poor, battered love. But you are safe now. And so are our children."

Our children.

Diana looked up into his eyes and smiled before she started crying again.

Epilogue

~~~~~~~~~~⌘~~~~~~~~~~

Yorkshire, England, March 1815

They were sitting in the drawing room after dinner. Vincent was studying the chessboard, playing a game against himself, honing his strategy. His wife watched while she sewed some fancy small garment. Suddenly he looked up. Diana lifted her head, too, listening. Hoofbeats, coming up the drive at the gallop.

Vincent stood and walked out into the hallway. A few seconds later Justinian Sudbury's long frame, muddy to the eyebrows, came running up the steps two at a time. "Lonsdale! Have you heard the news?"

Vincent ushered him into the drawing room. "What?"

"Bonaparte has escaped Elba." Sudbury shrugged out of his greatcoat and gave it to a hovering Durbin.

"Great God! How?" Vincent hurried to hand his chilled friend a glass of brandy.

"Don't know. Left Elba with twelve hundred men, but then the French army came up with him…" Sudbury tossed the liquor back in a single gulp, choked and held out his glass.

"What, man?" Vincent refilled the glass. "What happened?"

"The bastard rode out to the French army, threw open his coat and shouted, 'Let him that has the heart kill his Emperor!'" Sudbury sank down tiredly onto a stool by the fire.

"Bloody hell! The audacity." Vincent poured for himself.

Diana set her sewing aside. "What did they do?"

"Shouted, *'Vive l'Empereur!'* and came over to him—*to* a man."

Vincent could hardly credit it. He stared at Sudbury openmouthed. "All of them?"

"Even the generals. They are riding on Paris. The Bourbon king has fled." Sudbury wiped a blob of mud off his face. "Thought you would want to know."

"Then…we failed." Vincent slowly sat back in his chair. "After all the risk, the intrigue, the blood… We accomplished nothing—all we did meant nothing."

"Aye," Sudbury agreed glumly.

Vincent felt Diana's hand on his shoulder. "No, Vincent." She gazed deeply into his eyes. "The outcome does not change the meaning of what you did. You risked your life for your country. You abandoned your future to rectify your past. You fought for your honor and the safety of England. Nothing can change that."

Vincent sat thinking silently for a space. At last he nodded and said, "Thank you, Diana." He covered her hand with his and glanced at Sudbury. "I also learned who my friends are."

Justinian grinned and held out his glass. "Tolerable brandy, this."

* * * * *

MILLS & BOON®

Live the emotion

Historical
romance™

0606/04b

THE MERCENARY'S KISS
by Pam Crooks

Elena Malone was a woman of true grit…and Jeb Carson
respected her for it. He was a law unto himself, but this
soul-scarred beauty, intent on reclaiming her child, made
him hunger for something more. When she had been
attacked, Elena swore nothing could be as terrible –
until her baby boy was kidnapped. Now her only hope
for his rescue lay with Jeb, a dangerous man who lives
– and loves – by a code all his own…

REFORMING THE RAKE
by Sarah Elliott

REGENCY

To Beatrice Sinclair, after so many fruitless years on
the *ton's* marriage mart, life on the shelf seemed an
appealing prospect. Still, she yearned for romance –
bone melting, scandalous romance – and what she
really wanted, even for one mad moment – was a rake.
And Charles Summerston, Marquis of Pelham,
seemed only too happy to oblige!

On sale 7th July 2006

FREE!
2 Books
and a surprise gift!

We would like to take this opportunity to thank you for reading this Mills & Boon® book by offering you the chance to take TWO more specially selected titles from the Historical Romance™ series absolutely FREE! We're also making this offer to introduce you to the benefits of the Reader Service™—

- ★ **FREE home delivery**
- ★ **FREE gifts and competitions**
- ★ **FREE monthly Newsletter**
- ★ **Exclusive Reader Service offers**
- ★ **Books available before they're in the shops**

Accepting these FREE books and gift places you under no obligation to buy, you may cancel at any time, even after receiving your free shipment. Simply complete your details below and return the entire page to the address below. You don't even need a stamp!

YES! Please send me 2 free Historical Romance books and a surprise gift. I understand that unless you hear from me, I will receive 4 superb new titles every month for just £3.69 each, postage and packing free. I am under no obligation to purchase any books and may cancel my subscription at any time. The free books and gift will be mine to keep in any case. H6ZEF

Ms/Mrs/Miss/Mr ....Initials.................................
                                                                                                    BLOCK CAPITALS PLEASE
Surname ....

Address...

....

....Postcode ....

Send this whole page to:
UK: FREEPOST CN81, Croydon, CR9 3WZ